Opening the Floodgates

Catrina J. Sparkman

ISBN 13: 978-1-949958-02-7

Opening the Floodgates

Paperback Edition ISBN 13: 978-1-949958-02-7

Copyright © 2015 Catrina J. Sparkman

Published by:

The Ironer's Press
PO Box 1122
Madison, Wi 53701

Other works by Catrina J. Sparkman

<u>Non-fiction:</u>

Doing Business with God: An Everyday Guide to Prayer & Journaling

Intimacy the Beginning of Authority

Divine Revelation for a Twitter Generation: Growing in the Prophetic

Doing Battle with the Names of God

The Fourth Watch: A Watch for Prophets, Warriors, Intercessors & Love-Sick Believers

Intercession 101: The Heartbeat of God

Wired for War

The Dishwasher Anointing

<u>Fiction:</u>

Opening the Floodgates

The Fire this Time

DEDICATION

This book is dedicated to every child that has ever been hurt in the household of faith. For your body, for your mind, for your spirit—

A demand

This is what the Sovereign LORD *says:*

⁴ On the day you were born your cord was not cut, nor were you washed with water to make you clean, nor were you rubbed with salt or wrapped in cloths. ⁵ No one looked on you with pity or had compassion enough to do any of these things for you. Rather, you were thrown out into the open field, for on the day you were born you were despised.

⁶Then I passed by and saw you kicking about in your blood, and as you lay there in your blood I said to you, "Live!" ⁷ I made you grow like a plant of the field. You grew and developed and entered puberty. Your breasts had formed and your hair had grown, yet you were stark naked.

⁸ Later I passed by, and when I looked at you and saw that you were old enough for love, I spread the corner of my garment over you and covered your naked body. I gave you my solemn oath and entered into a covenant with you, declares the Sovereign LORD, *and you became mine.*

EZEKIEL 16: 4-8 (NIV)

Opening

the

Floodgates

CHAPTER 1

Whomp! *Whomp-whomp! Whomp!* Mike had dropped Joshua and Jabari off three hours ago, and for two and a half of those hours Joshua had been holed up in his home gym punching the man size hanging weight bag.

Joshua felt a fury in his soul that he hadn't felt in years. Playing basketball that morning hadn't spent the pent-up rage. The shower afterwards certainly hadn't cooled him down. This was the same edge that he would take out onto the court with him, every night as a professional ball player. If someone even looked at him wrong, crossed him in anyway, Joshua Keys would get physical. That's how he felt right now. Bella made him want to punch someone. His fist ached to connect with another man's flesh.

He had been able to find a relative amount of enjoyment in the time he'd spent shopping with his brother and the boys that afternoon. He'd even managed to smile a few times at Jabari's corny jokes. Seeing the joy on both the boys' faces, knowing that he was at least partly responsible for putting that joy there, made him glad. But there was still this undercurrent of anger running through his veins. Joshua punched the bag until sweat poured from every pore of his body and his lungs felt like they would explode. Still, no relief. That's when he heard the gentle voice of God tugging at the corner of his mind.

This kind can only come out by prayer and fasting.

He hadn't realized it until this moment, but unconsciously, he had been fasting. Yesterday, he had been too concerned about finding his family to eat. Then, when he'd found them, he'd been too excited. This morning, after making love to Bella, he'd been ravenous. Whether that was for her or for food, he couldn't tell, but after seeing the truth, he'd been too disgusted to eat. Even at the restaurant this morning, Mike, Jabari, and Marcus had collectively eaten enough food to feed a small village. Normally, Joshua would have been right along with them, but all he'd been able to stomach was a cup of herbal tea. Was this God's gift to him? Had God divinely put him on a fast to keep him from totally losing his mind? Yes, Joshua decided, He had. Even in this awful mess that had become his life, God's merciful hand was still upon him. The peace that he sought right now would not come from punching a sand bag, or even from having his fist connect with another man's face. The peace he sought would only come through prayer. Mike's words from earlier that morning vibrated through Joshua's soul. "What's God telling you to do? What does he want?" Joshua slammed his gloved fist into the padded wall.

"What about what I want!"

Joshua, these are the sins of the father, visited upon the child.

But Joshua wasn't trying to hear that. Not this time. Not again.

SPRING, 1997

CHAPTER 2

Tonya laid the bill from the bursar's office out on the bed and got down on her knees. *Lord, you know my desire. I really want to finish this semester debt free. My daddy's gone from this earth. He's up there with you. I'm trusting you to help me out.*

❧ ❧

"Hello, may I speak to Tonya, please?"

"Is this Michael?" the girl asked in a singsong voice.

"Is this Nisha?"

"It's me." Nisha closed her eyes and twirled an auburn hair extension around her fingertip, pleased he recognized her voice.

"Now Nisha, what other dude would be calling your house for the Blackbird besides me?"

"This is college. It could be anybody."

"Anybody like who?"

"Like a study buddy."

"It better not be," Mike muttered.

Nisha chuckled. "I missed that, what?"

"Nothing. She there?"

"Hang on. I'll get her for you." Nisha knocked twice before walking into Tonya's bedroom. Tonya rose from her position on the floor. "I didn't mean to interrupt your prayer time, but you have a phone call."

"That's okay. I'm finished. Is that Michael?" Tonya said, smiling and reaching for the phone.

Nisha ignored Tonya's outstretched hand, plopped down on top of the bed and grabbed one of Tonya's fluffy

4

pink throw pillows. "It's him. With his fine self." Nisha looked down at the tuition bill now scrunched up under her thigh. She pulled it out and handed it back to Tonya. "You praying about your school fees?"

Tonya nodded. "I'd like to finish my last semester debt free."

"You ain't got to pray about that. It's a no-brainer. It's called your very rich boyfriend. You know the one who plays for the Houston Rockets?"

"You mean the one who can hear everything you're saying right now because he's on the phone?" Tonya grabbed for the receiver.

Nisha laughed and held the phone out of Tonya's reach. "My hand is on the mute button. For now, anyways."

"I'm not asking Michael for money, Nisha. Now give me the phone."

"Why not?"

"Because I'm not."

"And when you can't pay your tuition or your rent, then what?"

"No worries, Nisha. My rent will be on time just like it has been every other month."

Nisha shook her head. "You're too holy for your own good. You ain't thinking right either. Doesn't Jesus say something about being meek and wise? You got the meek part down, I'll give you that much."

Nisha sucked her teeth and looked Tonya up and down. How in the world had her plain Jane of a roommate landed the most eligible bachelor in all of Houston? It was beyond her understanding. Nisha eyed her roommate enviously. The girl was a walking goldmine of untapped potential. Under all those loose-fitting clothes she preferred, Tonya had curves for days. With her flawless mocha skin, pretty face, and naturally thick long tresses that would make any weave connoisseur drool, she could be the hottest thing to ever hit their campus, the whole city even. If only the dumb chick knew how to leverage her assets.

"Wow, Nisha, I'm actually surprised you can say God's name without melting."

Nisha stuck her middle finger up at Tonya and hopped off the bed.

"Real classy, Nisha. Let me speak to my man."

"Actually, I was wondering if I could borrow him for a bit?"

"For what?"

"Well, I figure with you being such a holy roller now, he has got to be missing the wild thang. I don't mind helping him out in that department."

Tonya stared at her roommate in disbelief. In the three short years Michael Dutton had played for the Houston Rockets, he'd quickly risen to become the franchise's star player. You couldn't go anywhere in the city without seeing The Man of Steel's face or his trademark paraphernalia.

Tonya knew her friends thought Michael played around on her because number one, he never appeared anywhere with her in public. And number two, he was often seen publicly photographed with beautiful female celebrities by his side.

And although she knew the truth, seeing the photos splashed across the covers at newsstands and in supermarkets still made her nauseous.

Nisha gave Tonya the phone and sprinted for the door. "Geez, apparently you Christians don't have a sense of humor either."

"I have a great sense of humor, Nisha. I'm cracking up on the inside," Tonya said as she slammed the door in her roommate's face and unmuted the phone.

"Dang, girl, I didn't think you were ever coming to the line."

"Sorry, peanut gallery."

"Nisha got jokes, huh? What that girl talking 'bout now?"

"I ain't even about to repeat that crazy mess. When are you coming home?"

"Why, do you miss me?"

"You know I do."

"Well, I'm back and I have a surprise."

"Tell me now I can't wait!"

"I bought a spot."

Tonya gasped. "A house?"

"Yeah, and I want you to decorate it for me."

"You do realize that I'm a psych major, and not a design student, right?"

"Well, it's like this, I figure I could have my future wife do this, or I could hire some random decorator chick. You decide."

Tonya fell silent. There was a time when she would have been overjoyed to hear any words related to marriage cross his lips. That was before she recommitted her life back to Christ. It wasn't that Michael wasn't a Christian. He'd been raised in the church just like she had. He just didn't believe the *same way* she believed. Lately, the lack of unity in the area of their faith was the cause of most of their arguments. That and what he referred to as her stubborn, pigheaded refusal to let him help her financially.

"What if I told you the job pays?" Mike said, filling the silence between them.

"I'd say we're family and you don't have to pay me."

"Just cause we're fam doesn't mean I should take advantage. It's a big spot."

"How big?"

"Actually, it's two spots."

"Michael, why would you buy two houses when you only have one body?"

"One is the house I've always wanted. The other is the one you said you wanted. I figured since you won't move in with me, you could move into it, just until we agree on the next step."

Silence.

"So, you gon take the job or what?"

"How about I help you for free?"

"Tonya, the word help implies that you expect me to participate in some way. That won't happen."

"Why not?"

"Because I can afford to have someone do it for me. Time is money, girl. What's it gon be, you, or random decorator chick?"

Tonya smacked her lips, "How much you paying?"

"For you, twenty Gs."

"Funny how that just happens to be the same amount I owe in semester fees this year."

"Relax. Ain't nobody trying to take care of you. We both know how you hate that. The job actually pays more, but it's like you said, you don't know what you're doing."

"How much more?"

"Thirty grand more. But I figured you know me, you know my style. You can handle this, and I can save a little cash in the process. I'm kind of in a hurry. I need this place finished before the playoffs, in time for my victory party."

"Aren't the Hornets playing the Rockets in the conference finals this year?"

"If they keep winning they will."

"Hum, they've got Joshua now. Don't you think it's a little premature to be planning your victory celebration?"

"I see Nisha isn't the only one with jokes today."

Tonya laughed. "Hey, I'm just saying. Your brother is out there dominating on the court every night."

"So, you a Bad Boy fan, huh?"

"I have to admit I am, but I'm the Man of Steel's number one fan. Believe that." Tonya could almost see his smile through the phone.

"So, what's up? What we gon do?"

Tonya sighed, "Can I pray about it?"

"Whatever, Tonya, just do it quickly. I'll be there in an hour. I need my answer today."

CHAPTER 3

Mike and Tonya walked through the mansion hand in hand.

"What do you think?"

"It's amazing, but how do you expect me to get this place ready in time for the playoffs?"

"Well, it's like this, I figure one day, when you come to your senses—"

"And marry you?"

"That's right. You'll be responsible for managing all of this. Might as well learn how to delegate now, pay whoever you need to."

"We can save money if we paint ourselves."

"Baby, you know that's not gon happen. Now, I might help you paint that little shack out back during the off-season, maybe. But even that's a strong maybe."

"Hey, it's a cottage, not a shack."

"Yeah, but, baby, you gotta admit, compared to this, it's a shack."

"That all depends on what you like."

Mike smiled down at her. "So do you like it?"

Tonya waved her hand around the huge open floor space. "You mean all of this? It's alright, I guess. I could live here one day. If I really had to."

Mike laughed. "Yeah, so what about the cottage?"

Tonya closed her eyes and smiled. "It's like you picked the house right out of my dreams. The red door, the old-fashioned claw foot tub, a wraparound porch with a swing."

"I listen."

"You do."

"So you like it?"

"I love it but—"

Mike put his finger over her lips. "Then don't tell me you can't take it. When I first saw this property with the guesthouse out back and the monster garages for all my stuff, I knew this place would be perfect for us. The guesthouse is not a proposal, Tonya. Taking it doesn't mean you'll marry me. And you ain't gotta worry about me creepin' over there at night, invading your space. I'll only come when and if you invite me. In fact, move your girls in, Nisha and all the rest of your little roomies. Live there while you're in grad school or just until we figure out the next step. Okay?"

"And you're sure this isn't a proposal?"

"Girl, please, when I propose to you, my junk will be tight. Believe that. Take the guesthouse, Tonya. I'll probably just end up renting it out if you don't."

"Okay."

His dark, handsome face broke out into a full grin. "Yeah?"

"Yeah."

He pulled his cellular phone out. "Call your girls and tell them to pack."

Tonya scrunched up her nose. "Nah, that's okay."

Mike lifted his eyebrow in question.

"They ain't moving up in here with me."

Mike threw his head back and laughed. "Come on, I just have one more thing to show you."

⁂

"Michael, don't tell me this place has another garage."

"This is just a small one for the cottage." Mike pulled a remote control out of his pocket and pushed the button.

Before the garage door was fully up, Tonya began shaking her head. "Michael, no."

"It came with the house."

11

"No, this is all you. A Range Rover did not come with this house."

"Okay, it's an early graduation gift. If you live here, you'll need a car. I tolerated that, I-don't-need-a-car-crap while you were living on campus. But you won't be living on campus now and I can't do that anymore."

"It's too much."

"It's not nearly enough. But she's dependable and the technology in this baby won't be on the market for at least another ten years. She's a beast." Mike grinned proudly at the truck. "I had it armored. You can't even get a flat tire in this thing."

"You got me a bulletproof car? Don't you think that's a little over the top?"

"No, I don't," he said firmly. "If you were ever in an accident, or, God forbid, some psycho fan came after you, I need to know that you'd be safe."

Tonya folded her arms across her chest. "I would be safe because God's angels would protect me."

"Well, just in case they're off their game, the Man of Steel got you too."

"Michael—"

Mike pulled her into his arms. "My woman doesn't ride the bus."

"I never ride at night."

"My woman doesn't ride the bus ever."

Mike buried his face in her hair. "Tell me that you're still mine, Blackbird," he murmured. "Tell me I haven't completely lost you?"

"You haven't lost anything, Michael. I'm right here."

CHAPTER 4

Tonya, you outdid yourself. I can't believe what you've done to the place!" Bella exclaimed as she and Joshua followed Tonya and Mike on a tour of the mansion.

Joshua nodded, "You hooked it up, sis."

Mike beamed with pride as he ran his long fingers up the back of Tonya's neck and tangled them in the thick tresses of her hair.

Bella studied the deep curves of the furniture. "It's a very nice balance of the two of you. So much of the furniture has a masculine feel to it but I also see a feminine presence here too."

"Wait until you see my place." Tonya grinned.

"Another perfect blend?" Bella asked.

"Nope. It's all me."

"You can say that again," Mike added.

Tonya tilted her head backwards and looked into Mike's eyes. "You trying to tell me you don't feel comfortable in my spot?"

"It's not made for me, baby, with those midget walls—"

"He's being silly, you guys. I have nine-foot walls with crown molding."

"Nine-foot neon colored walls," Mike said.

Joshua grimaced.

"No, not neon, high energy colors. Colors that wake you up in the morning but also help you relax in the evening," Tonya said.

Mike leaned over and kissed her forehead. "My bad, what was I thinking?"

Bella smiled at her friend. "Tonya, that sounds so completely you. I can't wait to see it. I think a person's home should reflect their personality. I can't wait for it to be our turn."

"Yo, Josh, you hear that? The wife wants a house. When you gon do this, bro?"

"First time I'm hearing it." Joshua looked at Bella. "I thought you were happy with the condo?"

"I was. I mean, I am. But having a home we could decorate together would be nice too. I feel like I moved into your spot."

"You can redecorate, Bella. Change the whole thing if you want."

"I can do anything?"

"Yeah, baby, within reason. Just keep in mind that I'm not really a high energy color sort of brother." Joshua winked at Tonya.

"Can I knock out a wall and add a dining room?"

Joshua waited for the punch line, but Bella didn't crack a smile. "We'll call a realtor when we get back."

Bella flung her arms around Joshua's neck and squealed in delight. "Thank you! I love you."

"Yeah, yeah, yeah."

Mike gave Joshua a pound. "Now, what you need is a little spot in the country with some pastureland for a few horses."

Joshua shook his head. "Come on, man, you know that's not going to happen."

"Nope, never gonna happen," Bella sang.

Mike shuddered. "Aw, dog, I forgot all about that."

"I have no idea how you could have," Joshua muttered.

Tonya looked at Joshua. "I always pictured you on a ranch somewhere."

"Hey, me too, but my wife here doesn't do horses."

"Oh, Bella, that's easy. We just have to take you out riding on the trails one day. Josh is an excellent teacher. Michael and I aren't bad either. Between the three of us, we can cure your fear of horses just like that." Tonya snapped her fingers to emphasize her point. She looked to Mike and Joshua for their agreement, but they were both shaking their heads no emphatically behind Bella's back.

"We tried that. It didn't work out so well," Bella said, biting down on her bottom lip.

Joshua wrapped Bella into a bear hug. "And I love horses way too much to ever torture a creature like that again."

"Ha-ha, very funny, Josh. And for the record, I was the one who was traumatized, not the horse, okay?"

Bella tried to pull away from Joshua, but he held her tighter. "See what love will make you do, Tonya?"

Tonya smiled at the couple in front of her. "Remember when Josh use to say the only girl he was ever going to marry was Lady?"

"I was five."

Mike shook his head. "Naw, dude, you were at least eight."

Joshua covered Bella's ears. "Haters, baby. Don't listen to them."

"Oh no, after that horse crack, I think I need to hear this."

"Bella, my daddy was so concerned, he and Jack sat the three of us down for *the talk*," Tonya said.

Joshua groaned.

Mike sat down on one of the cushioned high back chairs that lined the upstairs hallway. He leaned forward, knitted his brow together, and pointed at Joshua. "Joshua, people mate with people and horses mate with horses. You cannot marry Lady, son. It is anatomically impossible. And Tonya, you are a little girl. You are not a bird," Mike said, pointing to Tonya and imitating the tone and pitch of her father exactly.

"But I am to a bird, Daddy. I'm a Blackbird, cause Mikey says I am," Joshua said in a high-pitched child's voice.

Both couples burst into a fit of laughter.

"Bella, I wish you would have gotten a chance to meet my daddy. He would have really loved you," Tonya said.

"Yeah, I'd say you're pretty much the answer to every one of his prayers for Josh," Mike said.

Joshua grabbed Mike and the two brothers tussled playfully.

"It's true, Bella," Tonya said, laughing. "Up until the day he died, my daddy was asking my mama about Joshua. 'Barb, that boy hasn't brought a woman home yet. You don't think he still got his eye on that horse, do you?' And Mama would tell Daddy that when Joshua brought home a girl, he would marry her."

"Tonya's parents are my godparents. So she has a ton of very embarrassing stories about me."

Tonya rolled her eyes at Joshua. "Oh, like that Blackbird story was one of my finer moments?"

Mike pulled her close. "What are you talkin' about? I love that story."

"Only because it proves I've always been a fool for you."

Bella encircled her arms around Joshua's waist. "I can't wait to hear all the stories from your past. I want to know every single thing about you."

Joshua lifted her chin up so that her eyes met his gaze. "Ditto."

"Okay, guys, now that you've seen everything, I want you to be absolutely honest; especially you, Joshua. I'm actually depending on your brutal honesty for a change. Even though this place is well . . . massive, I still wanted it to feel like a home. Did I succeed?" Tonya bit her bottom lip and waited for their response.

"It's very homey," Bella said.

Joshua nodded. "You laid it down."

"Tonya, seriously, I am super impressed. You've managed to make everything in here, including the home gym, feel comfortable," Bella said.

"Full regulation-sized court, baby!" Joshua said as he slapped his brother a high five.

"Not to mention the pool house and all twenty garages," Bella said.

Joshua looked at Mike. "I only counted three garages. Trucks, cars, and bikes, right?"

Mike smirked at Bella. "Right."

Tonya shook her head. "It's so sinful, Bella. He has one body and over twenty cars."

"Tonya, chill, alright? God is the blesser. We know where our help comes from," Joshua said.

Mike nodded. "Solomon was the richest man that ever was. God gave him everything he had."

"Yes, and he got in trouble for having too many foreign wives and too many foreign vehicles." Tonya folded are arms across her chest and offered the two brothers a look of finality.

Joshua shrugged. "Maybe God wanted him to buy local."

Mike gave Joshua a fist bump. "That's real talk right there. Build up where you come from. Put the money back into your own economy."

Tonya looked at Bella. "Wow, rich people."

Bella nodded her head in agreement.

Joshua grabbed Bella around the waist and spun her around till she let out a yelp. "Oh, you gon co-sign with your girl here, but you want me to buy you a house?"

"I sure do!"

Mike looked at Joshua. "Dude, she just called my spot massive."

"And she said it like it was a bad thing, dog."

Mike shrugged. "I mean it's not a shack."

Joshua looked up at the soaring ceilings. "No, my brother. This certainly ain't a shack."

"Okay, there you go again with that shack mess, Michael. I've got three bedrooms. Trust, okay? My place is no shack," Tonya said.

"I've got twelve," Mike countered.

Bella leaned her body back into Joshua's, delighting in the couple's playful banter. "So when y'all get married, where will the two of you live?"

"My place," Tonya and Mike both said together.

Bella and Joshua both laughed.

Mike shook his head and stood up. "Madness. Come on, y'all, let's go outside and get some fresh air. Blackbird's been sniffing paint fumes for too long."

Mike descended the deep, rich, cherry wood, spiral staircase. He held the front door open so that both Bella and Tonya could walk through.

"To answer your question, Bella, we gon turn her spot into the guesthouse. Yo, Josh, what do you think about me having a victory party here?"

Joshua put his hand on Mike's shoulder. "You'd do that for me?"

Mike smirked. "Do what?"

"Throw a victory party in my honor."

Mike knocked Joshua's arm away. "The paint fumes must be getting to you too. Your defeat, little brother, my victory."

CHAPTER 5

Bella leaned up against the rack as Tonya perused through the clothes. "Tonya, I'm concerned about the guys. This game is really important to Joshua."

Tonya looked into Bella's worried face. "It's important to Michael too. Don't worry. Those two are at their best when they're competing. I've only ever seen them get into one serious fight in my whole life."

"What happened?"

"They were racing through a meadow near our houses on horseback. I made the terrible mistake of declaring it a tie. As long as there is one clear cut winner, they'll be alright."

"Strange. That's exactly what Mel said," Bella murmured.

"It's true. If it'll make you feel better, I'll say a prayer for them tonight."

Bella nodded. "Mike is the most important person in the world to Joshua. It's hard to believe they are not brothers by blood."

Tonya held a lace peasant dress up to her chest for Bella's inspection.

Bella frowned. "This is the third resale shop we've been to. This ain't gonna work, mama."

"Bella, this is all I can afford."

"I thought you said Mike paid you to decorate the house?"

"It's gone. I paid my rent up on my old apartment and my tuition. It was just the money I needed to finish this year debt free."

"Okay, but we still can't shop here."

"Why not?"

"Because this is the NBA, and because your man is the star player for the Houston Rockets. Trust me when I say there are going to be groupies at this party, and you don't want them rolling up into your man's set looking better than you." Bella's eyes roamed slowly over Tonya's attire, taking in her colorful bangles and white cotton summer skirt. "I gotta give it to you, you work the heck out of the bohemian look. But for an event like this, we're gonna need chic and sexy."

"I hope we can find all of that right here, because my budget says Goodwill."

"It ain't here, sweetie. But don't worry, I got you."

"Bella, I don't feel comfortable spending Michael's money. I certainly wouldn't feel comfortable spending Joshua's."

"I don't like to be totally dependent on my man either. That's why I got a little side hustle. Today is on me. Just promise me you won't breathe a word of this to Mike. Joshua doesn't know I have my own money."

CHAPTER 6

Tonya's eyes bucked when she turned over a price tag in the upscale boutique Bella had taken her to. "Bella, I can't afford this place."

"Well, I can. So try these on." Bella pushed four dresses into Tonya's arms and led her into a large dressing room.

"Call me if you need help zipping," Bella said before disappearing back out onto the saleroom floor. A tall, average looking black man spotted Bella through the store's window. When he strolled inside the boutique, the two sales ladies stopped their work at the counter to whisper and stare.

"Bella? I thought that was you."

Bella didn't fluster at the nearness of the man, standing so close she could feel his breath on the back of her neck, nor did she bother looking up from the rack of clothes she was inspecting.

"You here alone?"

Bella picked up a turquoise, sequined pantsuit the exact shade of Joshua's Hornet's uniform. She had considered wrapping herself in a bow as a consolation prize should her husband's team happen to lose, but seeing her decked out in his team's colors would elicit a much better response. Bella quietly queried the man standing behind her. "Tell me something, is this business or personal?"

"It can be whatever you want it to be, baby."

"Wrong answer. It's always business, never personal." Bella turned, pinning the man with cold eyes. "Don't ever make the mistake of calling me 'baby' or 'Bella'."

The man backed away from her, holding his hands up in mock surrender. The corners of his mouth turned into an impish grin.

"My bad, Rosemary. When can I see you?"

"You know the rules, Brady. Nobody gets an interview twice."

"Bella!"

"Be right there!" Bella called back over her shoulder. "Oh, and, Brady, unless you want me to cut off that incredibly, unremarkable thing you call a magic stick and hand it to you in a paper bag, you won't ever approach me like this."

Bella tossed her hair over her shoulders and walked away.

Tonya came out the dressing room wearing the silver dress and the matching heels Bella had chosen for her. She did a runway walk and a twirl. "What do you think?"

"I think if you walk up into that party with that dress on, you gon hurt somebody."

Tonya frowned. "You think it's too much?"

"Are you kidding me? Tonya, it's just right. That dress is banging. You don't even have to try the rest of that stuff on."

Tonya looked up at the sound of the shop bell. "Hey, isn't that Michael's teammate?" Tonya snapped her fingers trying to recall his name. "Number eleven. I should know this one. He and Mike, they're kind of like a duo on the court."

Bella allowed her eyes to follow the man as he left the store. "You mean like Batman and Robin?"

Tonya smiled. "Actually, it's more like the Man of Steel and Robin. I don't know why I'm drawing a blank on his name, though."

Bella shrugged. "I surely couldn't tell you. I'm a Hornet's fan myself."

CHAPTER 7
Three Weeks Later

Bella sat across the table from Tonya in a famous Houston lunch spot, studying Tonya's hair as she munched on her salad. "I'm thinking we should go Foxy Brown for the hair. That would be perfect with those shoes and that throwback-era dress."

"Actually, Bella, I've been thinking about perming my hair."

Bella's eyes bucked. "No, you can't."

"Why not?"

"Hum, let's see. First of all, because Mike would kill me and second because, oh yeah, I remember now, Mike would kill me."

"Bella don't you think you're being just a little overly dramatic? It's just hair."

"No. I don't. Joshua and I have been hanging out with you guys for what, three weeks? And in the span of one hour, Mike runs his fingers through your hair an average of forty-two times."

Tonya shook her head, a tiny smile played across her lips.

"I ain't lying. I counted. Forty-two times per hour. That man loves your hair. Heck, your man touches your hair so much it motivated me to grow my own daggone perm out."

Tonya laughed so hard she cried.

"I'm serious, my new ambition in life is to get Joshua to run his fingers through my hair like that."

"What are you talking about? Joshua can't keep his hands off of you."

"Maybe, but he ain't massaging my scalp every chance he gets and he definitely isn't running his fingers through my hair."

Tonya shrugged. "It's no big deal, Bella. Mike and I aren't intimate, so we have to find other ways to show our affection."

"If it's no big deal, you shouldn't have a problem giving up this asinine idea."

"What about all those other women who are going to be fried, dyed, and laid to the side? I've never been seen anywhere with Michael in public. He's going to be introducing me to the world for the first time tonight. People are going to think I'm some kind of country bumpkin who can't afford a perm."

Bella stopped chewing for a moment and stared at her friend. "Tonya, I don't know what sort of personal crisis you're having right now, but your hair is beautiful and I will not be the one to introduce you to the creamy crack. End of story."

Tonya sat back in her seat. "You're right. What am I thinking? I've never done crack a day in my life. I guess I just got caught up in some my-man-just-won-the-championship-hype. I love my hair, and it's just one night, right?"

Bella breathed a sigh of relief. "That's right. One night."

"And the beauty of having natural hair is that you can wear it straight, curly, or kinky. You think I should at least flat iron it for the occasion?"

Bella reached across the table and lifted a handful of Tonya's long, thick marshmallow-soft tresses. "Actually, I have an even better idea."

CHAPTER 8

Tonya sat at the vanity table in her bedroom while Bella stood over her applying a coat of make-up to Tonya's face.

"What's college like?"

Tonya shrugged. "It's what you make it. Mostly it's about finding yourself."

"Look up towards the ceiling for me," Bella commanded. She expertly applied the mascara to Tonya's eyelashes.

"Why, you thinking about going?"

"Josh wants me to go."

"What do you want?"

Bella shrugged. "For him not to be ashamed, I guess."

Tonya frowned. "Joshua?"

Bella nodded. "Purse your lips together like this. He's not just a jock. He has a degree." Bella expertly applied the lip color to Tonya's mouth. "He reads, and let's not forget I married a brother who rides horses. When you get past the whole Bad Boy persona, there's a whole lot more to him than what meets the eye. His wife, on the other hand, barely graduated from high school."

"Okay, I'm a stop you right there because I see where this is going and I'm not sure I like it."

"Hold your head still."

"Joshua is not ashamed of you, Bella. Go to college because you want to. Don't try to go so you can measure up. Or make Josh happy. Go for you. Joshua just wants you to be happy. Happy people tend to be people with meaning and focus in their lives. So the question you should really be asking yourself is: What is it that I've always wanted to do?"

Bella handed Tonya a folded piece of tissue. "Press lightly between your lips."

"What about your side gig you were telling me about a few weeks ago?"

Bella laughed a humorless laugh. "I certainly don't want to be doing that for the rest of my life. What about you? Joshua said that after graduation you plan on going to graduate school?"

"Eventually . . . I mean he's right. That is the plan. It's always been my dream to become a child psychologist. But I'd like to spend some time overseas doing mission work first."

"How much time?"

"A year, maybe two. Depends on the program."

"What does Mike think?"

"He doesn't know. I haven't figured it out completely yet, so please don't say anything about this to Joshua."

Bella shrugged. "Your secret's safe with me. But Tonya, you do know that Mike wants to marry you. You not playing him, are you?"

Sudden tears filled Tonya's eyes.

Bella quickly grabbed a box of tissue.

"Sorry, you worked so hard on my face," Tonya murmured.

"We can fix it. Just dab, don't wipe."

"Bella, I have loved Michael my entire life. He's the only man I've ever been with, and if I have my way, he'll be my one and only. But it's not just up to me."

"Who else is it up to?"

"God. I've prayed about this. God told me that the man I marry will be His minister. I want that man to be Michael. I believe with all my heart that it is. But I cannot marry him, not until he answers the call. I'm sorry, Bella. I hope I didn't just make things really weird between us. Michael hates when I talk about God like that."

"Like what?"

"Like He's here with us. Like He's a person."

Bella raised an eyebrow. "Really? Cause he's gotta be used to it by now. His brother does it all the time." She handed Tonya another tissue. "You didn't make anything weird between us, Tonya. There once was a time . . . well let's just say, I wasn't always wicked."

Tonya's eyes met Bella's in the mirror. "Don't ever speak that way about yourself. Not in or out of my presence."

Bella shrugged. "Why not? It's true."

"It's not true."

"How would you know?"

"I know because I see God in you."

CHAPTER 9

Remind me again whose idea was it that we wear the monkey suits?" Mike walked along the cobblestone path that led from his home to Tonya's cottage with his father and brother following behind him. The three men looked quite dapper in their black tuxedos. Mike shot a look at his father over his shoulder.

"It's Tonya's idea, alright, so behave."

"Don't you worry about me, by the time we get there I'll be the perfect gentlemen. Just stand back and take notes."

❦ ❦

Bella looked warily into her mother-in-law's cornflower blue eyes. "Mel, please don't. I don't want to have to repair your make-up too."

"I promise I won't. I am just so proud of both my boys. I can't take credit for the amazing women that you turned out to be, but I am so proud anyways. My two boys and my two best girls; you both are simply breathtaking. I wish I could get my hair to stand up like that. Tonya, Bella, I don't know how my sons are going to be able to resist either one of you."

Bella grinned. "Well, that's the point."

❦ ❦

"You mean to tell me you own the place and you're ringing the doorbell. Don't you have a key?"

"For emergencies, yeah. But I don't just go barging into her space," Mike explained.

"You're whipped, you know that?" Jack said.

Joshua snickered under his breath.

"Shut up, old man." Mike looked at his brother. "You too."

"Man, I didn't say a word," Joshua said.

"Well, ring it again. For Pete's sake, you're gonna be late to your own party," Jack said.

Mike kissed Melissa on the cheek when she opened the door. "Mom, you look good."

Melissa's hand fluttered unconsciously to the strand of pearls around her neck. "Thank you, honey."

Joshua kissed her other cheek. "Yeah, Mom, you look great."

Jack surveyed his wife with hungry eyes. "These two idiots must be blind, sweetheart. From where I'm standing, good and great don't cut it. You look amazing."

A deep blush spread across Melissa's face. "Thank you, Jack."

"Mom, where's Tonya? Dad's right, we gon be late to our own party."

"She'll be out in a minute, Mikey. You boys come in and take a seat in the living room. Trust me, it'll be worth the wait."

When Tonya and Bella walked into the living room, Joshua was the first to stand from his position on the couch. First his eyes took in Tonya, who was wearing a flowing silver gown that perfectly complimented her deep mocha toned skin and called attention to every one of her usually hidden curves. Her hair had been braided into an intricate crown in the front, with a waterfall of spiral curls flowing down her back.

Next, Joshua took in Bella. Her long spiral curls hung wild and free just the way he liked, and she was wearing an incredibly sexy turquoise, flair leg pantsuit.

"Well, what do you think, Joshie?" Melissa asked.

"Wow, I think you both look…wow." Joshua's eyes settled on Bella, who turned around slowly, pulling her loose hair around to the front of her neck so he could get an unobstructed view of her honey colored skin. Joshua motioned for her to come. Bella walked into his arms and Joshua kissed her like no one else was in the room.

Melissa beamed. "Joshie's speechless."

Jack stood up next. He kissed first Melissa's hand, then Tonya's. "I'd like to kiss my daughter-in-law's hand too, but I guess I'll have to wait until my son stops mauling her." Joshua waved him away and both Tonya and Melissa laughed.

"I want you ladies to know that we have the privilege of escorting the most beautiful women in the world," Jack said.

"Thank you," Tonya said.

Mike stood leaning against the doorpost, his face an unreadable mask.

"Mikey, don't leave us in the dark, honey, tell us what you think," Melissa gushed. "Doesn't Tonya look amazing?"

"I'm really not sure what to think right now, Mom. This is all so complicated."

Joshua released Bella and stared at his brother.

Tonya lowered her head. "Complicated…wasn't exactly the reaction I was going for." She studied her feet and willed herself not to cry. Mike crossed the room and stood directly in front of her. He lifted her chin with two gentle fingers.

"Yes, complicated. You are far too lovely tonight and I'm the only man here not married."

CHAPTER 10

Mike held up a crystal wine goblet filled with champagne. "I'd like to make this next toast to my brother Bad Boy Joshua Keys, the New Orleans Hornets MVP!" Hornet ball players all over the room began to hoot with excitement. "For his first year in the NBA and for holding it down!" The room exploded in applause. "You deserve a ring, little brother, and you will see one. Just as long as you never have to play me to get it." The crowd broke into ruckus laughter and the two brothers embraced.

"Everybody enjoy the party, the music, the alcohol, and the food. *Mi casa es su casa* and all of that. You can dance with any girl up in here, except mine." Mike held his hand out to Tonya. "Come here, baby. Let all the fellas see you so don't nobody get hurt tonight." Tonya walked slowly onto the dance floor and joined Mike at the center. While she moved, the DJ began to play, "Isn't She Lovely."

Joshua nuzzled his face against Bella's cheek as they slow danced to Earth, Wind & Fire. "You know this outfit is making me crazy, right? I haven't been able to concentrate all night."

"What if I took it off? Just for a little while so you could clear your mind."

Joshua raised his eyebrow. "What, here?"

"Not down here, silly. We could sneak off somewhere."

Joshua kissed the tip of her nose. "I hate to bust your bubble, Bella, but you aren't really the sneaking off with type, baby. You're loud."

"We could go upstairs to our bedroom. I could bite a pillow or something."

Joshua glanced across the room at Mike who was slow dancing with Tonya. He shook his head. "Naw, if we both go up there at the same time, my brother will suspect something."

"Joshua, we're grown and Mike's grown. He knows what grown folks do."

"Yeah, and he ain't getting none either. I don't know if it was such a good idea putting Tonya in that dress."

"I think she looks ravishing."

"That's the problem." Joshua pulled Bella closer. "For real though, if I wasn't having sex, nobody under my roof would be having any either. You can believe that."

Bella stared up at him. "So you're saying we should respect Mike's house? That we shouldn't have sex while we're staying here this weekend?"

Joshua smirked. "Naw, girl. I'm saying you go up first and I'll meet you up there in ten minutes."

⁂

Bella smiled when she heard the soft click of the bedroom door. "That was quick. I'm glad you're here, my zipper's stuck."

"Yeah, you know what's up, don't you?"

Bella whipped around to see Brady. "Get out!"

"Stop playing. You knew it was me."

Bella's eyes darted nervously to the door. "Joshua will be here any moment. Leave."

"I ain't scared of your husband."

"Then you really are crazy, because if he finds you here, he will kill you."

"There you go with the empty threats. First you were gonna cut me. Now your man is gonna kill me. Which is it?" He grabbed her and slammed her up against the wall.

"Let go of me!"

"I ain't going nowhere! He said ten minutes. I heard him. That gives you just enough time to work my magic stick."

Bella kneed him in the groin. Brady backhanded her and threw her down on the bed. Bella struggled to get up, but Brady was on top of her, straddling her and using his full body weight to pin her to the mattress.

Bella screamed. Brady covered her mouth with one hand and unzipped his pants with the other. "$20,000 for one time. Ain't nobody worth that. You gonna earn my money today."

The door to the bedroom flew open. A massive hand reached down and grabbed Brady by the neck then flung him up against the wall like a rag doll.

Bella flew into Mike's arms. Mike pulled Bella close. "You alright? Did he hurt you? Did he—"

"No. Thank God, no!" Bella buried her head into his chest. Oh God, Mike. I thought you were Joshua. I thought… oh God."

"Yo, Mike, man. Rosemary and I just had a little unfinished business."

Mike released Bella and stalked towards Brady who was attempting to orientate himself and raise his body off the floor. "Who the hell is Rosemary?!" Mike bellowed.

Tears pooled in Bella's eyes. "Mike, please. He's drunk. He wandered in here by mistake. He's not worth the trouble."

"Get downstairs, now!"

The thunder in his voice made Bella recoil, but she remained frozen, glued to her spot.

Mike blew out a deep breath and ran one large hand over his face. When he removed it, his deep chocolate features were even, calm again. "I'm sorry. Sorry." He opened his arms wide to Bella. "Come here." Bella walked obediently into his arms. "This is not your fault. You hear me? None of this is your fault. I had no right to speak to you that way. No man ever has the right to talk to you like he's lost his mind or to put his hands on you like he's crazy. You feel me?"

Bella nodded. Mike kissed the top of her hair.

"Now, I want you to go downstairs and find Josh. Go dance with your husband."

"Please, Mike, come with me," Bella managed to squeak out. "I don't want you to get into trouble. I don't want you to go to jail."

Mike's dark, handsome face transformed into a pleasant grin. He watched his smile have the intended effect on her, which was to melt away any remaining tension.

"This is a victory party, baby, nobody's going to jail. Look, here's what happened, alright? My teammate got full. He mistook you for some other girl and he stepped to you wrong. It was a mistake. Things almost got out of hand, but I handled it. Alright?"

Bella breathed a deep sigh of relief. "Yeah, that's exactly right."

"Good, because that's exactly what you need to tell Joshua if he ever gets wind of any of this right here. Because Bella, if you don't say it exactly the way I'm telling you to say it, my brother will kill this low life piece of garbage and he will go to prison. Not jail. You feel me?"

Bella shook her head vigorously.

"In the meantime, I'mma deal with Brady, because mistaken identity or not, I can't let something like this slide. I gotta tighten him up. Now go. Find Josh before he comes looking for you."

Bella turned and ran out of the room.

CHAPTER 11

Joshua sat at the bar with his father. When Jack wasn't looking, Joshua caught the attention of the bartender and made the cut off sign as he pointed to Jack's glass.

"It's been great talking to you, old man, but I need to go find my wife and you need to sober up before your wife finds you," Joshua said, slapping Jack on the back.

Jack scanned the room looking for signs of Melissa. "You think I'm scared of your mother? I wear the pants in my relationship, Joshie. I'm not whipped like your brother and you."

"Yeah, alright. Now I know you're drunk." Joshua raised his arm and caught the bartender's attention again. "Get my dad a cup of coffee, please."

"I don't want coffee," Jack insisted.

"Coffee," Joshua told the bartender again firmly. "Put it in a glass so he can look hard."

The bartender smiled and slid the glass in front of Jack.

Jack took a swallow of the coffee and made a face. "This tastes about as bad as what you are drinking," he said, pointing to the ginger ale Joshua was sipping on.

"Yeah, but you'll have your wits about you in case something foul pops off and you still look hard."

Jack laughed and raised his glass in salute to his son. "I still look hard!"

One of Joshua's teammates approached the two men. "Yo, Bad Boy, I hate to interrupt a father and son moment, but Brady is upstairs getting a serious beat down."

"Good," Jack said, lifting his glass in salute to the ball player. "I never liked that Brady. I don't trust him. And don't think I didn't see him clip you out there on the court, Joshie. I thought it was real classy of you, showing respect for your brother and all, by not beating the crap out of his teammate."

Joshua shrugged. "You know how we do. Family first, right?" Joshua looked at his teammate. "Man, I know y'all ain't up there tearing up my brother's house over no beef that happened on the court."

"Dog, you ain't listening. The Man of Steel is upstairs breaking up his own stuff. He is beating the hell out of Brady. It's about six dudes from his squad and they can't keep him off em."

"Aw, crap!" Jack said. He and Joshua took off running towards the stairs.

CHAPTER 12

Y ou assaulted a female in my house!"

"You broke my nose, Mike! As far as I'm concerned, we're even." Brady pulled a handkerchief out his tuxedo pocket and attempted to mop up the flowing blood.

Mike lunged at the man again. "I'mma break your teeth in a minute!" Two of his teammates held Mike firmly by the arms. Two more gripped his torso. Another two clung to each of his legs.

"Come on, Mike, this ain't you and this fool ain't worth it," Deon said.

"I guess you happy now, huh?" Brady shouted.

"Somebody go get Bad Boy, and can somebody get Brady out of here?" Deon shouted.

Another Rocket ballplayer ran into the room. "Hey, D, we got a situation downstairs."

"We got 'em, D," called one of the men holding back Mike's arm. "Whatever it is, man. Just go handle it."

Deon released his grip on Mike's shoulder. He stepped outside of the room and closed the door behind him. Deon pointed his finger in the young man's face. "I put you in charge of crowd control, Rook. You told me you could handle it."

"I know and I can! I mean, I am!"

Deon blew out and exasperated breath. "Then what is the problem, Rookie?"

"Mike's woman is downstairs. She is insisting that we step out of the way and let her through. I'm thinking maybe we should. Maybe she can calm him down. I mean, can't nobody else do it."

"That's your problem right there."

The younger man looked confused. "What?"

Deon touched his finger to the man's temple. "Thinking. You don't get paid to think. You get paid to keep the bench warm while we go out there and make it happen on the court."

"Does that mean you don't want me to let her through?"

"Hell naw, don't let her through. You tell her that the Man of Steel is in a team meeting right now and that he'll come find her when he's through."

𝓡 𝓡

"Four years, Mike! And you play me like this? I've been a brother to you, man! You gonna treat me like this over some skirt?"

Mike barreled through the men holding him back. He grabbed Brady by the neck and slammed him down hard onto the floor.

"She's my brother's wife," Mike growled.

Jack ran into the room out of breath. He leaned up against the doorway to steady himself. "Mikey, let him go!"

Joshua was in the room next, pushing his way past the senior members of the Houston Rockets basketball team. He jumped directly into the fray. Joshua grabbed Mike from behind, using his powerful forearm to encircle his brother's neck.

"Come on, Mike. Let him up. You gon kill him, bro. Let him up."

At the sound of Joshua's voice, Mike immediately came to himself and released Brady. He stood up slowly, straightened his tux, and surveyed the damage to the bedroom. He took in the broken lamps, the toppled vases and flower petals strewn all over the floor, and the floor length mirror shattered into large, jagged pieces around the room. "Tonya," he muttered. Mike looked down at Brady, coughing and bleeding on top of a bed of glass on the floor. "We ain't

38

never been brothers, Brady. Now we ain't teammates either."
Mike locked eyes with his dad and then each one of his
teammates before he turned and headed out the door. He laid
his hand on Joshua's shoulder as he passed by him. "You and
Bella take one of the other rooms down the hall."

CHAPTER 13

Tonya sat perched on Mike's lap. Mike laced his fingers through her hand and nuzzled his face against her neck.

"You know what I want?

"What's that?" Mike murmured.

"I want to know what could be so important that you guys decided to have a team meeting in the middle of your victory party."

Mike ran his finger along the contour of her face. "Did I tell you how devastatingly beautiful you look tonight?"

"Yes. You've been using words like 'devastating,' 'complicated,' and 'excruciatingly painful' to describe me all night. Frankly, I'm starting to get a complex."

"I never said excruciating."

"You're avoiding my question."

"A minor problem with Brady. It's cool, we handled it."

Tonya's eyes lit up. "That's his name: Brady! Bella and I saw him while we were out shopping a few weeks ago. I couldn't think of his name if I had to save my life."

"Where'd you see Brady?"

"At a woman's boutique downtown."

Mike stood up abruptly, causing Tonya to have to stand too. "Is this fool following you?"

"Michael, no! I don't know why he was there. Bella and I were trying on dresses. We heard the shop bell ring and I happen to look up and see Brady leaving the store. Why would you think he was following me?"

Mike reached over and curled a tendril of her hair around his finger. "Were you trying on this dress?"

"Yes."

"So, Brady got to see you in all of this before me?"

Tonya stared at him.

Mike pointed his finger at her. "Don't look at me like that. You changed the rules the moment you put on that dress."

"There is nothing inappropriate about this dress and you know it. It's not too tight, you can't see through it, and I know it's not too short because the dang dress goes all the way to the floor."

"It's sexy, Tonya, and that's not you."

"Oh, so I'm not sexy. Well that's very good to know."

Mike groaned. "Blackbird, listen, you do demure. You do whimsical and colorful, quirky even, but not hot as hellfire. I can handle whimsy, alright? Whimsical on you is sexy to me. But I can't think straight around you when you look like this. I'm having a hard time respecting your boundaries, Tonya. It's taken every ounce of willpower in me not to take you up those stairs and make love to you. And I know if I'm having a hard time with this, so is every other brother up in here tonight. And the thought of that right there, is making me crazy."

"I don't know who this crazed maniac is that's standing before me right now, but can you send him away so I can have my boo back? Please?"

Mike stared at her with a frown.

"My man is always calm, you know. Never shaken. He's always poised, even under pressure."

Mike stroked his thumb against his chin. "What else?"

Tonya smiled. "He's handsome, dashing, confident, and excruciatingly beautiful, both inside and out."

"Is he complicated?"

Tonya threw her head back and laughed, "Baby, my man put the 'c' in complicated. But he's not easily intimidated.

Never has been, never will be. Not by anything or anybody. Not by a hot little dress, and certainly not by some fish-eyed ballplayer that plays back up to him on the court every night. And you know why?"

"Why?"

"Because he's smarter than that. He can read me like an open book. He sees what everybody else can clearly see: I only have eyes for him."

֎ ֎

Deon found Mike later on that evening at the bar. Mike held his fist out to Deon for a fist bump.

"We cool, Chief?"

Deon pressed his fist against Mike's. "Always, man. I'm just sorry you had to find out like this. But if anybody was gonna walk in on them, I'd much rather it be you than Bad Boy."

Mike studied the dark, amber liquid in his glass. He drank it down and then motioned for the bartender to pour him another one. "What we talking about here, D? We obviously ain't talking about the same thing. Cause see, I thought we were having a conversation about Brady's random womanizing ways. But it sounds like to me you saying something else. So why don't you fill me in on the parts I don't know." Mike stared at his teammate coldly.

Deon closed his eyes and muttered a curse. "Your sister-in-law runs an escort service. It's supposedly real high-end and exclusive. She's been hooking up with players from all across the league. From what I'm hearing, she's real expensive, real professional, and real careful."

Mike smirked at Deon.

Deon threw his hands up in surrender. "I'm just telling you like I heard it, man. She makes them submit medical records, drug tests, sign a contract, all of that, and she make sure they wrap their junk tight. And no matter what, she

42

don't mess with nobody twice. Now that I think about it, that could have been what set that obsessive fool Brady off in the first place. I got wind of this stuff between Bella and Brady about a month ago. I told that fool not to get involved. This was too close to home. But I guess he didn't listen." Deon laid his hand on Mike's shoulder. "Mike, I'm sorry."

Mike snatched his arm away. "You sorry? You knew about this. Knew she was playing my brother and you didn't tell me?"

Mike downed his drink in one swallow. He signaled for the bartender, who reached for his glass. Mike waved him away. "Just leave the whole bottle, man."

Deon waited for the bartender to walk away. "Before Brady it was just hearsay. You feel me? I didn't have any proof. Mike, think, because unlike the Rook over there, they actually pay you to think." Deon pointed to the new recruit who was on the dance floor surrounded by a group of women.

"If I would have brought some ill info to you about one of your family members, without proper proof, what would you have done?"

Mike lifted the glass to his lips. "Based on GP alone I would've had to tighten you up."

"Come on, man, this is me. I would never hurt you or your fam. You know that. So you tell me, how in the world was I supposed to tell somebody I love some crazy stuff like this?"

"You be a man about it, D, and you get lit!" Mike held the bottle of top shelf Remy up in the air. "That's what I'm gon do, 'cause I don't have your luxury. I gotta tell my brother."

Mike took the microphone from the DJ and walked out onto the makeshift dance floor. "Y'all havin' a good time tonight?" The audience released a hearty applause.

"Good. Good. I had them turn down the music because I have something very important to say tonight and I want to make sure that everybody I care about is in this room to share this special moment with me. Where's Tonya? Where's my brother? Yo, Josh, where you at?"

Deon quickly excused himself from his date and made his way through the crowded dance floor to Mike's side. He motioned to the DJ to cut the mic off.

"What up, D?" Mike said.

"You are, man. You high as a kite. I know what you bout to do. Mike, trust me. You don't want to do this here; not now, not like this."

"Man you don't know what you talkin bout. I'm the Man of Steel, baby, I got this. Back up." Mike tapped his palm against the microphone. When no sound came out he looked over at the DJ. "Turn it up. Yo, Josh where you at?" Mike said speaking into the squealing microphone.

Joshua, Bella, Tonya, Melissa, and Jack all made their way through the crowded dance floor. Suddenly Joshua was beside his brother, placing his arm around Mike's neck. "I'm right here, bro. We gon keep it breezy for the rest of the evening. Alright? So you just tell me what you need me to do to make that happen."

"I just need you to be here when I pop the question to Tonya."

Deon shook his head. "Aw, naw."

Joshua pressed his forehead against his brother's. "Mike, man, this is Tonya we talking about. This ain't no chicken head, bro. This is the girl of your dreams. Do you really want to propose to her while you're lit up?"

Mike looked at Joshua earnestly. "You think I'm lit?"

Joshua nodded. "Yeah, you tore up, man."

"In that case, you probably right. I should just go chill out somewhere."

Joshua chuckled and slapped Mike on the back as he walked off the floor. "Yeah, man, you do that."

Deon looked at Joshua and shook his head. "This you being the level-headed one and him being the hothead is messing with my mind. I need a drink."

❧ ❧

"Testing, testing one, two, three," Mike spoke into the mic. "Can y'all hear me out there?"

The crowd cried back, "Yeah!"

"I want to ask the most beautiful girl in the world to join me out here on the floor. Tonya, come to me, baby."

Tonya walked out onto the floor and stood next to Mike. As she moved across the floor, the DJ began playing Stevie Wonder's "Isn't She Lovely." The music stopped in a flourish when Tonya was standing by Mike's side.

Mike pointed to the DJ. "I like you, man. That's the second time you did that tonight and I like your style. That was tight, almost like we scripted it. But we didn't. You and I were just there."

The crowd roared with laughter. The DJ gave Mike a thumbs up.

"If this works, I'mma triple your salary. See my brother after the party, we gon hook you up, man. I want to tell y'all about this woman standing in front of me. I love her so much."

"Michael, you've been drinking; you've had a little too much fun for one night. I think you need to go sleep this off," Tonya said quietly.

"That's what you think I been doing? Having fun? I ain't been having fun, baby. This is the worst night of my life. Well, not the worst, it's probably a close second to my mama selling me to an undercover cop for drugs. I shouldn't be doing any of this. And I shouldn't be trying to propose to you right now, but I'm doing it anyway. Because somebody told me something tonight that was so incredibly f— up."

Tonya cringed and Melissa turned ghostly white.

Mike didn't catch the word until it was out his mouth. He turned around and looked at Joshua. "Josh, did I just say 'f—' in the middle of my proposal?"

"Yeah, bro, I'm afraid you did."

"Sorry, Tonya. Tonya's a holy roller, y'all. She don't like it when I cuss. Come to think of it, my mom don't like it too much either. Sorry, Mom. My mom and dad are here. They drove down from Dallas to celebrate with me tonight. The two white people over there in the back. By the way, she's not the one who sold me for drugs. My black mother did that."

Jack walked over and stood beside Joshua. "Why in the devil's name didn't you talk him out of this? Can't you see that this is going to end badly?"

"He's drunk, Dad. He's not exactly listening to reason right now."

"Well, are you gonna do something about it or not?"

"What do you want me to do? He in it now. No use in hating, might as well get behind him and support him."

"Support him? Don't hate on him? You sound as crazy as he does right now. That's not just my son up there, Joshie. That's my best friend's daughter up there too. That girl has loved him her entire life and she doesn't deserve this."

"He loves her too, alright? Don't count him out yet. That's the Man of Steel up there. He's been making lemonade out of lemons his whole life. He can still turn this around."

"Four hundred bucks says she turns him down flat," Jack said.

"You're on."

"Can y'all just give her a hand for being so beautiful? Isn't she beautiful? Give her a hand," Mike said.

The room exploded in applause for Tonya. Joshua put his fingers in his mouth and whistled loudly.

"She likes to tell people she fell in love with me first. But I have loved this pretty little Blackbird from the first moment I laid eyes on her."

Joshua grinned at his dad. "I told you, baby. That's the Man of Steel right there."

"I love this woman so much I paid her twenty thousand dollars to decorate this house for me."

Jack chuckled. "Not so smooth."

"Tonya, what I was trying to say a few minutes ago is that somebody told me something tonight that has totally shattered my faith in people and in love. I need you to help me believe again."

Mike got down on bended knee. All the women in the room released an audible gasp. He pulled a three-carat princess cut diamond from his pocket. "This ring is the first thing I bought with my signing bonus. I've been waiting for three years for the right moment to ask you. For a space in time when heaven would crack open and smile down on me. And you would agree to be my bride. Tonya, will you marry me?"

Tonya cupped his face in both her hands and leaned in and kissed him softly on the lips. "Baby, get up, please. Let's talk about this privately when all these people leave, okay? Please?" she whispered.

"No. I need you to say that you'll marry me. Right here and now."

"Michael, you're drunk."

"Yeah, Tonya, I know! I know I'm drunk, alright! Make a believer out of me. Say yes."

"I won't say yes to you like this!"

Tonya darted from the room and Bella ran after her.

Mike lifted himself off the floor. He stumbled, but his teammates were next to him in an instant, helping to steady him. He started out the door after Tonya.

Deon clapped Joshua on the shoulder as he walked by. "We got him."

"Man of Steel, my eye, pay up."

Joshua took a money clip out of his pocket and handed four crisp $100 bills to his dad.

"What the hell was that?"

The two men looked up to see a red-faced, angry Melissa standing in front of them.

"Mel, baby, calm down. Joshie and I are just horsing around."

"You think this is funny? Your brother, your son, just experienced the most devastating night of his life and the two of you are over here making jokes. Jack, I am ashamed of you. Joshie, I am ashamed for you. Jack, I expected you to be completely useless in this situation. But Joshua, I expected you to make this right."

"Mel, be reasonable. He can't make the girl marry the man. And what do you mean I'm completely useless?"

"Jack, please!" Melissa locked eyes with Joshua. "Michael has spent his whole life cleaning up after you. It's high time you figured out how to return the favor."

Joshua stared into Melissa's blue, but rather grey looking at the moment, eyes. He offered her his handkerchief from his inside breast pocket.

Melissa hesitated for a moment than took it.

"I apologize. The bet was crude and in bad taste." Joshua said.

"If it makes any difference, honey, Joshie had his money on Mikey."

"Dad, don't help me right now. Alright?"

"Fine." Jack dug his hands into his pants pockets and walked away.

"You're right, Mike has always been there to clean up after me. It's high time I returned the favor."

Melissa grabbed her son and hugged him tightly around the neck. "I should go find Tonya and check on her but these people need to be dispersed and the staff needs to be paid."

"Go look after Tonya. I'll handle everything here."

Melissa kissed Joshua's cheek and walked off.

Joshua turned around to see the DJ waiting to talk to him. He handed Joshua his bill. Joshua looked over the bill. "Six thousand dollars for a proposal accompaniment?"

"Yes, your brother said he would triple my salary."

Joshua shoved the bill back into the DJ's hand. "Man, if you wanna get paid, you better tear that up and come correct."

"But your brother said—"

"My brother was drunk and the girl said no."

CHAPTER 15

Mike didn't come downstairs the next day until three o'clock in the afternoon. Joshua was leaning up against the kitchen sink eating a bowl of cereal when Mike walked into the kitchen.

"You hungry?"

"What we got?"

Joshua pushed the box of cereal across the counter and held up the near empty carton of milk. "You gonna have to mix it with water, though, this is the last of the milk."

Mike peered into the refrigerator. "Dang, man, ain't no food left from last night?"

"Free food, free booze, about a hundred ballplayers up in this joint. What you think?"

Mike poured himself a bowl of cereal and sat down at the table while Joshua filled him in on the details he missed the night before.

"Thanks for taking care of that room situation. Tonya worked really hard on that. I would hate for her to think her efforts were in vain."

"Don't mention it."

"Who still needs to be paid?"

"Everybody's been taken care of. You might have to kick in for some of Brady's medical expenses, though. He was pretty banged up when he left here last night. You wanna tell me what you two were beefing about?"

Mike locked eyes with Joshua.

Joshua nodded. "Alright, I'mma let it ride for now."

"Where is everybody?" Mike asked.

"Mom and Dad left this morning and Bella got on the road about an hour ago."

"Tonya at the cottage?"

"I drove her back to campus last night."

Mike stood and dropped the empty cereal bowl and spoon in the sink. "If everybody's gone, Josh. Why you still here?"

"You're my brother, man. Where else would I be?"

CHAPTER 16

Joshua sat outside on the upstairs balcony of his brother's home talking on the phone to Bella.

"Sleeping Beauty awake yet?"

"Yeah, bout an hour after you left."

"How did he take hearing that Tonya had moved out?"

"Cracked into a million little pieces."

"Really?" Bella whispered softly.

"Naw, baby, I wish. Mike's more likely to implode than he is to explode. The thing with Brady last night was a complete fluke."

"When are you coming home?"

"In a few days. I'mma give my brother some time to talk."

"Don't stay away from me too long, Joshua Keys. I don't sleep so well without you."

CHAPTER 17

Joshua felt around for the ringing phone by the side of the bed.

"Hello?"

"Did you see the papers this morning?"

"No, Dad, I'm still sleeping."

"Well, Brady's been traded."

Joshua sat up in bed. "According to who?"

"*The Times, The Post,* and *The Daily. The Times* says he and your brother fought over a girl. *The Post* claims irreconcilable differences. You can't believe any of them, they're all a pack of liars. But it doesn't take a rocket scientist to see that your brother is definitely behind this. I thought you were out there trying to get a handle on this thing?"

"Let me call you back."

CHAPTER 18

When Joshua walked into his manager's twelfth floor office, the receptionist rose immediately to greet him.

Her hand fluttered self-consciously to her hair. "Bad Boy, we weren't expecting you this morning."

"I don't have an appointment. I was hoping Steve could make time to see me."

"He's in a meeting on the third floor, but if you'll have a seat, I'll page him for you. In the meantime, can I get you anything? Breakfast maybe? Water, juice, tea or anything else you might need?"

Joshua looked into the emerald green eyes of the salivating woman in front of him. "Naw, I'm good. Thanks."

Five minutes later, Steve Barnes appeared. Joshua rose from the chair and shook his hand.

"Joshua, good to see you."

"You got a minute to talk?"

"For you, anything." Steve held the door open to his office and allowed Joshua room to enter first. Joshua took a seat in front of the large oak desk.

"You don't look happy. I don't like it when my star clients don't look happy. What's going on?"

Joshua pulled a folded newspaper out his back pocket and threw it down onto Steve's desk. "You tell me. You couldn't give me a heads up about this?"

"I didn't broker this deal, Joshua. I swear. Mike went to management on his own. He didn't tell me, his agent, about it until after it was done. I'm guessing for the same reasons he didn't tell you."

"They just won the Championship. How could this happen?"

"Come on, Joshua. You know how these things work. He's the Man of Steel. Michael is the franchise. If he says he won't play with Brady, Brady's gone. It's as simple as that."

CHAPTER 19

Joshua returned to find Mike in his home gym shooting threes. A brief look of annoyance flashed across Mike's face when he saw his brother.

"If you want me gone, you can make that happen at any time, bro. All you gotta do is talk to me."

"You ain't bothering me none, Josh. I'm just trying to figure out why you're still here. Am I on suicide watch or something? You supposed to be my babysitter?"

"You need one?"

"Naw, I'm straight."

"Then why don't I believe you?"

Mike dribbled the ball then released it. *Swoosh!*

"Mike, what's up?"

Mike shot a three. Retrieved the ball. Then shot another one. *Swoosh!*

"Mike!"

He drove the ball hard to the net, Joshua leapt into the air and snatched the ball out the hoop. "Mike!"

"WHAT!"

"Talk to me!"

"What you wanna know, Josh?'

"When's the last time you spoke to Tonya?"

"The night of the party." Mike stuck his finger in Joshua's face. "The night you helped her move out. Next question."

"Did you call her?"

"Did I call her? What kind of question is that? Of course I called her! She ain't taking my calls, Josh!"

Joshua nodded. "I heard Brady got traded."

"That's not a question, that's a statement."

"Don't play me! You know what I'm asking you! What happened between you and Brady? If your teammate gets out of line, you tighten him up and you leave it at that. But this holding grudges and messing with people's careers, this ain't you, man."

"As usual, little brother, you don't know what you're talkin about. What happened between me and Brady, is some grown man business, son. So do me a favor *Bad Boy* and stay out of it." Mike thumped Joshua hard on the chest and walked away.

Joshua barreled his forearm into Mike's throat, slamming him against the wall,

"No! I know you! This is personal! You're acting like—" Joshua swore loudly. He released his brother and backed away.

"Like what? What am I acting like, Josh? You man enough to come at me like this, don't chump up now. Spit it out."

"You're acting like he slept with your woman!"

"Naw man, not my woman. Your wife."

CHAPTER 20
Houston, Texas, After Midnight

Mike pulled up in front of Tonya's apartment building and left his car running in the middle of the street. He took the stairs two at a time and pounded on the front door like a madman. Tonya came to the door wearing her bathrobe, with Nisha and her two other roommates following closely behind her. Nisha stood directly behind Tonya, gripping a baseball bat. Tonya turned the porch light on. She gasped when she saw the large purple bruise underneath Mike's left eye and waved her roommates away. "Go back to bed. I got this."

She opened the door and resisted the urge to fly into his arms. "What happened to you?"

"Josh and I had a fight."

She tried to draw him inside the apartment but he wouldn't bulge. "Michael, please come inside. You need ice."

"I don't need ice, alright? All I need is you. Tonya please. Baby, please. All I need is you."

Tonya looked at the car idling in the street, and back at the broken man standing in front of her on the porch. "Give me five minutes. I'll be right out."

CHAPTER 21

New Orleans, After Midnight

Bella opened the front door to find their home in shambles. Joshua was on his hands and knees feeling in between the sofa cushions for something. Bella's eyes scanned the apartment, doing a quick inventory of the damage. Every cabinet door stood open at attention with pots and cookware tossed haphazardly onto the granite countertops or hurled carelessly onto the floor. Even the freezer side of their subzero refrigerator had been left wide opened.

"Joshua, what—"

Joshua turned toward her, his eyes blazing with anger. That's when she saw the bruise on his face. Bella dropped her shopping bags in the doorway and ran over to him. She pulled his face between her hands, "Baby, what happened?"

Joshua pushed her away. "I got into a fight."

"With who?" Bella said, wondering who could have ever gotten close enough to strike his face.

"Mike."

"Your brother?"

Joshua tipped the sofa completely over onto its backside. He examined the base of a very expensive crystal lamp then sent it crashing to the floor.

"Let me get you some ice."

"No!"

"Okay," Bella said evenly. "Then why don't you calm down and tell me why you and Mike were fighting, and how this fight led to you destroying our home."

"How long, Bella?"

"How long what?"

"How long have you been cheating on me."
Bella swallowed hard. She stood there blinking rapidly, like a rabbit backed into a corner. Like the moment she had dreaded hadn't actually come.

Joshua held his arms out in question. "What? You gon tell me he's lying? You gon tell me that the one person who has always been there for me, is lying to me?"

When she refused to answer, Joshua moved into their bedroom with Bella following behind him at a safe distance. He ripped stuffing out of the pillows and flipped the mattress off the bed. When he made a move for her closet, she spoke. "I don't like people going through my things," she squeaked.

"And I don't like hearing that half the NBA has been inside my wife."

He ripped through her closet, pulling out clothes and shoes, until he found the thing he had been looking for: a small box in the far corner. When Joshua opened the box he found stacks of hundred dollar bills.

Joshua grasped the money in his fist and shook it in Bella's face. "Where did you get this?"

"It's mine."

"Where did you get it?"

"I earned it."

"HOW?"

Bella folded her arms across her chest and lifted her chin defiantly into the air.

Joshua turned away from her. He grabbed the money box and strolled out of the bedroom. Bella waited for a minute and when she realized he was not coming back, she ventured out of the bedroom. She found him in the kitchen. An angry red flame danced on top of the gas range as he dropped one hundred dollar bill after the next into the open flame.

A sob caught in Bella's throat. "You can't do that. That's mine. I worked really hard to get it."

"How did you earn it?" he asked, throwing more and more cash into the open flame.

"They pay me. All they want is sex. But I would never do it with anyone on your team."

Joshua froze. He stumbled backwards, literally knocked off balanced by her words. He backed into the subzero refrigerator and slid down to the floor.

"I never do it raw. They always wear condoms," she continued in a ragged voice. "Everybody I've ever been with has been tested."

Silence enveloped the kitchen for what seemed like an eternity. Then Joshua spoke.

"Did it ever occur to you that I could be traded? Or that one of those men you had sex with could be traded to my team. Are you trying to make me the laughing stock of the NBA?"

She looked at him earnestly, tears pooling inside her eyes. "No."

"Then what were you thinking? Did you even stop to think about what this would do to me? What it would do to us?"

"Baby, I swear, I...I never meant to hurt you. It didn't mean anything." She tried to go to him, hold him and be held like she had so many times before, but Joshua held out his arm to stop her. A clear warning for her not to come any closer.

"I just needed the money."

"For what?

Silence.

"What do you need that my money can't buy?"

Silence.

"What do you need, Bella Rose!"

"Just in case." She tried to back out of the kitchen, but Joshua was on his feet, grabbing her, pushing her hard up against the refrigerator. Caging her in-between his arms.

"In case what!"

"In case you leave! Or you put me out and I don't have no place to go!"

"Why would I do that? Why would you even think that?"

"Why wouldn't you?" Bella snatched violently away from Joshua, breaking through the cage that had been his arms and running into the living room.

"No. No. Tell me this isn't true. Tell me this is a bad dream, or a practical joke. Anything. But Bella, please don't tell me I married a whore."

Bella turned and faced him from her safe position in the living room. "I've been sleeping with men for money since I was fourteen years old."

Joshua's face turned beet red. He balled his hands into fist and walked towards her. When he got about two feet away, Joshua stopped dead in his tracks. Urine seeped from her body and splashed noisily onto the hardwood floor. Bella dropped to the floor and formed her body into a tight ball, as if to protect herself from any impending blows. All the anger seeped out of Joshua as he stood by helplessly watching. Bella squeezed her eyes shut and repeated the words to a simple child's prayer over and over again. "Now I lay me down to sleep. I pray the Lord my soul to keep. If I die before I wake. I pray the Lord my soul to take."

"My God. What happened to you?" Joshua asked.

Her father, that still, quiet voice said.

Joshua felt his mouth go dry, felt like the air had been knocked from his lungs. The still, quiet voice spoke again.

Her father did this.

That voice that had been directing him all his life. Speaking quietly into his ear, telling him, *"This is the way to go. This is the path to take. Not that one, take this one over here."* The voice had led him to Reverend LeBlanc's church over a year ago. Had told him that Reverend LeBlanc's beautiful daughter was to be his bride. Now this? No, there must be a mistake. He had misheard or misunderstood. Not the Reverend LeBlanc. Not the man who had become a spiritual father to him. The one who had identified the voice as God. That man couldn't hurt his own child, or any child.

"Bella," Joshua said, his voice hoarse with confusion. "I need you to come back to me and tell me who hurt you. Baby, please."

She rocked back and forth. Squeezing her eyes shut as if she was willing herself to disappear,

"Now I lay me down to sleep, I pray the Lord my soul to keep. Now I lay me down to sleep. I pray the Lord my soul to keep. Now I lay me— Now I lay me— Now I lay me."

Don't abandon her, Joshua; the sins of the father are being visited upon the child.

Something about Bella's rocking was familiar to him. It reminded him of a foster kid that the Kennedy's had taken in named Molly. Molly had been molested since the age of three by her father. When she was afraid, the little red-haired girl would go inside herself, just like, Bella, was doing right now. She'd sit in the corner and rock for hours at a time. Molly didn't pray, but she would repeat one simple phrase over and over again. Nothing could bring her out of those states. One day, Joshua watched this girl, who shared no history with him, but yet had become his sister, and he prayed three simple words. *Lord, release her.* And suddenly, she stopped. This is what he did for Bella right now. Joshua got down on his hands and knees and crawled on the floor over to her. He remembered his mother saying how unsafe it was for him or Mike to ever touch Molly when she was in one of her states. But Joshua grabbed hold of Bella anyway. Joshua buried his face into her hair. She smelled awful, a putrid combination of urine and fear, but even after all of this, he realized he still loved her. *Lord, please, release her from this agony.*

As he prayed, Joshua felt her body go limp. He crooned soft, gentle words into her ear until he felt the slowing of her heart rate. Finally, after some time, Bella's breathing returned to normal again.

"Sometimes if I prayed, he wouldn't touch me." Unbidden tears stung Joshua's eyes. He knew the truth, but he had to ask anyway.

"Who?" he whispered hoarsely. She shook her head and tried to push him away, but Joshua held on tighter. "Tell me who hurt you, baby."

"Why, so you can tell me it's not true? Take his side like my mama did when I told her? Go ahead, pick him over me!" Her fists flew wildly at him. Joshua didn't block any of her punches. He sat there quietly and took every blow. "Go ahead, call me a liar like my mama did! Say it!"

When her energy was spent, he grabbed her face, and looked directly into her eyes. "I already believe you. Okay? You can tell me the truth, because I already believe you."

"My daddy. I was eight years old when he started taking me into his church office."

Joshua closed his eyes and pulled her to his chest. He tried with all of his might to wrap her inside his love. "I swear before God, Bella Rose, he will never hurt you again."

❧ ❧

Joshua lifted Bella off the living room floor. He led her into the bathroom, peeled off her wet clothes, and gave her a bath. Later that night when Bella fell asleep on the bare mattress, Joshua got up and put in a call to his agent. "I want you to demand a trade." Steve Barnes sat up in bed and tried to wrap his mind around the words that were coming out of his client's mouth.

"Talk to me, Joshua. Where is this coming from?"

"I'm moving to Texas."

"Can I ask why?"

"No. It's personal."

"Joshua, you signed a contract, you can't—"

"That's not the answer I want to hear, Steve. I need you to make it rain."

Steve sighed. "I'll make some calls. The Rockets just lost their shooting guard, I'm sure they'll be thrilled to have you."

PRESENT, 2005

CHAPTER 22

Bella spent the afternoon watching Jabari model his new clothes. The tension between her and Joshua was thick enough to cut with a knife, yet somehow, Jabari remained blissfully ignorant of it. When the two of them had arrived home that afternoon, Joshua had taken one look at her, muttered something about needing to work out some more, then made a hasty escape to his home gym. But not before Jabari got him to grudgingly agree to a family movie night.

"Come on, Dad, please. It'll be just like old times."

The hard lines in Joshua's face softened as he gazed at his son. "Alright, champ, after dinner."

Bella cooked dinner, but when she sent word through Jabari saying that dinner was ready, Joshua sent word back telling them to eat without him. Later on that evening, when Bella popped popcorn and handed Joshua a bowl, he muttered a thank you but never ate so much as a single kernel.

This piece of rejection hurt the most. Cooking for him was the one thing Bella always seemed to be able to get right. Was she now so filthy that he couldn't eat from her hands?

Jabari sat between them during the movie marathon. He and Joshua laughed at all the funny parts, while Bella tuned out and contemplated her next move. One thing was for certain, she would not be married for much longer. Joshua's attitude towards her made that abundantly clear.

Jabari fell asleep midway through the third movie. Joshua clicked off the television, shaking Bella from her reverie.

"You take the master. I'll sleep in the guestroom tonight. We leave for my parent's house at ten tomorrow."

"Josh?"

"What?" His voice was annoyed, or resigned, or… she couldn't really tell what it was.

"Don't you think we should talk?"

"No." Joshua picked up Jabari, cradling him in his arms, the exact same way he had done when he was a little boy, and carried him up to his bedroom for the second night in a row.

Just 24 hours ago Joshua had carried her up those same stairs. Bella waited, giving Joshua enough time to settle in for the night. Then she made her slow ascent up the stairs alone.

CHAPTER 23

Mike and Marcus arrived at Joshua's house at 10 o'clock sharp. One look at Joshua's face told Mike that his brother's mood hadn't much improved from the previous day. "Y'all ready?" Mike asked.

"I'm ready," Jabari said cheerfully, dropping his overnight bag by the front door, next to his dad's.

"Where's Bella?" Mike asked.

"I thought you said your mama was ready?" Joshua said, avoiding his brother's eyes.

Jabari shrugged. "She is. Well, she said she was."

Bella appeared at the top of the stairs tussling with an oversized suitcase. The sight was so comical Mike couldn't help but smile.

"Uh, Mom, we're just going for the weekend. We're not moving in."

"I know. I just wanted to be prepared," Bella explained.

Mike looked at Joshua, "You gon help her with that?"

Joshua stared up at Bella but made no attempt to move towards her. Instead, he stuck his earbuds in his ears, hoisted his own bag onto his shoulder, and walked out the front door.

"Jabari, man, go help your mom," Mike said, staring after Joshua.

"I got it," Marcus said, climbing the steps two at a time. "Let me get that for you, Ms. Rose."

"Thank you, Marcus," Bella said. "That's very kind of you."

When they got outside, Joshua was sitting in the back seat, brooding. Marcus and Jabari climbed in beside him and Bella took her seat on the front passenger side.

Mike loaded Bella's bag into the back of his Land Cruiser and closed the trunk. He walked back around to the driver's side and opened the door. "This is gonna be a long ride," he muttered.

CHAPTER 24

Mike pulled onto their parent's property at three o'clock. As soon as the truck had turned onto the property, Melissa and Jack ran out to greet them. Jabari flew into his grandmother's arms.

"Oh my, look how you've grown!" Melissa exclaimed. "You can't imagine how long I've waited to do this," she said, squeezing Jabari tight. "And Bella," Melissa pulled her into a tight hug. "Look at you, you're as stunning as ever!"

Bella took in both of her in-laws. Melissa's blond hair was braided in a long, thick braid down her back. Jack's hair was almost completely white, but it made him look distinguished and not a day older. "Me? Look at you two. You haven't aged a bit. I'm so jealous!"

Jack set Jabari back down on the ground and held out his arms for Bella to walk into them, "Look, Bella, pants. Just for you!"

Mike and Joshua both found themselves chuckling, despite the day's tension in the car.

Melissa wasn't a short woman, not at 5'8" but she had to stand on her tiptoes as she kissed each of her boys, first Mike and then Joshua, on the cheek.

Joshua frowned when he saw tears in his mother's eyes. He wiped them away with his thumb. "Hey, cut that out. You know I don't like it when you do that."

"I know you don't, honey. I'm just so happy to have my whole family here at once," Melissa sniffed. "I'll try to stop."

"You must be, Marcus?" Jack said, shaking Marcus's hand vigorously.

"Yes, sir, I am."

"None of that 'sir' stuff, ya hear? Makes me feel old. Call me Jack."

"And I'm Melissa," Melissa added, taking both of Marcus's hands firmly in hers. "I can't thank you enough for saving my family," she said, her voice quivering again.

"While you're here, Marcus, my Mel's certainly gonna try," Jack said.

"That's right. I hope you didn't eat on the road? Mikey, you didn't stop, did you?"

"No, Mom, per your instructions we didn't stop. Thanks to you, everyone is hungry and mad."

"Well, I didn't want you boys to ruin your supper."

"Your mother put out a big spread," Jack said.

"Yes, everybody come on inside. Marcus, I hope you like rhubarb pie," Melissa said.

"Yes, ma'am, I like all pie," Marcus said.

Everyone laughed.

"Good, because I baked one in your honor," Melissa said, walking towards the main house.

Mike opened the trunk of the car, "Jabari, Marcus, come grab a couple of these bags before you go in."

"Leave them. Stu's here. He'll bring your things in," Melissa said.

A look of displeasure passed between Mike and Joshua.

"No thanks, I'll bring in my own things," Joshua said. "Bella?"

Bella's head snapped up when she heard Joshua addressing her for the first time. He was eyeing the expensive leather handbag on her arm. The one he had purchased for her in Italy, the summer he and Mike both had represented the US in the Olympics.

"Watch your purse."

Bella nodded to him and hoisted her handbag up on her shoulder.

Jack chuckled quietly under his breath.

"Hey you two," Melissa said, scolding both Jack and Joshua, "Not funny!" Melissa held the door open for Bella, Marcus, and Jabari to enter the house.

"Bella, please try to ignore them. Stu's in the kitchen, he'll show you and the boys to your seats."

"You're right, it's not funny," Mike said. "Neither is almost losing this ranch and your entire life savings on his little crooked investment scheme. I thought we agreed Stuart wasn't allowed back here anymore?"

"Honey, I know, but he showed up three days ago with nowhere else to go. What was I supposed to do? Cast him out into the street?" Both Mike and Joshua stared at her. The expressions on their faces clearly said, yes, that was exactly what she was supposed to do.

"He's been really repentant about the whole situation and he's so excited about seeing you boys again. He's been helping me in the kitchen all day. So do me a favor, all three of you," Melissa said, pointedly staring at her husband, "Be nice."

"What are you looking at me for? I've been here putting up with the little twat the whole time!" Jack said.

"Jack! How many times do I have to ask you not to speak that way in front of the children?" Melissa turned quickly on her heels and marched into the house.

"Aw, Mel darling, don't be mad," Jack spoke to her retreating back. When he was sure she was completely out of hearing range he added, "The children are grown men."

Joshua, Mike, and Jack broke into a fit of rowdy laughter.

CHAPTER 25

Joshua, Mike, and Jack, filed into the dining room. A grinning Stuart held his hand up in the air. "Hey, bros, what's up?"

Marcus and Jabari shook their heads in disgust while Bella closed her eyes, waiting for Joshua, who was already on the edge, to finally explode. Much to her surprise, both he and Mike filed past Stuart without a word.

"Don't be a jackass, Stuart. Sit down," Jack said.

"I'm sorry, was that offensive?" Stuart asked.

"Uh…yeah, dude, it was," Marcus said.

Stuart shrugged, nonchalantly. "I didn't mean 'bros' in a cultural sense. I meant bros because we grew up together."

"We didn't grow up together, Stuart," Mike said. "You stayed at our house for two weeks when your aunt put you out."

"Really? It seemed much longer than that," Stuart said.

"Yeah, for us too," Joshua said.

Melissa looked at Jack anxiously. "Jack, please bless the food." Jack exhaled deeply and bowed his head. His voice was a low rumble that rippled across the now completely silent table.

"Dear Lord, I ask for a blessing on this food and a blessing on my lovely wife who prepared it. Let it bring nourishment to our bodies. I ask for a special blessing on this gathering this weekend. Lord, you know all our hearts. Some of us are tired, and some of us are stupid. Be in our midst, and don't let anybody get hurt. Amen."

A dark smile crossed Joshua's lips briefly as he and the others around the table echoed an, "Amen."

"That was a lovely prayer, Jack, and very apropos," Melissa said as she began to pass platters of food around the table.

"Yep," Bella muttered.

Stuart tapped his silverware against his water glass. "I have something to add, well not add exactly, it's more like something I need to get off my chest." Stuart's eyes met Melissa's. "Mom, I was thinking this would be as good a time as any, if you don't mind."

"Go ahead, Stuart," Melissa encouraged.

Stuart's eyes skirted first to Joshua. When he saw absolutely no sign of encouragement there, his eyes quickly darted to Mike's, whose expression was unreadable. "Mike, I want to apologize to you and Joshua for that whole investment fiasco last year. I've apologized to both Mom and Dad—"

"You've apologized to Mel and Jack," Jack corrected.

Stuart's eyes flew to Jack. "What? Oh, yes, sorry, Jack." Stuart shifted his pleading gaze back to Mike. "Mike, I swear, I had no idea my partners were into anything illegal. I can't thank you enough for not pressing charges. I am forever in your debt. Please, please, please, accept my apology."

Everyone around the table seemed to be waiting on the edge of their seats for Mike's response. Only Joshua appeared relaxed.

"I'll accept your apology, Stuart. Once. But if anything else were to happen, anything that would even remotely remind me of that unfortunate event, if anything of my parents' were to come up missing while you're here, if my mom so much as misplaces—"

"A hairbrush," Joshua said, seamlessly completing his brother's thought.

Mike nodded. "Or an ink pen."

"A 20-cent plastic fork," Joshua added. Mike leaned in close and smiled a smile that didn't quite reach his eyes.

"You should remember that the statute of limitations isn't up, Stuart. If we have any problems out of you this weekend, I will personally make sure you are prosecuted to the fullest extent of the law. I hope I'm making myself perfectly clear."

"That's some real talk for you, *bro*," Joshua said, winking at Stuart. Stuart gulped hard and nodded. Bella, who hadn't realized she'd been holding her breath, breathed a sigh of relief.

Melissa smiled lovingly at her sons. "Well, I'd say that went as well as could be expected, don't you, Jack?"

Jack grunted in response and shoved a forkful of parsley potatoes into his mouth.

Melissa reached her hand across the table and patted Stuart's hand reassuringly. "Very brave, Stuart."

"Or suicidal," Jabari said.

Marcus snickered.

Bella flashed her son a chastising look. Lord knows he didn't need to give this situation anymore gas. "Mel, thank you so much for doing this for us. The table is so beautiful and the food is delicious," Bella gushed.

A chorus of thank yous and agreements went up from the table, mostly from Marcus and Jabari.

"Well, I didn't do it on my own. I had help," Melissa said. "Stuart did all the floral arrangements and he actually made those napkin rings."

Bella held the intricately designed silver ring up. "You made these? They're lovely."

"Stuart, Bella does jewelry also and she's very good at it."

"Thank you, Mel."

"Don't thank me, honey, it's true."

Stuart looked at Bella, his interest peaked. "Handmade?"

"Yes, nothing as elaborate as this. I've always wanted to try my hand at metalworking. Just never really had the time." *Or the money, for that matter.* Bella thought.

"Where can I see your work, do you showcase anywhere?"

"I had a cart on Bourbon Street in New Orleans. But Katrina came and I lost everything."

Joshua was staring at her. Bella could see him out of the corner of her eye. She had been extra careful to keep her voice neutral and airy, but even when no one else could see it, Joshua had always been a master at uncovering her pain.

Stuart smiled. "I just figured out a way to make restitution around here. I'm going to show you the metal making process while you're here."

Bella's breath almost caught in her throat. "Really?"

"I'd be glad to. In fact, there's a big jewelry makers convention in town this weekend. I'm going tomorrow and you're more than welcome to tag along. Josh, you can come too if you like."

Joshua grunted. "I'll pass."

Mike and Jack chuckled.

"Bella, this show is going to be incredible. You can get tons of ideas and some new tools to start again."

Bella looked over at Joshua, hopeful. "Josh, do you mind?"

Joshua shrugged, still refusing to meet her eyes. "Nope. Do you."

"Cool, artist day!" Stuart squealed, bouncing up and down in his seat. He held his hand up in the air and slapped Bella a high five. Bella pasted a weak grin on her face.

"When we get back, I'll give you your first metal working lesson in the barn."

Bella's voice rose an octave higher then she had intended. "The barn?"

"Well, the stable. It's really the best place to do this type of work. Why, is there a problem? You aren't allergic to hay or anything like that are you?" Stuart asked.

"My mom doesn't do horses," Jabari said.

"Really, never? You're so missing out. Horses are like . . . the most remarkable animals in the world. Joshua was quite the equestrian when we were kids."

"Joshie is excellent with horses. He's been riding bareback since he was how old, Jack?" Melissa asked.

"Three," Jack said.

"Wow," Marcus said, genuinely impressed.

"My dad and Uncle Mike are taking us out on the trails in the morning. That is, if you're not afraid," Jabari said.

"Me? Naw, I ain't scared, Shorty," Marcus said.

"I'm riding bareback. You game?" Jabari challenged. "I've never been on a horse before," Marcus explained. "It's not that I'm afraid it's just—"

"A moot discussion, because you'll both have saddles," Mike said firmly.

"Aw, Dad, can I?"

Joshua, clearly not paying attention looked at Jabari. "Can you what?"

"Ride bareback tomorrow?"

"No."

"But, Dad—"

"I said no, Jabari."

Jabari slouched down in his seat.

Joshua looked over at Mike. "Can you believe this kid?"

Mike shook his head. "I tried to tell him, man."

Joshua smiled at his dad. "What kind of unfit parent let's their kid do something like that?"

Jack grinned and raised his hand. "Me."

"See, Grandpa did," Jabari grumbled.

"Kids were a lot less breakable then," Jack said.

"Jabari, your uncle and I grew up with horses. By the time I was your age, I'd handled them every day of my life. When's the last time you even saw a horse?" Joshua asked.

"Last time I was with you, I guess but—"

"That's my point."

"But you promised," Jabari grumbled.

"I promised to take you riding, not get you killed." Joshua said, the finality in his voice clear. Jabari's face fell.

"Son, if riding bareback is a goal that you'd like to work up to, we can talk about how to achieve that goal safely. But for now, you gotta learn how to crawl before you can walk. I just got you back, Jabari. I'm not trying to lose you over no foolishness. You understand me?"

"Yes, sir."

"Good, so it's settled. The boys will have saddles and helmets tomorrow," Bella said anxiously.

Laughter erupted around the table.

Jabari groaned.

"Don't they get the little riding hats?" Bella said.

"That's English style, we ride western around these parts, darling," Jack said.

"You need a helmet to ride a bike. Why not a horse?" Bella said.

"She's got a point," Melissa said.

"No, there are no helmets in horse riding," Jabari moaned.

Mike chuckled. "Relax, little man. We won't play you to the left like that. They'll both be fine, Bella, I promise."

"Wow, this is interesting. Bella, you hate horses and Joshua loves them. I find that totally fascinating," Stuart said.

Bella forced a smile. She hated it when people did that. Made it seem like they were just so different from each other, that they just didn't make sense together.

"She's never stuffed a ball into a hoop for living either, Stuart. What's your point?" Joshua said.

Bella threw him a grateful glance.

"Oh, nothing, nothing. I'm just thinking about how the old saying is true, opposites do attract."

"For the record, I don't hate them, Stuart," Bella said. "I think they are wonderful, majestic creatures. I'm just mortally afraid of them."

"Well, I'm certainly not judging anybody. I know what it's like to be mortally afraid of something. Well, in my case, someone. My metalworking tools were the only thing I was able to flee with when I was running for my life."

Joshua's fork clattered to the table. "Someone is hunting you and you come here, to my parent's house?"

Stuart looked around the table dismayed. "Oh, I guess Mom didn't tell you?"

"No, *Mom* didn't. Enlighten me," Joshua said, a hard edge creeping into his voice.

"Stu, I didn't say a word, I figured that was your business to share or not," Melissa said.

Stuart sighed. "Well, I might as well get it out in the open. I'm a victim of spousal abuse."

Jabari slapped his hand to his forehead. "Oh, I knew it, you're gay. Right?"

Bella's face flushed in embarrassment.

"That would explain the flowers and the jewelry and stuff," Jabari said.

Mike, Jack, and Marcus tried unsuccessfully to choke back their laughter.

"Boys, behave," Melissa warned.

"Jabari, apologize," Bella said quietly.

"For what? All I did was ask a question."

Bella sighed in frustration. "Joshua, aren't you going to correct him?"

Joshua's eyes met Bella's directly for the first time. "It's a fair question. Besides, Stuart brought it up."

All the males at the table shifted their eyes to Stuart.

"Josh, is right, Bella, it is a fair question and a common misconception. I'm an artist, yes, but I'm totally straight. My wife beats me."

Mike laughed out loud. "With what?"

"Her fist," Stuart said coolly.

"The little redhead?"

"Janice," Melissa said.

"Beat him like he was Lionel Richie," Jack said.

"You gotta be kidding me, man. That girl can't be a hundred pounds soaking wet."

"That's the thing about spousal abuse, Mike, that no one seems to really get. There's a lot of emotional stuff that happens behind the scenes before the abuser ever throws the first punch," Stuart said.

"Well, we're all very glad you broke the cycle," Melissa said. She reached across the table and patted Stuart's hand. Joshua stood and threw his napkin down on his untouched plate.

"Joshie, you done already?" Melissa asked.

"Oh yeah, way done. I'm going to bed."

"Oh, honey, that reminds me, Stu's been bunking in your old room, so I have you and Bella set up in the guest room for the weekend. I hope you don't mind?"

Neither Melissa nor Jack missed the brief moment of hesitation that passed before Joshua said, "We'll make it work."

CHAPTER 26

Bella stayed up late into the night, catching up with Jack and Melissa and talking jewelry with Stuart. She had been watching Jack and Mike teach Jabari and Marcus how to play chess when she fell asleep on the living room couch. Melissa woke her when she announced that it was well after midnight and time for everyone to go to bed.

Truth be told, Bella had been ready to retire hours ago, but she had forced herself to stay up in the hopes that when she arrived back to their room, Joshua would already be in a deep sleep. Much to her dismay, Joshua was up and the shower was running in the adjoining bathroom.

Bella, who had been dead on her feet a few minutes ago, found herself suddenly awake. She busied herself, setting out her clothes for the next day and getting herself mentally prepared to face Joshua when he got out the shower. She had planned to take up residence on the sleek leather couch that flanked the wall in the guest room and give Joshua the bed, but the neatly made up couch with the pillows and the folded coverlet told her that Joshua had already determined their sleeping arrangements. Her things had been placed on top of the bed and his things sat on the floor next to the couch. Bella was considering this when she heard a gentle knock on the door and before she could say "come in," Stuart poked his head through the door.

"Is he asleep?" Stuart whispered

"No, Stuart, what can I do for you?" During her talks with Stuart that evening, it was easy for Bella to see why people disliked him. He pushed past boundaries that normal people respected. Not in an innovative, trendsetting sort of way, but in an, in-your-face-way-too-close-for-comfort kind of way. Like the annoying way he'd started calling her Bells. He was very knowledgeable about jewelry, she'd give him that much. But there was no way around it, the man was a pest with a capital P.

Bella understood why Joshua had escaped to the sanctuary of the guest room tonight. Because even if, as her friend Maggie had suggested, Joshua had "found religion" everything about Stuart would drive the most spiritual of persons— Gandhi even, to the dark side. Heck, Joshua could barely tolerate having her in his space tonight, the last thing he needed was to come out of the shower and find, of all people, Stuart. It was time to nip this in the bud, quick.

"Stuart, it's late and Joshua will be out any minute. Perhaps you didn't notice, but he wasn't in the most cordial of moods tonight. I don't think it would be a good idea if he found you in here."

To her horror, Stuart pushed the door open and walked all the way into the room.

"Did I notice? Bells, of course I noticed. I'm just glad he isn't sleeping. He was such a gloomy gus at dinner, I'd hate to see what happens if somebody disturbs his rest."

Stuart looked around the room curiously, taking in the whole space. His eyes settled on the made up couch, then flew back to Bella in alarm. "You guys aren't together? On YouTube it looked like you were together."

"We're fine, Stuart" Bella said quietly, her eyes darting quickly to the bathroom door.

"Then why is he sleeping on the couch?"

"Joshua's very tall. The two of us in a full sized bed, well, that wouldn't be very comfortable for either one of us," Bella said quickly.

"But I don't understand, after being separated from you for so long, doesn't he want to hold you, Bells? I mean if you were mine I would—"

"It's complicated, Stuart," Bella said icily. "And I really, really, don't want to talk about this with you. So what do you want?"

"I just stopped by to give you this brochure. I thought you could read up on the vendors, that way if there were booths that caught your eye we could make them a priority tomorrow." Stuart held the brochure out to Bella. Bella stood there for a moment glaring angrily up at him. Finally, she took it from his outstretched hand.

"Thanks," she muttered.

"Look, Bells, I wasn't trying to offend you. It's just…well, there's a king size bed in my room. Why don't you sleep in there with me tonight? Give Joshua the bed, that couch can't be comfortable." Bella took a step backwards away from him. Stuart stared at her innocently, like he hadn't said anything in the least bit inappropriate at all.

That's when Bella heard Joshua's deep baritone laugh. Something was off about the sound. She thought she heard a note of madness in his voice. Bella whipped her head around to see Joshua, handsome as ever and bare chested, in the bathroom doorway. He was clad in pajama bottoms. The veins in his neck were almost bulging and his chiseled chest muscles were so tight he looked like a huge mountain lion ready to spring.

"There's gotta be a hidden camera in here," Joshua said, his gaze slowly surveying the room. "That's the only plausible explanation for you standing in my parent's house, asking *my wife* to sleep with you. I'm being punked, right?" His eyes shot daggers through Stuart as he stalked deliberately towards his prey.

Instinctively, Bella was at Joshua's side. She wrapped one arm protectively around his waist and laid what she hoped to be a calming hand on his chest.

Stuart, as if suddenly understanding the seriousness of the situation, turned beet red. "No, no, Josh, you misunderstand me." Stuart slapped the palm of his hand hard against his forehead. "I don't know how I keep offending you! I don't mean sexually. Of course, Bells is desirable—"

"Get out," Joshua said calmly. Too calmly. The calm in his voice made Bella hold on to him tighter.

"I was just thinking we could stay up and talk jewelry all night, like one big slumber party," Stuart finished in a rush. Bella blinked at Stuart, trying to see him, to really discern him for the first time. Was he joking? Was the man mentally insane? What if Jabari had been right all along and Stuart really did have a death wish? *Out of the mouth of babes.* "Stuart," Bella said patiently, but firmly, as if she were talking to a misbehaving child, "If you want to wake up tomorrow in the land of the living, I suggest you leave now."

Stuart did an about face and quickly walked out of the room. Bella didn't release Joshua until she heard the soft click of the bedroom door. The fire was still smoldering in Joshua's big brown eyes. "Thanks," he murmured. Bella nodded and slipped past him into the bathroom.

CHAPTER 27

Joshua woke long before the breaking of the day, the proximity of Bella making it nearly impossible for him to sleep. He sat on the leather couch in his parent's guest room, watching her. In the pre–dawn stillness Joshua couldn't lie to himself, and he found himself face to face with the most tormenting of truths. He'd hoped that this fast he'd been on, ever since Bella's return, would give him the strength to make a clean break, to do what his rational mind told him he so desperately needed to do. To be done with her, because she was hazardous for his health, in more ways than one. But the more he abstained from earthly pleasures, the more forgiveness grew in his soul; the more the callous shell that he'd erected to surround and protect his vital organs began to break away. The anger, raw and unrelenting before, began to ebb and fade away. He was still angry. Still didn't completely trust himself not to hit somebody, but the anger that was once loud and searing was now a dull ache. And that, he knew, was because of Bella. When she laid hold of him last night, albeit, to keep him from killing Stuart, he felt an unbelievably cool balm fill his soul. Her touch, her arm gripped tightly around his waist, her hand pressed up against his chest, was like a prayer. *I know you've come to the end of your rope,* her touch said, *but I've got you. I won't let you fall.* It's what he'd been asking the Father to do for him all along. It was why he had even been fasting in the first place. But for the long awaited answer to come through, of all people, Bella . . . *How can the source of so much pain be the bearer of your healing?* Joshua asked quietly, bitterly, to the only one who could hear his thoughts.

Look at Paul, came the quiet response. **Look at you. Let me do for Bella what I have done for you.**

She's a free agent. I won't stop you.

There was no doubt about it, Joshua loved this woman. The truth he'd uncovered less than 48 hours ago didn't change that. What he couldn't understand was if this type of irrational love, this self-deprecating love, was from God or just some major flaw in his psyche. Joshua clasped his head between his hands and slid onto the floor. If nothing else, he would try to bargain with the Maker of his soul. *If I help her, will you take these feelings away from me?*

You want me to stop you from loving Bella?

Can't you see I'm in agony?

I won't stop you from loving Bella. Just like I won't stop myself, can't stop myself, from loving you.

Strength surged through Joshua's entire being. And for the first time since Bella had come back to him, it was well with his soul.

SPRING, 1997

CHAPTER 28
Houston, Texas

Mike and Tonya reclined on the living room couch together, listening to the sounds of Thelonious Monk being piped throughout the mansion's state of the art stereo system. Mike's head rested in Tonya's lap while Tonya applied ice to his bruised face. They sat like this for over an hour, with Tonya developing a pattern of removing the ice every few minutes or so. Inspecting the wound. Taking a new measurement with her index finger and thumb. Remove. Inspect. Measure. Remove. Inspect. Measure. She spoke to the wound through the rhythm of her movements, telling it to back away from his spirit, to back away from his soul, and to back away from his heart. Because now having heard the whole story, Tonya was convinced. This wound was more than skin deep. It was as lethal as snake venom seeping into his heart. He had known it too. The moment he'd learned the truth about Bella and Brady, he knew he had been bitten. He'd asked her to marry him thinking she could be his antidote. *You will not die from this. Do you hear me, Michael? You will heal from this. My touch will be your antidote.* Remove. Inspect. Measure. Remove. Inspect. Measure.

Mike complained at first, saying how pointless and silly it was applying ice to an old wound. Tonya declared that her God was a healer, so he laid his head in her lap and allowed her to ice his soul.

Tonya lifted the ice bag from Mike's face and smiled triumphantly down at him. "Ha! Old wound my toe. I was right, admit it."

She pulled out her compact and angled it so that Michael could see his face.

"I'll admit you got skills." Mike stared up at her, a crooked smile danced across his lips. "But if I had known that a shiner was all it took for you to talk to me, I would have paid somebody to hit me three days ago."

Tonya pushed him up off her lap and stood abruptly from the couch. "That's not funny, Michael."

Mike laughed and sat up. He grabbed her hand and pulled her back down onto his lap. Surprised to see unshed tears in her eyes. "Yo, Blackbird, you serious?"

Tonya shook her head and tried to force the tears back. "No, I'm fine."

He cupped her heart shaped face in between his two large hands. "How long have we known each other?"

She squeezed her eyes shut. "Michael, I told you I'm fine."

"Humor me, alright?"

"Our entire lives."

"Look at me when you say that."

Tonya blew out a breath and opened her eyes. The tears she'd been holding back began to fall. "We've known each other our entire lives."

"That's long enough for me to know when you're lying. So don't tell me nothing is wrong, when I can clearly see it in your eyes. Baby, what's wrong?" He wiped her tears away with the pads of his thumb. "Talk to me."

"Just the thought of somebody being able to hurt you makes me feel like I can't breathe. You're the Man of Steel. You're not supposed to get hurt."

Mike released a heavy sigh and pulled her closer, wrapping her in his arms.

"Don't believe the hype. That's just a nickname created to sell tickets, baby. I'm a man, I bleed like everybody else."

"I know," she murmured into his chest. "That's why I'm so mad at Joshua right now. He should be thanking you for telling him the truth, not getting into a slugging match with you."

Mike pulled back and lifted her chin to meet his eyes. "Blackbird, this is not Josh's fault."

"Oh really, because according to the story I just heard, he threw the first punch."

Mike shook his head. "I couldn't figure out a way to tell him, so I drew him into a fight. I know my brother very well. I hit him long before he ever hit me."

Tonya folded her hands across her chest, "I don't care what you say. It still doesn't give him the right to put his hands on you."

"You gave me some advice about Bella a little while ago. Looks like you gon have to do the same thing for Josh. Remember what you told me?"

Tonya rolled her eyes. "Yes, forgive. I know. And I will, but right now I just want to stay mad."

His handsome face broke out into a grin. "Look at you, acting like you're in love with me or something."

"You know I am."

"Are you?"

"Michael, why would you even ask me that?"

"Why'd you say no?"

"Oh, you mean besides the fact that you were drunk?"

Mike lifted her up and sat her on the coffee table directly in front of him. "Yeah, besides the fact that I was drunk."

"I wanted to say yes. But I couldn't, because God said not yet. Not until you answer the call and become the man that He has ordained you to be."

Mike ran his hands over his face. He stared up at Tonya. "God told Joshua to marry Bella."

"I know."

"You see how well that turned out."

"Michael—"

"Yeah, so forgive me if I'm not too big on what He says concerning matters of the heart these days. Why would your God do that, Tonya? Why would He tell my brother to marry a whore?"

"Don't do that."

"Don't tell the truth? Oh, so what, we lie to each other now?"

"Not that. Don't call Him my God, as if you're not a believer. As if you didn't walk down that aisle at St. Mark's Holy Cathedral when you were nine and give your life to Christ. I was there, remember?"

"That was a long time ago. I don't know what I believe anymore. What I do know is that my brother got a really raw deal."

Tonya rolled her eyes. "Boy, please. You think your brother is the first person God ever spoke to and told to marry a prostitute? What about Hosea in the Bible? God caused Hosea to fall in love with the prostitute Gomer. And He used their lives together as a metaphor for His undying love for his rebellious and adulterous people."

"And you don't think that sounds twisted at all?"

"No. Hard maybe, but not twisted. God's ways are not our ways. His thoughts are not our thoughts. I don't know what greatness God has in store for Bella, or Joshua either, for that matter. All I know is if God told Joshua to marry Bella, then I'm not about to count her out. It ain't over until God says it's over."

Mike nudged her leg playfully. "After everything I told you, you still got mad love for Bella. I really admire that about you, how you love so fiercely."

"You still got mad love for Josh. Why is it so unusual that I would love Bella?"

"Let's not forget that Josh is the victim here."

"No, Michael, Bella's the victim. Your story pretty much confirmed it, but for a while now I've suspected that she suffered from some serious childhood abuse."

Mike considered her words for a moment. "You think she was molested?"

"I don't have proof, but everything in my spirit says that's what happened to her. Think about it, nobody chooses this kind of life for themselves. It chooses them. Nobody wakes up and says, 'I want to be a prostitute when I grow up.' When you're four and you're playing with your dolls and you dream about the fairy tale, you don't dream this. You think about the house you are going to live in. What your wedding day will be like. Whether you'll own a dog or a cat—"

"Or a unicorn?" Mike added.

Tonya smiled at the memory. Yes, he had even managed to give her the impossible once. For her tenth birthday he'd given her a unicorn. He had fashioned a horn for her horse, Pepper. Had used his dad's lathe to make it look just like the ones the horses wear in the movies. He even fitted it with an elastic string and tied it around Pepper's head. And from that day forward, her white mare became a unicorn.

"Do you know that, hands down, that is still the most amazing gift that anyone has ever given me?"

"We do aim to please. You don't strike me as the unicorn type anymore. What does the fairytale look like for you these days?"

"We weren't talking about me. We were talking about Bella."

"We were talking about why you said no. The conversation shifted to God, then conveniently to Bella. But my original question still remains."

Tonya stood abruptly. "I'm going to go put this up before it starts to leak all over everything and make a big mess." She grabbed the ice bag next to him off the couch and ran off. Mike followed her into the kitchen. Her back remained rigid as she unwrapped the dishtowel and untied the plastic bag that now only held ice water and poured it into the sink. Mike leaned up against the kitchen counter, studying her profile as she worked.

"I'm not going to grad school like we talked about in the fall. I've decided to take some time off and do some missions work overseas."

Silence. In fact, the silence lasted for so long that Tonya had no other choice but to turn and face him. She tried desperately to gage his reaction, but his face remained placid, a smooth, chocolate mask.

"Please, Michael. This is hard enough as it is. Don't shut me out. I need to know what you are thinking right now."

"When do you leave?"

"In a month."

"Have a nice trip." He walked out of the kitchen. Tonya followed him. She watched as he climbed the long, spiral staircase leading to the second floor of the mansion.

"Michael, wait." He stopped at the top of the staircase, his back toward her.

Tonya started up the stairs behind him. "This isn't forever. It's a two-year program. My dad's insurance policy isn't paying out. Not in the way it was supposed to. It's not enough for my mom to run the ranch and pay for my schooling too. But the Peace Corps will pay for grad school."

Mike turned to face her. "So this is about money. You'd leave me over something I could easily do for you?"

Tonya shook her head. "The money is only part of it. This is what I want."

"Then do it." He walked down the hall to the master bedroom. "Fly away, Blackbird. Have an amazing life."

⁂

Mike was sitting in the window seat removing his shoes when Tonya burst into his bedroom. "That's it? That's all I get! You just asked me to marry you three days ago. Now it's, 'fly away, Blackbird. Go have an amazing life!'"

"Is there anything I could say that would change your mind?"

"Yes, Michael, there is."

"I don't have a playbook for any of this, Tonya. So can you please just tell me what that is?"

Tonya walked over to the window seat. She wrapped her arms around his neck and pressed her cheek against his cheek. "You could answer the call of God on your life."

His body grew stiff as a board. "I can't do that, Blackbird. Not even for you."

Tonya stepped away from him. She cocooned herself in her own arms. "It's late, I'd better be going."

"Stay, spend the night with me."

"Michael—"

"You just told me that you're leaving for two years. Going to Timbuktu or someplace like that."

"It's Peru."

"Right. The least you could do is let me hold you for one more night." He wrapped his finger through a belt loop of her jeans and pulled her towards him. "When we got too old for sleepovers, there was the hayloft. Don't you remember slipping out of the house in the middle of the night to sleep under the stars with me?"

"I lost something in that hay loft."

"Not at first. For years we just held each other. And you weren't the only one who lost something in that hayloft."

Tonya placed her hands on her hip and glared down at him. "Don't even try it, Michael."

"What?"

"You did not lose your virginity to me. You were fourteen and you did it with Colleen Miller's much, much, older sister, Sheree, in their parent's basement."

Mike stood up, making a time out motion with his hands. "Whoa, first of all, she wasn't that old and second of all, who told you? I know Josh wouldn't—"

"No, he wouldn't, would he? Because while you were going all the way with Sheree, he was at second base with Colleen."

Mike fell back down on the window seat and released a long hearty laugh.

"What's funny?"

"You. Acting like a woman scorned. Like I cheated on you or something."

Tonya plopped down on the window seat next to him. "I'm not delusional, Michael." She pulled her knees up and wrapped her arms around them. "When you were fourteen, I didn't even exist for you."

"We were just kids, practicing, Blackbird. Would it help if I told you I was practicing for you?"

"You slept with old lady Sheree for me? I'm flattered, really I am, because I'm genuinely a better person because you did that."

"Ah, you got jokes."

She rolled her eyes. "Apparently so do you."

"Oh, so you don't believe me?"

"You were a horny teenage boy. End of story."

His dark handsome face broke out into a playful grin. "Now that's true. Very true. But I'm still going to prove it to you."

"You're going to prove that you did old——"

He put his hand up to her mouth. "Please don't say that again. What I'm going to prove is that there's never been a day that you didn't exist for me. Do you remember how old I was the first time I asked your dad for your hand?"

Tonya pursed her lips together. "Ten."

"Go ahead. Give it up. Give credit where credit is due."

"You had a crush on me for a hot second when you were ten and then you spent the next eight years ignoring me. What does that prove?"

"What about the next time I asked him?"

"I didn't even know there was a next time."

"Exactly. That's what I'm trying to tell you. I asked your father for your hand in marriage every year after that first time. Every year, until he finally said yes and gave me his blessing."

Tonya looked up at him, stunned. "When did he say yes?"

"Two weeks before he died."

"We were broken up when my dad died. Why would you ask him for my hand?"

"Because my heart was the thing I lost in that hayloft with you. I lost it the very first night you met me there. I meant what I said, Blackbird. I want you to have an amazing life. If a trip to Timbuktu is what you need to make that happen then . . . do what you gotta do."

"It's Peru, I think Timbuktu is a little further east," she said, trying to draw a smile from him.

"Go back to the beginning with me. Let me hold you until morning. Just for tonight."

Tonya closed her eyes and willed the words to come forth. Words that would help her to explain why this wasn't the best idea for either one of them. How if she climbed into his arms tonight, she might never climb back out. But when she opened her mouth to speak her heart betrayed her. "Clothes on?"

"Yeah."

"Alright, just for one night."

CHAPTER 29
New Orleans, Louisiana

Bella, wake up, we're leaving." A groggy Bella sat up in bed and looked around the completely demolished room. Her eyes landed on Joshua, who was sitting beside her on the bare mattress. "Okay, just let me pack our things."

"No. We leave everything. From here on out, we make a clean start."

Bella visibly stiffened when Joshua pulled the car into the church parking lot.

"Everything you told me was true?" She nodded her head vigorously like a child convinced she'd seen the boogieman.

"I believe you, and I believe in you. You don't have to destroy your life because of someone else's choices."

"What are you going to do?"

"I'mma have a little talk with the Rev." Joshua pulled Bella down a long corridor that lead to the main office. Sister Monroe sat at her usual perch outside her father's office, sorting mail.

"Oh, hello, Joshua," Sister Monroe said warmly. "Bella," she added, like the name was distasteful on her tongue. "It's good to see you in the house of the Lord. I don't think I've seen you here since your wedding day."

"Is the Rev in yet?"

"He's going over his notes for Sunday morning service. I can buzz—"

"Wait right here," Joshua said to Bella before barging into the office. Sister Monroe looked at Bella and shrugged.

"I guess not."

❧ ❧

"Joshua, my son, how are you?" Reverend Leblanc's face froze when he saw the look of anger and betrayal on the younger man's face. "Joshua, what's the matter? What's this about?"

"You tell me. I found a box of money in my home. Bella has been sleeping with men for money. When I confronted her about it—"

Reverend Leblanc's dark face turned ashen. He went limp and fell into his chair. "Oh, God, Joshua, I'm sorry. We should have…I should have warned you."

"To your own flesh and blood?"

Leblanc collected himself quickly and jumped up. He walked around the desk and stood in front of Joshua. "Now wait a minute, Joshua, whatever she told you is a lie. She's a liar, son. Joshua, listen to me. Bella deceived you and she deceived me. She is a liar."

"I watched her go into a trance and piss on my living room floor. Nobody can act that well!" Tears rolled down Joshua's face and he wiped them away furiously. "To an eight-year-old baby?" he asked hoarsely. "Your own little girl?"

Reverend Leblanc let out a wounded cry and dropped to his knees. "We are just men, Joshua. We wrestle not against flesh and blood, but against spiritual forces of evil in the heavenly realms. There is a strong spirit of seduction on Bella. A siren spirit. I tried to fight it, God knows I did, but it was too strong for me. Now I know why God sent you to us. We must fight it together, in prayer. You and me." Reverend Leblanc reached out his hand to Joshua, beckoning him to kneel also and join him in prayer. Joshua backed away from the older man in disgust.

"Don't ever come near either one of us again. If you ever try to see or contact her, I will not be responsible for what I do to you."

"Joshua, please, if we just bend our knees in prayer together we can rout this thing." Reverend Leblanc grabbed ahold of Joshua's pants leg. Joshua tried to shake him off, but the Reverend held on for dear life.

"No. You don't get to pray something like this away." Joshua yanked Leblanc up off the floor by his collar, stood him up straight, then punched him so hard he went flying through the private door that led directly to the pulpit. Reverend Leblanc crash-landed like a missile onto the altar.

"You should have cut your own hand off first!" Joshua roared. He stepped through the door into the pulpit and glared down at the Reverend. "Isn't that what the good book teaches us, Rev? If your hand—even your stronger hand—causes you to sin, cut it off and throw it away." Joshua bit out as he punched the Reverend again and again.

The praise and worship team stopped singing and moved out of the way as seven armor-bearers rushed the stage. Each one tried to pull Joshua off of the Reverend, but Joshua picked them off one by one like they were nothing more than annoying houseflies. Bella and Sister Monroe were in the front office when they heard the crash and screams. They came running into the sanctuary just as Joshua told Reverend Leblanc in front of a stunned congregation of two thousand people. "If you ever come near my wife again, so help me God, I will kill you."

The entire church stood frozen with mouths agape. That's when Sylvia Leblanc noticed that the cameras were still rolling and that the world was watching.

"Cut the cameras!" Sylvia called to the cameraman. "Cut the cameras this instant, goddamn you!"

Joshua walked off the stage, grabbed Bella's hand, and marched down the long red-carpeted aisle and out the front doors of the church.

CHAPTER 30

Michael turned up the volume on the television when he saw the breaking news footage. "Bad Boy Joshua Keys has struck again, this time the pastor of a large mega church. Reportedly his wife's father. Mr. Keys was not available for comment," the reporter continued.

The next image that appeared on screen was that of Reverend Leblanc standing outside his church holding a press conference before a crowd of reporters. "Joshua Keys is an angry, troubled, young man. He was abandoned as a small child by his biological mother, no doubt a drug addict, who walked into a hospital off the street and handed him over to a nursing attendant."

Mike unleashed a string of curses at the television.

"We have tried to embrace Joshua like a son," Reverend Leblanc continued as the cameras flashed, "But the wounds from his childhood were just too great. We have faith that one day God will do a work in Joshua and he will be able to receive our love. As for my daughter, despite her Christian upbringing, she too has lived a troubled life. I've done my best to keep that side of our personal lives out of the media, but I cannot protect my daughter's reputation any longer at the great expense of the cause of Christ. All I can say is that the devil always comes after the preacher man's child."

"Reverend LeBlanc, will you be suing Mr. Keys?" one of the reporters asked.

"Our Bible tells us not to sue our brethren in the Lord. Joshua is my son. I have fully forgiven him."

As Mike flipped through the channels, he found the footage of Joshua punching the pastor playing on every network.

Mike picked up his phone and saw five missed calls from his agent and nothing from Joshua. Mike dialed his brother's number. The phone rang once and went straight to voicemail. "Yo, Josh, pick up. Where you at?" The phone beeped signaling he had a call on the other line. Mike clicked over.

"What's up, Steve?"

"Mike, where have you been? I've been calling you all morning."

"Yeah, I see that. I turned the ringer off last night. What's up?"

"Are you kidding me? Have you seen the news, have you picked up the morning paper, or turned on a computer? Talked to your frickin' neighbors!"

"I'm watching it right now, okay?" Mike responded calmly. "I see we got a fire blazing, what I can't understand is why you're wasting time calling me. You're the rainmaker, so make it rain."

"Rainmaker, okay. What is it with you and your brother, huh? Mike, if I made it rain for 40 days and 40 nights, I could not begin to wash this fiasco. He hit a pastor!"

"I wasn't there. Neither were you. As bad as this looks, I'm sure Josh had his reasons."

"You do realize that the League is going to issue a fine."

"That's the least of my worries. What I need is for you to calm down and do what we pay you so very well to do." Mike hung up the phone just as Tonya walked into the bedroom.

"Michael, is everything okay?"

Tonya glanced at the footage of Joshua playing on the big screen television. Her eyes grew big as saucers and her hand flew to her mouth.

"I have to go find my brother."

"Of course."

Mike kissed her cheek. "Will you stay here until I get back?"

"No way. I'm coming with you."

The doorbell rang.

Mike took the stairs two at a time with Tonya following closely behind him. When he flung open the door, Joshua and Bella were standing on his front doorstep.

"Is this a bad time? You look like you're on your way out," Joshua said.

"Yeah, I was just coming to find you."

CHAPTER 31

The brothers fell into each other's arms. Bella and Tonya looked on in relief and cried. "We'll be at the cottage if you need us," Tonya said when the two brothers finally parted. Joshua and Mike watched the two women walk down the front stairs and along the winding path that led to Tonya's cottage, arm in arm.

"You two straight?"

Mike closed the front door and motioned for Joshua to follow him into the living room. "She's leaving for Peru in a few months. When she comes back, we'll see where things end up."

Joshua took a seat on the sofa next to Mike. "I'm sorry. I know you'd never lie to me, I just couldn't believe Bella could—"

"Josh, we good. You gotta figure out what your next move is as far as your marriage is concerned. But you and me gon always be good."

"You sure about that, Mike?"

Mike stared into his brother's bloodshot eyes.

"I won't let her go. You're the only brother I got. If you can't get past this, I understand, but God gave her to me and I won't let her go. She was just a baby, Mike." Joshua's voice broke. "She was just a little baby and that son of—" Joshua lowered his head between his legs and sobbed like a child.

Mike grabbed his brother and held on tightly. "We're family and we gon always be family. Bella too. Whatever comes, we ride or die."

CHAPTER 32

The footage of Joshua punching out Reverend Leblanc played over and over again, on every network for months. Reverend Leblanc seized the spotlight any chance he got. The preacher appeared on major talk shows across the country, talking to anyone in the press who would hear him. Each time publicly announcing to Joshua that he forgave him and harbored no ill will towards him. And when it seemed like all the media attention would finally die down, like Lazarus from the grave, Reverend Leblanc would resurrect it again.

Mike turned the station to get away from the drama on one network only to be confronted by a now all too familiar sound bite on another network.

"As for my daughter, despite her Christian upbringing, she too has lived a troubled life. I've done my best to keep that side of our personal lives out of the media, but I cannot protect my daughter's reputation any longer at the cause of Christ." The commentators on this particular station were discussing amongst themselves what the phrase, "troubled life" could possibly mean.

Mike stood up. "God knows I hate this mother—" He stopped himself short, his eyes flying over to Bella. "Sorry, he's still your pops."

"Don't be. My sentiments exactly." Bella looked at Joshua. His face was a carefully composed mask that told her absolutely nothing. But Bella knew deep in her soul that Joshua was hurting. When Joshua walked away from Reverend LeBlanc that day, he also walked away from the church. Ever since they'd made the move to Houston, Joshua hadn't so much as set foot inside of a church. And these days, both on and off the court, Joshua was getting into even more fights.

The event surrounding Reverend LeBlanc had become a media circus, complete with people choosing sides and whispers of sexual abuse. Stories circulated about a young teenaged Bella being impregnated by her father. But no matter what anybody said, Bella was the hot button. Joshua completely lost it if the media approached her. She stopped coming to his games; she and Tonya opting to watch the brothers play on television at home, because Bella got more press coverage then the players.

The media crucified him, but Joshua remained steadfast, her chief intercessor, her bulwark. Standing in the gap for her, feeling all of the things she should have felt had she been able to feel anything at all. His fist connecting with faces on her behalf. While her father seized the limelight anytime he could and spoke about Joshua constantly, Joshua, true to his word, remained silent about Reverend Leblanc.

"This is a private family matter, not open for public consumption or debate," Joshua had told the gaggle of reporters who were staked outside the gate of Mike's mansion on that first day they arrived.

"Joshua, you do realize that Reverend Leblanc is on national television right now, telling his side of things. It behooves you to give us your side. Your fans deserve to know."

"That's all I'm going to say on the matter," Joshua said before rolling the car window back up and being ushered through the gate by the guard.

Now if a reporter began with the statement, "Reverend LeBlanc said," Joshua would say, "This interview is over. Get that camera out of my face."

"Why? Are you gonna hit me like you hit the pastor?" one reporter brazenly asked.

"You'd like that, wouldn't you?" Joshua retorted. "If I punch you in that smart mouth of yours, I'd make you a rich man."

The fans loved it. Joshua was already a favorite son of Houston, and now that he had returned home to play for the Rockets, he had groupies everywhere. Bella's father even managed to make his way onto the once popular talk show, *Larry King Live*. Bella and Tonya were enjoying a spa night at the cottage the night the special aired.

"Why did he just up and hit you?" Larry asked.

"He's a violent man, Larry. What can I say?"

"I've known him to get a little aggressive on the court from time to time, but never without provocation. Reverend, people in your congregation reported hearing Joshua say, 'If you ever come near my wife again, I will kill you.' Members also reported hearing the following shouts coming from inside your office. 'How could you do such a thing to a little girl, to your own child?' There are whispers of abuse. Were you abusing your daughter?"

"Larry, I am a man of God. I resent you even implying that."

"Is that a no?"

"Of course it is!"

"Do you think the controversy between you and Mr. Keys has affected his game?"

"I think being out of God's will has affected Mr. Keys' game. The Bible is very clear about these types of things, Larry. Touch not my anointed and do my prophet no harm."

"But you can't deny he's playing better than he ever has before. Doesn't look like God's punishing him to me. If he keeps this up, he'll be inducted into the Hall of Fame before he's 40."

Steve, Joshua's agent, decided to have Joshua appear on *Sports Center* to get the public's focus back on Joshua's game. But when the interviewer flipped the script and asked the forbidden question, "Why did you hit Reverend Leblanc?" Joshua stood up on national television and walked off the set.

The next day Joshua's attorneys put out a press release saying that Joshua had called a moratorium on the press. Unrelenting as ever, the media changed their tactics. If Joshua wouldn't talk to them, then they would talk to people Joshua knew. Mike switched to another station.

"Right now, we are outside the home of Jack and Melissa Kennedy, Joshua's adopted parents," a reporter announced.

Bella's hand flew to her mouth. Bella watched as a smiling Melissa opened the door. The reporter asked a few questions about horses and what it was like running a ranch. Once Melissa and Jack were laughing and relaxed, the reporter moved in for the kill.

"This is a very extraordinary home. You have raised not just one, but two high profile, pro basketball players, Michael Dutton the Man of Steel, and Bad Boy Joshua Keys. You adopted them both, correct?"

"That's correct," Melissa said.

"Yet neither one of them has your last name. Why is that?"

"Both our boys decided to take Kennedy as their middle name and keep their last names to honor their heritage."

"Their African American heritage."

"That's correct, yes."

"Tell us about, Joshua. Was he a violent child growing up?"

"Of course not. What kind of question is that?" Jack snapped.

"What's the matter with you people? You come in here pretending to do a special on horses only to denigrate my son!" Melissa said.

Jack stood and looked directly at the camera. "Come on, buddy. Get your stuff, it's time for you to go." He turned to the reporter. "You too."

"Has Joshua instructed you not to talk to the press?" the reporter fired quickly.

"He didn't have to instruct us to do anything," Jack said as he grabbed the reporter by the arm and pushed him through the front door.

"But what do you think about Joshua hitting a pastor? Sir, a pastor!"

"If Joshie socked him, then he must have had it coming!"

"Sir, I just have a few more questions for you and your wife."

Jack slammed the door in his face.

Bella sat there staring at Joshua, waiting for anything at all. A break in his calm. Mike picked up the remote control and shut the television off.

"Yo, Josh, man, you alright?"

Joshua stood up from the couch. He smiled painfully down at Bella. "I'm fine. Let's go play some ball."

CHAPTER 33

Tonya sat on the sofa in her cottage looking through an old picture album. She stopped and ran her fingers across a photo of her and her horse Pepper. The photo had been taken at her tenth birthday party. The day Michael made Pepper a unicorn.

Aunt Katie had watched Tonya's face break out in joy when Mike led the new and improved Pepper to her from the barn. "You hold tight to that one right there, baby girl. That's what you call a forever love. Forever only comes along once in a lifetime."

Tonya shook her head. "We're just friends, Auntie Katie. He ain't studying me like that."

"The boy showed up at your party today with a mythical creature that doesn't even exist. Trust me, he's studying you."

Mike reached over in the dark groping for the ringing phone. The alarm clock read 1 AM.

"You asleep?"

"What's wrong, Blackbird?"

Silence.

He yawned. "You wanna talk about it?"

She wanted to tell him that she was afraid that her Aunt Katie was right and that she was about to make the biggest mistake of her life. Instead, she said, "Could you just come over and hold me?"

"I'm tired, baby," Mike said stifling another yawn. "I can't sleep in that little bed tonight. Come over. I'll get dressed."

CHAPTER 34

Tonya opened the door to Mike's bedroom and looked both ways. She spotted Joshua walking towards the spiral staircase and quickly closed the door.

Mike looked up from his morning paper. "What?"

"They're up. Josh is out there walking around."

"Tonya, why are you whispering? I told you the walls in the master bedroom were sound proofed for privacy. You could scream to the top of your lungs and no one would hear you. So, if you were inclined to break a brother off with some real lovin', nobody would know."

Tonya rolled her eyes at him.

Mike shrugged. "Can't blame me for tryin'."

Tonya fell back down on the massive bed beside him. "You need a fire escape or something. We can't keep doing this."

"You're not sinning, Tonya."

Tonya looked up at him doubtfully.

He smirked at her. "Trust me, sinning feels way better than this."

"I know, but I still feel convicted. Now that Joshua and Bella are staying here, I feel like we should stop. I don't want this to affect my witness to either one of them."

"Which part, sleeping in here or getting caught?

Tonya bit her lip. "Getting caught."

"That's a little hypocritical don't you think?"

"I know. It's just, how can I be an example to Bella of sexual purity if it looks like I'm having sex?"

"I can't help you with that one, Blackbird. You gotta do whatever you need to do to feel better about this. Even if that means we stop not sinning."

CHAPTER 35

Mike awoke the next morning to the smell of Tonya's lavender scented hair on his pillow. In his state of semi-consciousness, he reached for her in the darkness. She wasn't there. Mike sat up in bed and turned on the lamp beside him. He found a note on the pillow next to him.

I figured it out. I can avoid the appearance of ungodliness if I leave each morning before dawn. See you tonight.

Love, Tonya.

Mike got up out of bed and headed to the bathroom for a cold shower, a morning ritual now that Tonya had taken to sleeping in his bed. Thirty minutes later Mike padded into the kitchen with bare feet. He grunted a greeting to Joshua, who sat at the kitchen counter eating a bowl of cereal.

Mike grabbed the box of cereal off the counter, attempted to pour, and came up empty.

"Sorry, we're out. There are other types in the cabinet."

"Why didn't you eat those other types?"

Joshua shrugged. "I wanted this."

Mike sat the empty box of cereal in front of his brother. "Whose face is that on the box?"

Joshua grinned. "Yours."

"That's right, mine. My endorsement. My cereal."

Joshua reached into his back pocket and pulled out his wallet. "You need me to leave some scratch on the table?"

Mike smirked and pushed Joshua's hand away. "Whatever, dog. You can help yourself to anything up in here. You know this. All I ask is that you don't break the code."

"Okay, what's the code?"

"The code is simple, Josh. You can't eat the last of the cereal if your face ain't on the box. Get your own endorsement."

"That's cold, bro."

"No, see out in the cold is exactly where you gon be if you don't stop letting all this fighting affect your game. You should have had two or three endorsement deals by now."

Joshua studied his brother for a minute. "You seem stressed. I saw Tonya sneaking across the courtyard before dawn. She seemed happy. Why aren't you?"

Mike opened the refrigerator door and peered in. "Cause it ain't what you think, alright? And don't say nothing to her about that. She'd be mortified if she knew you saw her tipping out of here this morning." Mike pulled a carton of orange juice out of the refrigerator. He removed the top than hesitated before lifting the container to his lips. He looked around the corner. "Bella up?"

"Naw, you good."

Mike turned the jug up to his lips and gulped the juice down. "I'm a grown man, scared to drink juice in my own home. Living with your wife is like living with Mom," he growled.

Joshua chuckled. "Dude, for real. For somebody who had a woman in his bed last night, you ought to be a lot more relaxed than this."

"There is nothing relaxing about sleeping with Tonya, Josh. We sleep with our clothes on. Tonya has a no horizontal kissing rule. A no fondling rule and a damn sure no entry rule."

"You sleep together with your clothes on?" Joshua nearly fell off the kitchen stool laughing.

"Shut up, man. I knew I shouldn't have told you."

"I'm sorry, dog. I can't help it." Joshua laid a hand on his brother's shoulder. "You love this girl for real, bro. It's obvious, and it's obvious that she loves you. So what's the problem? Other than that very wack wedding proposal. Tonya's not the type to hold a grudge. Why don't the two of you just get married?"

"Because your God told her not to marry me."

Joshua's face suddenly grew serious.

Mike closed the refrigerator and leaned up against the counter. "She keeps waiting for me to become something I'm not. I can't compete with that and I won't come between her and her faith."

"So what you gon do?"

"I'mma figure out a way to break this thing between us for good."

CHAPTER 36

Bella sat on Tonya's bed as she packed. "What am I going to do without you for two whole years?"

"Don't say it like that. I'll be home for the holidays. And every week we'll talk on the phone. It'll just be like I'm in another city."

"Except you'll be in another city in another country." Bella paused, making sure that the next words coming out her mouth would sound, easy, and carefree. "What does Mike think about all of this?"

Tonya plopped down on the bed next to Bella. "Honestly, I don't know, Bella. He won't talk about it. Not one word. Whenever I try to make plans for the holidays, he just changes the subject. I'm scared to death that I may be losing him."

"On my wedding day, my mama said to me, 'Bella, this is your one chance to turn your life around, so don't mess it up.' But she was wrong, because here I am sitting here with another chance."

The two women sat in silence as they both contemplated this.

"Tonya, did God tell you to do this?"

"Yes, I think so."

"Then trust Him."

CHAPTER 37

ike was dressed in some slacks and a sports jacket when Tonya met him in his room later that night. "That's a little dressy for bed, don't you think?"

He didn't smile. Or laugh.

"What's up, Michael?"

"Look, Tonya, we can't do this anymore."

"Didn't you get my note? I figured it out. I'm going to leave before dawn. That way nobody sees me."

"It ain't that. This little arrangement worked when we were kids, but I'm a grown man who is used to having what I want, when I want it. I don't have the same conviction of my faith that you do."

"Michael, what are you talking about? You're a believer just like I am."

"Yeah, but I don't let Christ inform my every waking decision the way you do. What I should eat, what I should wear, and who I should love. How I should express that love. You, on the other hand, do. Tonya, on a physiological level, this is killing me. I don't want to hurt you. But I don't want to lie to you either. I called one of my standbys. I got a date tonight."

Tonya blinked. "One of your standbys. What does that mean, Michael?"

"Come on, Tonya. Don't act like you don't know. You went to a revival one weekend and ended our relationship. That was two years ago, remember? And I'm just supposed to fall in line."

"I'm still here! I'm right here!"

"You know what I mean. Do you even care how excruciating it is for me to lay next to you night after night, knowing how it feels to be inside of you?"

"It was your idea," she hissed.

"One time. Once! You've made this an every night thing."

"I thought you could handle it."

"I can't. Sorry. I'm just a man. I'm not made of steel. I'm not God."

Tonya watched him pocket a set of car keys and his wallet. "What's her name?"

"Does it matter?"

A sob caught in Tonya's throat. "So that's what I've been to you all this time? Just a place holder, a stand in!"

"You're the love of my life, Tonya. You're just too stupid to see it."

"I don't understand you. Why are you doing this tonight? Why now? I leave for the mission field in three days."

He nodded and walked out the door. "Yeah, I know. Have a good trip."

CHAPTER 38

Joshua loaded Tonya's suitcase into his brother's Yukon. He held the passenger door open for Bella and Tonya both, and the two women climbed into the far backseat. Next Jack climbed into the front passenger seat and Joshua walked back into the cottage to retrieve Melissa and Barbara.

"I don't mean to rush you, but we have to leave now if we gon beat the traffic."

"We're coming, I just had to get my camera," Melissa said.

"Joshua, where's Michael? I couldn't believe it when Tonya told me he wouldn't be here today," Barbara said.

"Something came up, Auntie. He couldn't make it."

Melissa and Barbara shot each other a knowing glance. Melissa opened her mouth to protest, but Joshua stopped her.

"I'm sure they'll talk to you both when they're ready. But for right now, we have to go. Otherwise we gon miss the flight."

CHAPTER 39

"Upgraded?"

"Yes, ma'am, to first class."

"Send it back, please. I don't want an upgrade." Tonya slid the ticket back across the counter. Joshua shifted restlessly from one foot to the other, jingling change in his pants pocket. He seemed oblivious to both the potential drama about to break out at the ticket counter and the group of onlookers pointing and gawking at him. Jack ran his hand through his hair and muttered something under his breath. Melissa and Barbara both wondered aloud about the ticket.

The ticket agent blinked at Tonya as if she didn't understand the words that were coming out of Tonya's mouth. "It's a non-refundable upgrade. Ma'am, it's a really long flight. You're going to Peru. Trust me, you want the upgrade."

"I don't want it."

"Well, I'll have to call my supervisor. No one has ever turned down a first-class ticket before."

"You do that," Tonya said curtly.

Bella stepped forward. She smiled warmly at the ticket agent. "That won't be necessary. We'll take the ticket. Thank you."

"Bella, I don't want his ticket," Tonya protested.

"Yes, you do. You are not so mad that you're gonna turn down a first-class ticket. Now come on, let's go find your gate."

⸙ ⸙

"If you cry, I'm gonna cry. So don't," Tonya said.

Bella wrapped her arms around her. "Okay, then I won't. But it's so hard because I already miss you." As Bella and Tonya held each other, Melissa and Barbara surrounded the two younger women, forming a hedge of protection around them.

"Traveling mercies to you, daughter," Barbara said.

"Yes, traveling mercies," Melissa echoed.

"Mel, are you and Barb gonna pray right here in the airport? You prayed back at the house and in the car, not to mention on the four-hour trip down here. God's not deaf, ya know. I think she's covered," Jack said.

"Of course she is. I have an idea," Melissa said, drying her eyes. "Why don't we stop all this crying and praying and get a few more photos. Tonya, come stand in between Joshie and Jack, honey."

The group of onlookers had followed them all the way to Tonya's gate. They shamelessly took pictures of Joshua.

"It's a good thing your brother didn't come, this would have turned into one hell of a circus," Jack said to Joshua quietly over Tonya's head.

"Smile, Tonya, your public is watching. And make it good, because one of these adoring fans is going to sell this photo to one of those seedy grocery store tabloids," Joshua said.

During his second year in the league, when his brand was just beginning to blow up, Michael, his agent Steve, and Joshua sat Tonya, her family, and Jack and Melissa down to explain the story they were launching of the Man of Steel as the consummate playboy with nobody special in his life.

121

Michael would be publicly photographed with a string of beautiful female celebrities. The goal being to create a juicy enough public persona so that the media never came searching for Michael's real private life. Tonya's father had immediately liked the idea. He didn't want Tonya in the spotlight or the cross hairs of any crazed fan any more than Michael did. The women in the family had been a harder sell. And Tonya, well Tonya sat quietly with adverted eyes the whole time, thinking how naive she had been to think he had assembled them all there for a marriage proposal.

"Say something, Blackbird. At the very least look at me."

Underneath his carefully perfected calm, Tonya could detect a note of panic in his voice. But she couldn't look at him, not just yet. Not till she could be sure that the disappointment and raw rejection would not show.

"I'm not playing you. I'm not ashamed of you. And I certainly wouldn't ask our whole family to be a part of some elaborate scheme to deceive you. I love you. Do you hear me? Girl, I love you."

The greatest irony of all was that now he was on the floor beside her, on bended knee. Cupping her smaller hands in between his two larger ones and speaking a flurry of desperate words, but not the four words she wanted to hear. Will. You. Marry. Me.

"Baby, the camera changes everything. Once you have them in your face, your life is not your own anymore. It's like being in a fishbowl. I don't want that for you, Blackbird. I don't want that for us."

A camera flashed in her face, shaking Tonya out of the past. "Nobody's ever seen me before, so who will they say I am?"

"My guess is either long lost sister or jilted lover."

Tonya wrinkled her nose in disgust. "That's crazy. Bella's standing right over there." Joshua shot her a look that said, *like that matters*. Then Tonya remembered a tasteless piece she had seen at the checkout counter once, about Joshua and Bella and their so-called "open" relationship. Joshua leaned over and held up two fingers that resembled bunny ears behind Tonya's head, while Melissa and the onlookers snapped pictures. "If you smile big enough, I think I may be able to get you cast in the role of long-lost sister."

Tonya pasted a broad grin on her face. Through her teeth she said, "I'm so glad I'm about to be outta here. You rich men are hazardous to my health."

"Don't worry. If they print something tasteless about you, I'll sue, alright?"

Tonya sighed. "Don't bother suing on my behalf, Josh. Save your money for the punch fund."

Joshua raised an eyebrow at her. "The what?"

"Well, that's what your brother calls it," Tonya blurted. "Oops, guess that was an inside joke. You know, punch fund, as in money set aside for your out of court settlements every time you punch somebody out."

"Yeah, yeah, I get it," Joshua said dryly.

"Jack, now let's get one of you and Tonya alone," Melissa said

Jack pulled Tonya close and placed a wad of money in her hand. "Don't talk to any rich creeps in first class. My son may be an idiot, but you're still spoken for. Call as soon as you land. And every week after that, you understand? You call me collect."

"I will, Jack."

"Which part?"

"The calling part. Not the talking to rich guys in first class part."

"That's my girl."

"Alright, now just Barbara and Tonya."

Tonya and Barbara pressed their almost identical heart shaped faces together. "I love you, baby girl."

"I love you too, Mama."

"If you need anything—"

"I know, Mama. I will."

"Now, Bella, you and Tonya together."

The two women smiled as Melissa took the photo.

The flight attendant's voice spoke over the loud speaker. "We will now be loading first class for flight 234 International to Peru."

Tonya hugged her mother then Melissa one last time before she turned to Joshua. "First class. Guess somebody can't wait to get rid of me, huh?"

Joshua frowned down at her and lifted her chin to meet his eyes. "My brother loves you. Don't ever doubt that."

"Look around, Josh. Everyone who loves me is here. I don't see him, do you?"

The tears she had been holding back began to fall and Joshua wiped them away with his thumb. "You and I know him better than anybody. Don't we? If he were here, do you think he would let you get on that plane?"

A sad smile played across her lips. "Not without causing a scene."

"And you know the Man of Steel don't do public displays?"

Tonya rolled her eyes. "Why, because that's your department?"

Joshua grinned. "You know how we do." Joshua's face suddenly grew very serious. "This is my brother's way of loving you, Blackbird. He's setting you free. Don't ask him to do anything else. Anything else would be too hard." Joshua pulled her close and kissed the top of her head. "Try to hold on for a little while longer, alright? Do that for me."

I'm sure gonna try, is what she thought. *Lord knows I'm gonna try to hold on to that man as long as my heart can stand it.* But what she actually said was, "You hold on to Bella for me too. Hold on tightly, Joshua. Don't try, do."

PRESENT, 2005

CHAPTER 40

Mike studied his brother intently. His mood had improved considerably, and what's more, the change seemed to have happened overnight. Joshua was completely back to his old self, laughing and joking with Marcus and Jabari. It could be the horses, of course, Mike thought. Even when they were kids, Joshua had always been happiest when they were on the trails. Joshua loved fast horses the way Mike loved fast cars. The boys were riding with them this morning and they were going much too slow to give Joshua the freedom buzz he enjoyed while racing through their family's meadow at breakneck speeds. No, Mike was willing to bet that this change of mood had something to do with Bella. Mike made sure Jabari and Marcus were well out of ear shot before he spoke her name. "I gave her some money and a phone. Told her to call if there was a problem."

Joshua smiled but said nothing.

"What?"

"Nothing, I just had a feeling you'd do that."

Mike stared at his brother, waiting for him to continue.

"I'm glad you did. She wouldn't have taken anything from me."

"You think it was a good idea to let her go?"

"She won't run. She'd never leave Jabari."

"I'm talking about Stuart, Josh. The guy is a trouble magnet. What if he gets into an altercation with someone and puts her in harm's way?"

"He's not a brawler, Mike. You heard him. He's a victim of spousal abuse. He's taking her to a jewelry show. What's the worst that could happen?"

Mike shook his head. "How in the world were you able to keep a straight face last night?"

"I ain't gon lie, man. That was hard." Joshua tilted his head slightly and peered earnestly into Mike's eyes. "We're just so glad you broke the cycle, honey," Joshua said in an almost perfect imitation of their mother last night.

The brothers both howled with laughter. Their laughter was cut short by the sound of Jabari's voice. Jabari and Marcus had brought their horses to a stop on the path up ahead.

"Dad, I'm worried about Mom. I don't like that Stuart guy. I don't like the way he looks at her."

Joshua and Mike looked at each other again. This time all traces of laughter were gone. Mike steered his horse alongside Marcus's, and Joshua brought his horse in step with Jabari's.

"I don't want you worrying about your mom anymore. I'm here now, and that's my job, alright?" Joshua said.

"Alright, but, Dad, aren't you even a little concerned?"

Joshua smiled at his son. "No, wanna know why?"

"Why?"

"Because I know your mother better than anyone else does, including you. She ain't no punk. She's tough, and if Stuart does anything your mother doesn't like, she will clean his clock."

Jabari burst into a fit of giggles. "Dad, that's hilarious. Did you get that from Grandpa Jack? That sounds like something he would say."

"Naw, that's your Grandma Mel right there." Joshua looked over at his brother. "What would Dad say, Mike?"

Mike winked at Jabari. "Your Grandpa Jack would say that she'd hand him his lunch."

Marcus and Jabari both snickered at that one.

Joshua nodded. "True dat."

"Look, I don't know about y'all, but I'm tired of riding like a bunch of old ladies. Who wants to race back?" Mike said.

Joshua grinned.

"You'll let us go fast, for real?" Jabari asked incredulously.

"Yeah, man, but whatever you do, don't fall," Mike said sternly.

"We won't," Jabari and Marcus said in unison.

"Uncle Mike, please let us ride fast. I swear we won't!" Jabari said.

"You'd better not, otherwise your mama will be trying to clean my clock."

CHAPTER 41

Bella spent the entire day with Stuart. He was right about one thing, the conference had been inspiring. There were so many things that Bella couldn't wait to try once she got settled into her new home. And thanks to Mike who'd slipped her a cellphone, his credit card, and a wad of cash before she left, she didn't have to depend on the generosity of Stuart.

"Call if you have any problems whatsoever out of this joker," Mike had said, glaring at Stuart. "I'll be there quicker than you can shake a leg. And make sure you get everything you need to start again. I mean it, Bella. Everything."

"Mike, I can't repay you."

"I don't want you to," he said, smiling a crooked smile that made her heart ache because it reminded her so much of Joshua. "Just make me some man jewelry or something. You're the only sister I've got. So take this money and stop trippin'." He kissed the top of Bella's head and ushered her into the car.

Stuart had overheard Mike's directive to Bella, and every time Bella had hesitated even the slightest bit over an item she wanted or thought she might need, Stuart was there to throw Mike's words back in her face. "He said get everything you need. Geez, Bells, he's rich. He's not worried about the money. I don't know why you are."

"She'll take two of these," Stuart told the salesgirl, pointing to the needle-nose pliers Bella had been eyeing. "You can never have too many of those. I can promise you that these will feel like butter in your hands. Get the best, that way you won't have to replace it anytime soon," Stuart coached.

Bella bought an assortment of beads, stones, clasps, and charms. As well as a top of the line tool set and a rolling storage container for everything, since she didn't know how long she'd be staying at Joshua's. She and Stuart laughed and talked as they wandered from booth to booth, stopping every now and again to do a couple of hands on demonstrations.

After the conference, Bella and Stuart had a late lunch at a little café in town. They were headed back to the ranch and Bella was even starting to reconsider her prior assessment of Stuart, when he made the colossal mistake of putting his foot in his mouth.

"You're really easy to talk to, Bells. I feel like we have so much in common, what with our love for jewelry and our relationship problems," Stuart said as he pulled onto the expressway.

"Our what?"

"Bells, face it, honey, we are both in love with a couple of hotheads."

"Stuart, Joshua is not a hothead."

"Really, so was that his evil twin that was ready to rip me a new one last night?"

"You mean after he walked in while you were propositioning his wife? No, that was him, Bad Boy Joshua Keys, in all his glory. Excuse me, not quite all his glory, because after all, you are still alive."

"Bells, you know I didn't mean it like that. And if he reacts to me that way, I can't help but think how he must respond to you when you displease him."

Bella laughed hard. So hard that tears began to roll down her face.

Stuart took his eyes off the road and peered at Bella. "What's funny about this, Bells? Hum? Because you're really starting to scare me. I feel like we need some type of intervention right now."

"You're funny, Stuart, because you don't know what you're talking about. Joshua is not now, nor has he ever been, an abuser. Read. My. Lips. Not mentally, not verbally, not physically. Any abuse that has happened between us, I can assure you has been entirely on my part."

Stuart gasped. "Oh, I thought—well, the papers said—"

"Maybe you shouldn't believe everything you read."

Bella turned her head toward the window and enjoyed the silence for the rest of the way back to the ranch.

CHAPTER 42

Stuart drove onto the Kennedy property and parked the car. He turned in his seat and looked over at Bella. "Listen, Bells, I'm sorry. I should have never compared what you and Joshua have to my problems with Janice. I really like you, Bells. So what do you say? Can we put that whole awful conversation behind us?"

Bella sighed. "Yeah, okay. Sure"

Stuart beamed. "Why don't you go put your things up and meet me in the stable for your jewelry lesson?"

❧ ❧

Bella heard laughter coming from outside of the house. She rolled her purchases around back to see Jack, Joshua, and Mike sitting on the back porch, talking.

"Hey, everybody," Bella said, careful not to let her eyes fall on Joshua.

"Bella's back," Jack said, rising to enclose her in a bear hug. Mike rose as well and grabbed the rolling case from her hand. Jack released her. Mike lifted an eyebrow at Bella. "This doesn't feel like starting over."

"A jeweler's supplies aren't that heavy. I got everything I need for now." Bella heard the screen door close softly and realized that Joshua must have gone inside. She forced herself not to look in the direction of the door. "Where are the boys?" Bella asked.

"Out back brushing down the horses."

"So, how did it go today, with the boys, I mean?"

"For a couple of city kids, they did pretty good," Mike said.

"Yeah, you should have seen them galloping across the field," Jack said.

Bella's eyes widened. "Galloping?"

"It was more like a trot. How was the show?" Mike asked quickly.

"It was great."

"Stuart didn't get on your nerves too bad, did he?" Jack asked.

Bella laughed. "Not too bad."

"I'm going to go put my stuff up, and if anybody wants me, I'll be in the stable with Stuart for my metal working lesson."

"Alright, hon, have a good time," Jack said.

CHAPTER 43

Stuart ran out of the barn to meet Bella with a yellow bandana in his hand.

"What's that for?" Bella asked skeptically.

"Just a little icebreaker for you. A team building exercise." Stuart tied the cloth around her eyes. "Hold your hand out." Stuart poured a handful of corn into Bella's hand.

"Okay. . ."

"Bells, just go with it, please." He led her over to a stall. "Now hold your hand out again."

Bella did as she was told. She felt a mild tickling sensation and realized that something was eating out of her hand. "Oh, sh—."

"Don't panic. Just go with it." Stuart stepped behind her and untied the bandanna. "There. See."

Bella stared in amazement at the tiny foal eating from her hand. "It's just a baby," she cooed. She reached her hand up to pet the foal gently.

"His name is Tyler."

"Tyler," Bella repeated.

"Not too bad, right?"

"No. But what does this have to do with metalworking, Stuart?"

"Everything. I told you it's an exercise in trust building. The best jewelers trust themselves and their art intuitively. That's what I'm trying to get you to do. I have one more exercise I'd like you to try. This one will require a little more trust. But I know you can do it." Stuart led Bella to the next stall. He opened the door and led out an already saddled black mare. "Bella, this is, Lady. Lady, meet Bella." The horse raised her head and blew out a loud whoosh. Bella jumped back.

"It's okay," Stuart laughed. "She's just saying hello. Go ahead, pet her."

"No way."

"Oh, Bella, don't be a scaredy-cat. She won't hurt you, she's a senior citizen."

Bella reached out her hand to touch the beautiful black mare.

"I'm surprised you've never met her."

"Stuart—" Bella began, annoyed.

"I know, I know, it's just that this is Joshua's horse. He was crazy about her when we were kids. The two of them were inseparable. They used to jump competitively. See." Stuart pointed to the winner photos of a young Joshua and a much younger Lady that hung on the walls in front of Lady's stall.

Bella ran her fingers lightly over each photo. Joshua looked bright eyed and innocent, his love for the horse clear.

"Nobody rides this girl anymore. She's retired. But I saddled her up so that you could sit on her."

"Then you must be out of your cotton-picking mind."

"Bells, trust. Remember?"

"If I sit on the dang horse then are we going to make some jewelry?"

"Scout's honor, all trust building activities over."

Bella took a deep breath and put one foot in the stirrup while Stuart held the reins. She swung her body up onto the saddle, gripping the horn for dear life.

"Not bad, that was pretty good. Now let go of the horn, Bells, and take the reins."

Lady stepped forward then backwards.

"I don't think I can do that," Bella said, agitation building in her voice.

"Just relax, okay? You're in charge, you've got to direct her where to go."

Lady took another step backwards, this time knocking the tray of metalworking tools onto the floor. The crash startled both Bella and Lady. Bella shrieked, and the horse took off, making a mad dash out of the stable door.

"Bella!" Stuart screamed.

CHAPTER 44

D ad! Dad! Help!" Jabari ran towards the house, screaming. Tears ran down his face, nearly blinding him. Jack and Mike jumped up and ran towards him.

"Jabari what happened?! Are you hurt?!" Mike said grabbing him.

"It's my mom! Stuart put her on a horse and it just took off!"

"Listen to me, son, do you know what horse your mom is on?" Jack said.

"Lady!"

Mike swore and took off running towards the stables. Jack cupped Jabari's face in his hands. "No, no, look at me, that's good," Jack said. "She's an old gal, now. More than likely she'll just tire herself out."

Stuart rode up on a stallion. He nearly fell off the horse trying to dismount. "I…I tried to catch them, but Lady was moving too fast for me!" Stuart huffed.

"Which direction?" Jack asked

"South pasture," Stuart said. Joshua and Melissa stepped out onto the porch.

"Jack, what's all the commotion about?" Melissa asked.

"Stuart put Bella on Lady and she bolted," Jack said. "She's headed for the south pasture."

Joshua leaped over the porch railing and tore down the driveway. He mounted the waiting stallion and rode like his life depended on it.

CHAPTER 45

Joshua rode so hard and fast that the landscape whipped by in a blur. He moved instinctually, his body becoming one with the fluid movements of the stallion. He dug his heels into the stallion's sides, pressing him to go faster. One thought filled his mind: Bella. He caught sight of Lady and a downed log a half a mile up ahead, and he knew with everything in him that Lady wanted to jump it. "Yah! Yah!" Joshua pressed the horse forward, intent on one goal: reaching Lady before she reached the log. Next thing Joshua knew, Mike was racing beside him on a horse as well. Mike moved in alongside Lady's left and Joshua rode in close on her right. The two brothers boxed the horse in on both sides. Joshua grabbed the reins with one hand, making sure to steady his own horse in the process.

"Easy girl. Easy, easy," Joshua called to the horse in low tones. "That's it," he said as Lady slowed to a trot. "Good girl, Lady. That's my very good girl." The horse came to a stop and Joshua dismounted the stallion. Mike also dismounted and tried to persuade Bella that it was now safe to come down. Bella kept her eyes squeezed shut, crying hysterically, her hands were glued to the horn of the saddle. The two brothers took turns, one trying to calm Bella and the other trying to soothe and steady the horse, but no amount of coaxing from either Joshua or Mike could make Bella let go.

Mike wiped his brow, "She's not coming down."

Joshua stared up at Bella. "Doesn't look like it. The two great loves of my life finally meet and I can't tear them away from each other."

"It's gonna be dark soon, how you want to handle this?"

"Take the stallion. I'll meet you back at the ranch." Joshua hoisted himself up onto the saddle behind Bella, his strong arms wrapped around her while he reached for the reins simultaneously. "Easy, baby," he said, talking just as calmly to Bella as he had to the horse. "I've got you."

Bella's breathing came out in quick short puffs.

"Take deep breaths, Bella, and relax your grip."

"W-w-what?"

"Your legs, you're holding her too tightly. As long as you grip her like that, she's going to think you want to go fast. You don't want to go fast again, do you?" Joshua asked teasingly.

"No!" Bella moaned, her head falling lifelessly back onto his shoulder.

"It's okay. Just show her what you want. Let your legs go limp."

"Okay," Bella said shakily.

"That's it. You're doing great." Joshua turned Lady around and headed slowly back towards the ranch. Joshua listened to the breathing of both Bella and Lady, letting him know they'd both calmed down considerably. He cooed encouragement to them both all the way. "You're a natural at this, you know that? You rode Lady and you didn't fall off. If you can ride Lady, Bella, you can ride any horse on this ranch."

"Stuart called her a s-senior citizen."

"Stuart's an idiot. I'm surprised you haven't figured that out by now. Lady is the baddest horse on this ranch. You just made history today, Bella Rose. Nobody has ever ridden this horse without being thrown."

"N-Nobody?"

Joshua kissed the top of her head and pulled her tightly to him, thanking God for protecting her from the many ways this situation could have gone dreadfully wrong.

"Nobody but me."

CHAPTER 46

When they got to the stable, Zack, the stable manager, came running out the greet them. Joshua slid effortlessly off the horse. He grabbed Lady's face and laid his head against her graying muzzle. The horse licked Joshua and snorted in delight.

"Thank you, old friend, for being so good to my Bella," he whispered.

Joshua patted her once more before handing the reins over to Zack. "Make sure she gets a good rub down and be sure to check her for wounds." Joshua held his arms out for Bella. "Ready?"

She nodded and slid down off the horse into Joshua's waiting arms.

CHAPTER 47

Relief flooded through Jabari when he saw his father coming through the fields carrying his mother. His Uncle Mike had arrived about twenty minutes ago with the stallion his father had ridden in tow, and the report that both Lady and his mom were fine, just a little shaken. But nothing for Jabari was like seeing them for himself. Jabari stood frozen, along with his grandpa, grandma, and Marcus, each of them tasting the air around his dad, everyone assessing his mood. Only Stuart was foolish enough to walk towards them. His dad never broke stride as Stuart approached. He just spoke one word in a low, hard voice, "Run."

Stuart ran into the barn, grabbed his tools, and broke camp. Grandpa Jack hurried and got the door and Grandma Mel ran into the house ahead of them, saying something about needing to turn down the sheets in their room.

"You'd better pray real hard, mister, that nothing happens to Bella and nothing happens to that horse." Grandpa Jack had growled at Stuart after his dad had ridden off on the stallion. He even let a few cuss words fly, and Grandma Mel didn't bother correcting him.

"They'll find them. You'll see," Grandma Mel had said, gripping Jabari too tightly. "That horse may tolerate everybody else, but she loves your dad. She'll see him riding across that clearing and stop dead in her tracks. You wait and see. Bella will be fine. Please, God." She whispered.

"Why the hell did you have her on a horse in the first place?" Grandpa Jack paced back and forth, screaming at Stuart, who was blubbering and crying some crap about team building.

"Two hundred and fifty horses on this ranch and you put her on Lady? What were you thinking?" Suddenly Grandpa Jack's eyes narrowed suspiciously at Stuart. "You're trying to make my boy catch a case, aren't ya?"

"No, no, Jack!"

"What's the matter, Stuart? Not enough black men in prison for ya? Well you won't have to worry about Joshua killing ya. If anything happens to that girl or that horse, I'm gonna shoot you myself. You have my word on that!" Grandpa Jack had just ended his tirade by telling Stuart to pack his stuff and get the hell off his property when Uncle Mike rode up saying that everything was all right.

Even Uncle Mike, who never lost his cool, was majorly pissed. Jabari had never heard his uncle swear, either on or off the court, and in the matter of one hour Stuart had his uncle cussing twice in one day. Stuart had tried to explain himself as Uncle Mike dismounted the horse. Uncle Mike told Stuart to back up off him and get the *bleep* out of his face. Stuart, at least, had the good sense to walk away.

Jabari couldn't see his mom's face right now, she was clinging so tightly to his dad's neck and her head was buried in his chest. He knew he'd feel more settled if he could just look into her eyes. Jabari followed his parents into the house.

"Dad?" he whispered when they made it to the door of the guestroom. His dad turned around and the confidence Jabari saw in his eyes dissolved the wad of tension that had been building in his chest.

Joshua flashed Jabari a knowing smile. "My job now, remember?"

Jabari nodded, remembering their talk on the trails.

"She's fine. Just needs to rest."

"Alright," Jabari smiled back. "Good night."

CHAPTER 48

Exhausted, Bella slept past noon the next day. She woke to the unfamiliar sound of quiet coming from the Kennedy house. That's when she realized that everyone must be out back. Bella yawned and sat up in bed; she checked the clock, wondering why no one had bothered to wake her and then remembered. Embarrassment, then anger, rose in her belly like a tidal wave. Last night, after Melissa had helped her into the bed, Bella couldn't stop trembling. So Joshua had climbed in beside her and held her close all night. Late into the night she had whispered something to him in the darkness.

"Joshua, I rode a horse today. I'm still alive. The thing I always thought would kill me didn't."

He'd kissed the back of her neck then, sending just the slightest quiver up her spine.

"I didn't know it until I saw you and Lady in the meadow today. You're still my air."

It was like a dream, a delicious dream, and now that she was awake, she couldn't tell whether it had been real or not. Had he really called her his air? Bella took her time showering and getting dressed, trying to compose herself. She had to make an appearance sometime, either that or Joshua would come looking for her, and that was the last thing she wanted right now. When Bella walked out onto the back porch, everyone tried to act normal, everyone except Jabari. He ran to her and buried his head into her stomach and she hugged him deeply.

"There's a plate of food waiting for you in the kitchen. I'll go warm it up," Melissa said, disappearing into the house.

Next came Jack enfolding her into his arms. Mike was next, cocooning her in his. "You okay?" he whispered.

"Yeah, I'm fine."

Marcus jumped up from his seat at the outdoor table, next to Joshua. "Ms. Rose, take my spot."

"Oh, okay. Thank you, Marcus." Her eyes met Joshua's for the briefest moment and to her relief, he just smiled. He knew her best. Knew that though the family meant well, all this attention was making her feel self-conscious. Melissa came out of the house and set a plate of steaming hot food in front of Bella. Everybody watched her anxiously until Joshua turned the conversation back to sports. Bella was happy to tune out the chatter around her as she ate her food. She only looked up again when the conversation abruptly stopped. Five pairs of male eyes glared at the individual approaching the porch.

"Oh dear, not good," Melissa muttered under her breath as Stuart made his way up the walk.

"Now, Jack, just hear me out. I know you said never come back here, but I just couldn't go too far without seeing about Bella." Stuart walked up the steps but stopped at the top of the porch. He held his arms open wide to Bella. "What do you say, Bells, can we let bygones be bygones?"

Bella smiled at Stuart and his face visibly relaxed. She pushed herself up from the table, removed the napkin from her lap, and walked over and stood in front of him.

"That a girl—"

Bella punched Stuart hard, aiming her knuckles for the soft fleshy part of the eye. The way Joshua had taught her once.

Stuart staggered backward and tumbled down the front stairs.

Mike threw his hands up in the air and slapped Jack a high five. "Lunch has been served!"

Bella spun on her heels and ran into the house. Melissa ran in behind her.

"She hit me!!" Stuart stuttered, holding his eye. She really hit me!"

Jack laughed.

"Look on the bright side, Stuart," Jabari said.

"What bright side!"

"Now my dad doesn't have to do it." Stuart's eyes flew warily to Joshua.

Joshua smirked at him, shook his head, and walked inside the house.

CHAPTER 49

Melissa set a bowl of ice in front of Bella. "Put your hand in this."

"Mel, I am so sorry. He just made me so mad."

"Don't apologize. It was long overdue. I'm just glad it was you and not Joshie." Melissa looked up when she heard the kitchen door open. "I'm going to go monitor the situation outside. Last night your father threatened to shoot Stu with the gun."

Joshua walked around the kitchen island and grabbed a tea towel and a Ziploc bag. He put the ice inside the bag and wrapped it in the towel. He lifted Bella's hand gingerly from the bowl.

"Josh, don't, it's fine."

"We both know that I'm clearly the expert when it comes to this."

A tiny smile crossed Bella's lips. "Which part, the slugging or the icing?"

"Both." Joshua frowned as he examined the small cut on her knuckle. "What'd I tell you about aiming for the meat?"

"I tried, he didn't have any. Felt like punching a skeleton."

Joshua wrapped the towel neatly around her knuckles. "Better?"

"Yeah, much. Thanks."

"So much for a relaxing weekend in the country. You ready to go home?"

Home, the word sounded so sweet coming from his lips, she wanted nothing more.

"Yeah."

"I'll grab our things."

CHAPTER 50

Bella awoke to find herself in her own bed. For a moment it felt like a dream; but then she felt a wave of nausea and along with it a heavy dose of reality. Yes, she was home, in her and Joshua's bed, but there was no reason to celebrate; she was pregnant by another man. Didn't matter what had transpired between them on the farm this weekend, nothing could change that. Bella fought back the unbidden tears and drug herself into the shower. After she had showered and brushed her teeth, she walked into her closet to see what she would wear. Bella loved her closet. It was the one room in the house, besides her dining room, that made her feel like a queen. A teardrop chandelier hung right over her vanity table, and Joshua had the room decorated to suit both their taste, so in the end the designer settled on shades of golds, pinks, tans, and cream. As a result, the room had a feminine touch with a decidedly masculine feel as well. It was a delicate balance of both of their styles. Bella leafed through her summer clothes looking for something to wear. She pulled out a kelly green sundress. One of her favorites. She held it up to herself in the full-length mirror and tried to remember where she'd bought it. Was it in Houston or Milan?

The year they'd moved to Houston, Joshua had asked her what she wanted for Christmas. Bella hated going anywhere with Joshua because they were constantly being approached, darn near mauled, if not by the media, then by his fans, especially the females, who would walk boldly up to them, press their phone numbers into his hand, as if she wasn't standing there. In the early days of their marriage, Bella had her fair share of heifer-don't-make-me-take-my-earrings-off moments.

So when he'd asked her what she wanted for Christmas, she told him, "To be alone with you in a crowd." So they flew to Milan to walk the streets and tour the shops, hand in hand, unmolested, and undisturbed. Who knew there was a whole sect of beautiful, statuesque, Italian women who loved American basketball and American ball players? Joshua Keys had fans in Milan. No, they hadn't bought the dress in Milan; it was when they returned. When they had returned, Joshua had rented the Foxwood Plaza, had it opened up after hours, then he invited all the Houston Rockets and all the Dallas Cowboys and their wives, children, and girlfriends to go shopping. Because, he said, it wouldn't be what she'd asked him for if there wasn't a crowd.

"I'm sorry about Milan, Bella," he said, as he kissed her long and passionately by the mall's wishing well fountain. And because all the people there were professionals, nobody bothered them, nobody took their picture, and nobody pointed or stared. No one said a word. Bella sighed sadly. *Wear it now, girlfriend, because in a couple more months it may never fit you again.* Bella slipped the dress over her head, and as she did, she realized it wasn't the most beautiful thing in her closet, but that it was the sentiment behind it that made it her favorite. She also realized that the best thing she could do was stay out of Joshua's way until she could figure out her next move. Bella opened the door to the upstairs bedroom and listened intently for sounds of Joshua and Jabari. When she heard the garage door open and then close, she made her way quietly downstairs.

CHAPTER 51

Joshua was sitting at the breakfast nook with the morning paper obstructing his face when Bella tipped-toed into the kitchen. *Dang it.* Bella lifted the heel of her foot and attempted to quietly back out of the kitchen.

"Bella?"

She froze. She had become a master at tipping in and out of places. She'd had a lot of practice avoiding her landlord. So she was sure Joshua hadn't heard her, it was more like he had felt her. There was a firm, but an unmistakable gentleness in his voice.

"Stay, please."

"I thought you guys had left," Bella mumbled.

Joshua lowered his paper and patted the chair next to him at the table.

Bella sat down at the kitchen table. Joshua peered intently at her, while Bella studied the table, the walls, the floor; anything and everything but his eyes. "Where's Jabari?" she asked.

"Upstairs getting dressed. We're getting ready to go shoot some hoops. What about you? You need anything before we leave?"

Bella shrugged and tried to appear as nonplussed as possible. "Nope, just the want ads. The sooner I get a job, the sooner I can be out of your hair."

"I'm not going to put you out, Bella, but I do want a divorce."

The word divorce hurt, but she swallowed the pain and tried to sound as casual as possible.

"That's very big of you."

"You can stay here until your baby is born, as long as you agree to my conditions. I'll help you through this pregnancy. I'll have your back 100%, just like I did with Jabari. I'll be in the birthing room with you holding your hand. I'll even do the Lamaze classes this time. And after your baby is born, I'll help you find a place of your own. I'll cover housing, alimony, and your medical expenses, as long as I get proper visitation with my son."

"You said there were conditions. What are they?" Bella said, finally daring to meet his eyes.

"First, no more running. You have to promise me that in the future, when we have problems, we'll talk them out like two rational adults. You can never take Jabari and disappear on me again."

"I can agree to that."

Joshua paused for a moment before he continued, "I also expect you to attend church with me every week."

"You're kidding, right?"

"No, I'm not kidding. When I go, you go. Church on Sunday, Bible study on Tuesday, and——"

"Let me guess, YPWW on Thursday," Bella said sarcastically.

"I want you to join an accountability group. The group I have in mind for you is called Broken Vessels, it meets on Tuesday evenings at the same time as my Bible study class. The group's leader is a woman by the name of Anna Parks. I contacted her this morning. She's looking forward to meeting you at church this Sunday." Joshua handed Bella a brochure.

She didn't take it. "Forget it," Bella spat. "I don't do church. You know that. As far as I'm concerned, the church house is full of hypocrites."

"Church is non-negotiable, Bella. Everyone who lives under my roof goes."

Bella jumped up from the table. "I guess I'll be needing those want ads, because I'm not going! And I will never, ever, expose my child to those people!"

Bella made a dash for the door, but Joshua was much faster and blocked her pathway.

"Let me through, Joshua!"

"Not until you hear me out. Do you really think, even for a moment, that I would ever let anybody hurt you or our child? I know church has been a source of unspeakable pain for you. I get it. But I also believe with all my heart, that this can be a place of healing for you too. If you'd let it. I've prayed about this, and this is the direction I feel led to go. God hasn't been wrong about you once, Bella Rose. He was the one who told me to send the PI to New Orleans to look for you in the first place. You just made me a promise a few minutes ago. You promised that from now on, we would work out our problems like adults. So I need you to sit back down and listen."

Reluctantly Bella walked back over to the kitchen table and sat down.

Joshua pulled his chair away from the table, flipped it around, and sat it directly in front of hers. He straddled the chair, leaning his torso up against the back of it. "Have I ever lied to you or misled you? Even once?"

Bella thought for a moment. Then she shook her head no.

"What about when things were really bad between us? When I was clubbing, drinking, and fighting. Could you trust me then? I mean, trust my word at least."

"You were always brutally honest," Bella said.

"Close your eyes, Bella."

"Why?"

"Because if you could trust me at my worst, it stands to reason you can trust me now."

Bella sighed and closed her eyes.

"Now, I want you to think back to the last time you went to church. It wasn't so horrible, was it?"

A wicked smile played across Bella's lips.

"Well, was it?"

"Actually, it was quite entertaining. You punched my father out and called him a perverted bastard."

"Okay, well forget about that time. What about the time before that?"

The memory hit her like a freight train and tears moistened the corners of Bella's eyes. She hid her face in her hands.

Joshua gently pried her hands away from her eyes. "What happened the time before that, Bella my Rose?"

"I married you," she croaked.

"That wasn't so bad, was it?" He wiped the tears falling from her eyes.

"The best thing that had ever happened to me."

Joshua stood then and pulled her into his arms. He held her until her crying stopped. But when her mouth searched hungrily for his, he pulled away gently, breaking their connection and replacing what had always been just the two of them with his faith. Suddenly Bella hated his faith.

Joshua picked up the brochure from the table and pushed it firmly into her hand. "I promise you, this is not to harm you, this is to heal you. You have a doctor's appointment scheduled today at three. Can you drive yourself, or would you like for me to drive you?"

"It's okay. I can do it."

Joshua nodded, stepping even further away from her this time. With each step he took away from her, Bella felt her heart breaking more and more.

"I see your clothes still fit, at least for now, but if memory serves me, I think you donated all your maternity clothes to charity."

Of course she had. Even when she'd been pregnant, he'd dressed her like a queen. She'd needed to get rid of them because they were a painful reminder of the sin surrounding the birth of Jabari.

"We'll have to go out and get you some more things soon."

Bella smoothed her hand down the front of her favorite kelly green sundress. "Do you remember where we got this?" Bella said, searching for something, any kind of connection between the two of them. "I was trying to remember if it had been when we got back to Houston, or if we got this outfit in Milan."

He said nothing, but his eyes told her that he did. They told her that, like her, he remembered everything about them.

"Don't forget about your doctor's appointment. I wrote all the information on the back of that pamphlet." Joshua walked out the kitchen and Bella tossed the Broken Vessels brochure into the trash.

CHAPTER 52

Phase one: *join his church. Phase two: accept his God. Phase three: gain his family's approval. Phase four: make him love me.* Selena walked through the offices of Home Court Advantage feeling like a million bucks. Her boss/soon-to-be-husband had given her a much-needed vacation which had given her the mental space and clarity to think about the progression of her life plan. And although the trip home had not been as successful as she'd hoped, she'd left with a resolve in her spirit. With or without the old woman's help, it was time to initiate stage four of her plan. When she got to her desk, Joshua wasn't there. This was, of course, uncharacteristic for him, but she figured he was running late. She decided to pass the time by checking her voice mail and answering some emails. The first email was from her cousin Leslie and marked urgent. Selena chuckled softly to herself. "What kind of dirt has this girl dug up on some poor, unsuspecting, fool now?" She clicked open the email with the subject line: You won't believe this. It was a link to a YouTube video entitled: Joshua Keys's Passionate Pleas for His Family. Selena opened it and watched aghast as the man of her dreams shed tears on national television for a woman who obviously couldn't give a rip about him. Selena jumped up, grabbed her purse, and headed for the door.

CHAPTER 53

Joshua was coming out the shower when he heard the doorbell ring. He picked up the television remote control and turned to the security camera station. That's when he saw his secretary standing outside at his front door. Joshua had left a message on her voicemail on Tuesday telling her that he'd be working from home for the next couple of days. She must not have checked her messages, he reasoned. Joshua zoomed in on the package in her hand, a take-out bag from a local deli that served great soup. Maybe she thought he was sick. Odd, but apparently no one in the office had told her about Bella and Jabari's homecoming. Selena rang the doorbell again and this time Bella answered the door. Joshua turned up the sound. Selena stared at Bella, open-mouthed.

"Can I help you?" Bella asked.

Joshua heard the attitude rising in Bella's voice. He pulled the t-shirt over his head and quickly slipped on a pair of sweatpants.

"Is Joshua here?"

Jabari stuck his head inside the bedroom doorway. "You almost ready, Dad?"

"Yeah, let me put my kicks on and I'll be right there."

"Was that the doorbell I heard a few minutes ago? Wow, cool! Is that a security camera?" Jabari said walking all the way into the room.

"Yeah. Jabari, I need you to run a little interference for me. Go downstairs real quick and tell your mom I'll be right there."

"He's unavailable at the moment," Bella was saying, "Who shall I say stopped by?"

Selena laughed coyly. "Well I'm his...wow, this is really awkward."

Awkward, what in the world had gotten into her? Did Selena have a death wish? On first glance Bella looked like a delicate flower, real prim and proper, but if you spent any quality time at all with her, you quickly came to realize that she had a side to her that was definitely street.

Joshua spoke to the monitor even though the women couldn't hear him. "You're my secretary, Selena."

"I'm Selena Monroe, his secretary. And you are?"

Bella now had her hands on her hips. "His wife."

Jabari came bounding down the stairs. "Hey, Mom, Dad heard the bell and he said to tell you he'll be right down."

Bella put her arm protectively on Jabari's shoulder. "This is our son, Jabari."

Selena reached out and touched Jabari's short curly hair. "Hello, Jabari, my name is Selena. You sure are a handsome young man. I think you look just like your dad."

Jabari's chest swelled with pride. "Thank you!"

"And you must be Bella, right?"

"Mrs. Keys."

An awkward pause.

"Oh, okay. I didn't mean to sound rude, it's just from everything Josh has told me, I gathered that the two of you were separated."

Bella's body stiffened.

Joshua appeared behind Bella then, wrapping his arms around her. He kissed her cheek and willed her body to relax. "Jabari, go wait in the truck for me."

"See you later, Mom. Nice to meet you, Ms. Selena!" Jabari waved.

"Bye, Jabari," Selena said.

"Babe, I see you've met my secretary. Selena's been away on vacation for a few days. I guess wherever she was, she didn't get a chance to hear the good news about my family's safe return."

"No, actually, I didn't. I went to visit my aunt who lives in the Gullah Islands. We barely have running water out there. My aunt won't even consider getting a television."

"You're from the Islands?" Bella asked.

"Born and raised."

Bella sucked her teeth.

"I only saw the clip of your press conference this morning, and when you didn't come into work today… well you seemed so upset on camera, I just wanted to make sure for myself that you were okay."

Bella's eyes narrowed with understanding and Joshua began to apply slight massaging pressure to the muscles in her neck, shoulders, and arms.

"But now, I just feel like a complete idiot," Selena said.

"Don't," Joshua said. "We appreciate the concern. Don't we, babe?"

Another awkward pause.

Joshua cleared his throat. "Well, Selena, thank you for stopping by. I'll be working from home for a while, so any questions you have can be directed to Mike."

"Oh, okay, sure." Selena held out her hand to Joshua, "This is for you. Soup."

Bella took the bag.

"I always like soup when I'm feeling down," Selena said.

Joshua released Bella after she closed the door. He followed her into the kitchen. "I saw the whole thing play out on the security camera upstairs. I didn't like her implying that I'd discussed our relationship with her. I'd never put our business out there like that."

"Yeah, I know you well enough to know that," Bella said as she poured the soup into the garbage disposal.

"You didn't have to do that," Joshua said.

"Just trying to protect you. I was born and raised in New Orleans. Believe me, Voodoo is real. She might act all sweet and innocent, but you'd better watch your back."

"The power of God is much stronger than that."

"Well, that ain't my experience. So, does your secretary always make house calls?"

Joshua rubbed the back of his neck. "Actually, this is a first."

"I guess home visits are reserved for when she thinks your wife and son have been swallowed up in a deadly hurricane."

Joshua leaned against the countertop. "Guess so."

"So, do you eat lunch together?"

"Nope."

"What about dinner?

"Negative."

"She kind of looks like your type."

"And what type might that be, Bella?"

"Pretty, educated. She's obviously smart; she made it over here by herself. Looks like a college girl."

"I sent you to college too, remember?" Joshua stopped himself abruptly. "You know what, forget it." He walked out of the kitchen.

Bella followed him into the hallway. "Go ahead and say it," Bella bated him. "You sent me to college and what?"

Joshua shook his head, "You obviously want to pick a fight and I'm not going to do this with you."

"No, I'm curious, Joshua, what were you about to say?"

"You have no right to be jealous."

"She's in love with you, Joshua. The woman basically stood in our doorway and told me she's been screwing you while I've been away."

"Stop."

"Hey, listen, I'm a big girl. I get it, okay? I've been gone for five years. For the record, I didn't expect you to live like a monk. I just want to know if you love her. I want to know if she's the reason you sent the detective to New Orleans instead of coming for me and Jabari yourself?"

Joshua pointed his finger in her face. "You left, remember? When you did, you gave up the right to question me."

"Just answer the question!"

Joshua ignored her and pulled a gym bag from the hall closet.

"Who's the one running now, Josh? Fine! I see that the rules of engagement only apply to me. I'm the only one not allowed to run. I guess your non answer is my—"

In one swift move, Joshua caught her in his arms and pressed her up against the wall. He kept his hands on both sides of her body, caging her in. He didn't hurt her, but the suddenness of his action stole Bella's breath and caught her off guard. "Let me be very clear, Bella Rose," Joshua began in a voice that was uncharacteristically calm for the situation.

A voice that Bella noted was surprisingly absent of anger and bitterness, but not devoid of truth and pain. In fact, it was the pain in his voice, and the raw truth behind the words that he spoke, that washed over her body like huge shock waves, threatening to drown her, to choke her, to rock her to the core, to cleanse her.

"I want a divorce because you left me. I loved you with all my might and you violated our covenant time and time again. You did that. You, Bella, all by yourself. I'm not sleeping with Selena. I'm not in love with her. There is no one else. As long as we are married, as long as you wear my name, whether you live in my house or not, whether you sleep in my bed or not, there will be no one else."

Joshua removed his hands, picked up his bag, and walked out the front door, leaving a silent Bella barely able to breathe in a room so filled up with pain.

CHAPTER 54

Selena hit the steering wheel and screamed in frustration. After what she had just endured, there was no way she was going back to the office. She made a beeline to her cousin's apartment.

"Ah ha! You thought you was gonna snag that rich ball player but his wife is back. And that trick ain't havin' it!" Leslie sang.

Selena glared at the computer screen as Leslie played the second video of Joshua tenderly enfolding Bella in his arms, kissing the top of her head, and carrying her away from the Astrodome.

"Why didn't you send me this video first? Before—"

"Before what?"

"Before I went over to his house and made a complete fool out of myself!"

"Don't even try to put this on me! You should have read the whole email. I sent you two links."

Selena fought back the anger that was growing inside of her. She had worked hard, so very, very hard. Things were finally beginning to look up for her and now this.

"What about the old lady? Did she open The Book for you?"

Selena thought back to the conversation with her aunt this weekend. She had literally begged for the spell that would bind Joshua's soul to hers forever. Selena shuttered at the thought of the old woman's eyes which never quite looked at you, more like looked through you, penetrating your soul.

The old woman had stared at her great-grandniece who was kneeling before her in feigned humility. The Americanized one.

"You do not love him," the old woman pronounced. "Your hunger is money. It is foolish to tie yourself to the shadows for money."

"It not just he money, Auntie. Joshua is a good man. Him honest and true," Selena said, slipping effortlessly into her native island patois.

"Watch out, gurl. Him got powerful magic he ownself, if you believe that. How many Christians you know are honest? How many more true?"

"He no warlock, Auntie. His faith is real. Him love his god for true."

The old woman studied her for the longest time, making Selena think that she might be actually willing to change her mind.

"I hid the wife and chile for you. Now do the rest. The old fashion way."

"But Auntie, I don't have time. The wife and chile are no longer cloaked. The spell broke."

The old woman looked imperiously down her nose at Selena. "Impossible."

"Him found he family, Auntie. It's true."

"My spell broke and him no witch? Him true?" The old woman began to tremble and Selena watched her rich cinnamon toned skin turn an ashen gray.

"Yes, Auntie," Selena said, laying her hand upon the old woman's shoulder. "Now you see what we are up against. Why I need you to open up the family grimoire and read the ancient scrolls."

"No, it is over. The Ancient of Days is fighting for him now. There is no spell that can help you. I will do one last thing. Perhaps . . . it may absolve you. Tomorrow I will offer tribute."

Selena's eyes lit up. "To Baphomet? So that he will help us?"

"To the Living One, so that He will spare you," the elder hissed. The old woman rose to her feet, signaling that the meeting was over. Selena rose too. "You chose the wrong Christian, gurl. You overstepped the boundary lines."

Selena's face contorted with anger and confusion. "So that's it? You have power untold at your fingertips and this is your answer? You're going to go pray to the Christian god?"

The old woman slapped Selena hard across the face. "Blasphemous chile, you know nothing about how the Universe works."

Selena rubbed her cheek. That had been days ago and still Selena felt the humiliation of the old woman's slap.

Selena looked at Leslie and shook her head. "She wouldn't budge."

"Then you gotta find something on the wife. Been gone for five years. Gotta be a whole lot of dirt under that rock she done crawled out from. Something that would put the nail in the coffin of their relationship for good."

"And how am I supposed to find all of this so-called dirt?"

Leslie side-eyed Selena then sucked her teeth. "It amazes me how you ever even found a job. I guess Bad Boy is just like every other man, a sucker for a pair of legs and a pretty face." Leslie pushed away from her desk and strolled into the kitchen.

Selena followed behind her, choosing to ignore, for the moment, her cousin's obvious hater-aide. Leslie could be cute too. And she'd be able to pull a half-way decent man herself if she stopped looking at that dumb computer screen all day, took a jog around the block, and stop stuffing her fat face. "Les, listen. This could pan out for both of us."

"How you figure?"

"If I marry Joshua, I'm set, and if I'm set, you're set. Have I ever left you hangin', even when we was kids?"

"Naw, we both ate."

"That's right. We both ate. And since I know you a little low on ends these days, I'mma give you the little stash I had already broken off to bless the old woman. Just think of it as a down payment on our future."

Leslie reached into the fridge and handed Selena a beer. "I'll start with an internet search. All I gotta do is plug in the right information and the Universe will tell me everything I need to know about Bella Keys, aka, Rosemary Leblanc."

CHAPTER 55

After spending two nights on a short, lumpy mattress with his feet sticking over the edge of the bed, Joshua decided to return to the master bedroom. The master suite had been designed for extravagance and comfort, with its soothing spa green colors, soaring vaulted ceiling, the splendid four-poster bed, and custom mattress to fit Joshua's pro-ball player size.

The guest room, on the other hand, had been designed to be accommodating but not too welcoming. Because in the early days, when Joshua and Bella had first fled to Houston, privacy was the thing that had been in shortest supply. It was also the thing they valued most.

If the decision had been left solely to Joshua, there would have been no guest bedroom at all, but Bella insisted, having been raised in the South. She said that it was rude and improper to have such a large home and not have at least one bed available when guests came to call. The compromise, they decided, was to design it together. Joshua chose for the room lower thread count sheets and Bella decorated the room with whimsical flea market finds.

"I think I want a bright sunny yellow that makes our guests feel right at home," Bella said when they were picking out paint swatches.

"How about a yellow that wears on the nerves a little bit and after three days says, 'go home'," Joshua had replied.

In the end, they settled on good paint and a cheap night's sleep. The walls were painted a bright butter yellow that said, "We're so glad you're here." But when a body sank down on the economy mattress Joshua picked out, the bed would groan and dip just a little bit in protest, as if to say,

"I'm good for a night or two, my friend, but whatever you do, don't stay too long."

Bella, who clearly was no longer welcome in the master bedroom suite, took up residence here.

Since she had way too many clothes for the small closet to accommodate, Joshua had workmen build a door in the wall leading back to the master closet. So now, even though they no longer shared a bedroom, Bella still had access to the master bathroom and closet.

Joshua knocked on Bella's bedroom door Sunday morning at 8 AM sharp. It took a moment for Bella to recognize where the knocking was coming from, but when she opened the closet door, she found Joshua, dressed in a suit and tie and standing on the other side.

"You know what you're wearing this morning?"

Bella flopped back down on the economy mattress. "No."

Joshua grabbed her hand, led her into the walk-in closet, navigating her through the rows and rows of beautiful clothes. He chose a silver scoop neck dress with a saucy flair and held it up for Bella's inspection.

Bella shook her head. "I always feel like people stare when I wear that."

"That's because you look stunning in it."

Bella made an icky medicine face. "Really?"

"Yeah, really."

That was the thing Joshua found most infuriating about her. She didn't seem to understand who she was in the world. If she would let him, he would treat her like a priceless jewel. Instead, she allowed strangers to claw at her body like she was nothing more than a two-bit hooker. Joshua had always enjoyed buying clothes for Bella, and whenever he dressed her, he dressed her like she was a queen.

Bella picked up two pairs of shoes. "Silver or black? The silver match better," Bella said as she held the shoes up for Joshua's inspection.

Joshua stooped down and examined Bella's ankle. Although she had injured it escaping Hurricane Katrina it was now almost completely healed. "The black are more practical. Put a pair of slippers in your purse too. I'mma get Jabari started. Meet us downstairs in a half an hour."

CHAPTER 56

When they walked into the huge sanctuary of New Horizons Christian Training Center that morning, Bella was somewhat comforted by the fact that this was a mega church. Mega churches were great places for hiding. They could always sit in the back, slip in and slip out, and no one would ever be the wiser for it. No harm no foul, and best of all, she would be keeping her word to Joshua. But to her horror a white-gloved usher led them all the way to the very front of the auditorium. Not just the front, but to the very first row—the one reserved for the muckety mucks. The usher held out her gloved hand, motioning for her and Jabari to enter the pew first. "Josh," Bella whispered. "That woman is telling us to sit there. The sign clearly says reserved." The last thing Bella wanted was to call any undue attention to herself by sitting in some pompous spiritual dignitary's seat, only to have to be later ejected. Reserved seating was set aside for church royalty. *Lord, help this woman,* Bella thought. She was un-churched and even *she* knew that.

"It's okay, Bella," Joshua said. He placed his hand on the small of her back and guided her into the row.

The gloved woman's next question to Joshua almost stopped Bella's heart. "Will you be sitting in the pulpit today, Pastor, or will you be sitting with your family?"

Pastor. Pastor. She called Joshua, her Joshua, Pastor. Bella didn't really hear too much more after that. At some point, she thought she heard somebody call her name, perhaps the stately older man giving the sermon, who she deduced to be the senior pastor at New Horizons. Next, she heard Joshua whispering in her ear, asking her to stand. When she did, the whole congregation stood to their feet and in one voice the entire assembly released a mighty roar. People were cheering, clapping, and crying. The organist started playing a shouting song and some of the women abandoned their high heels and took off running.

Bella gripped Joshua's arm in fear.

"It's okay, Bella," Joshua whispered. "They're praising God. Many of these people have been praying for a long time for your safe return home to me."

"They know about me?"

"Only what the media has said."

The media had said that she ran away because she couldn't take having them in their business. That she was tired of the fake paternity suits, tired of the cameras, and the reporters constantly invading their lives.

After church, Joshua introduced Bella and Jabari to the ministerial staff of New Horizons. The youth pastor, a Korean man named Dave, hit it off with Jabari right away. And Bella had to admit that she was pleasantly surprised at the kindness shown to them by everyone. She was used to people loving Joshua, but the head pastor and his wife embraced her like she was their long-lost daughter. One of the assistant pastors even referred to her as Joshua's better half.

He actually said, "It's good to finally meet Joshua's better half."

Bella snickered silently to herself. Maybe he was calling those things that are not as though they were. *Lord, if these people only knew the truth!*

After the service, Jabari attended a youth group meeting and Joshua, her Joshua, stood in line next to the senior pastor and his wife and four other assistant pastors and their wives, shaking hands with the members of the church. Joshua had explained to her that this was a part of a system they'd developed to put names and faces with all the people at New Horizons.

"It's kind of a lengthy process, that's why we only do it once a month," Joshua had said. Joshua had left her sitting in the pew and instructed her to put on her house shoes. The next thing Bella knew, the little white gloved usher lady from earlier was standing next to her with a pillow in her hand, never speaking, just motioning impatiently for Bella to lift her leg so that Bella could elevate her foot. Bella did as the woman asked without getting an attitude, but only for Joshua's sake.

Joshua seemed right at home in the limelight, smiling and greeting all of the people, and just like during his ball playing days, Bella began to feel out of place in his world. Alone, and very small. Watching Joshua and the other pastors took her back to a memory in her childhood. She was standing next to her mother and her father, like she had on so many other Sundays, greeting new members in their church's receiving line. But on this particularly sweltering day with the air conditioning system broken, Bella couldn't stop fidgeting with her hair bows, or complaining about her feet hurting, and about having to shake so many fat, sweaty hands. Sylvia Leblanc had leaned over to Bella with her first lady smile plastered perfectly in place. "I know you're hot, I know you're tired, but this is really good practice for you. Your mama had the most remarkable dream about you the other night, Bella Rose. I saw your future just as clear as day. You're gonna grow up and marry a preacher. So you stand right here, darling. You watch and you learn, because mama's gonna teach you how to keep every sanctified whore in the house underneath your feet."

Apparently, the pastor's wives at this church knew the same thing her mama knew, because they stood right next to their husbands, welcoming and greeting the long line of people that snaked out the door. Bella jumped when she felt a hand on her shoulder.

"How's that foot feeling?" Joshua said.

"Oh, you scared me."

"Sorry, didn't mean to."

Bella looked at the long line of people that seemed to go on forever. "Why aren't you still up there with the rest of the spiritual dignitaries?"

"I wanted to check in on you. You looked kind of lost sitting over here by your lonesome."

"Just remembering my mama. That's all."
Joshua studied her face intently for a moment.

"Josh, really, everything's fine," Bella whispered. "I'm fine. In fact, if anything, all this attention is making me feel uncomfortable. I've been walking around the house now for days and my ankle has felt fine."

"I know, but today's the first time you've worn heels. I wouldn't want you to have a relapse."

Bella rolled her eyes. "I won't relapse."

Joshua raised an eyebrow skeptically.

"You've prayed for my leg a billion times. Don't you believe in the power of prayer?"

Joshua grinned. "Okay, I see you're trying to call a brother out."

"I'm just saying, I'm in church, the one place on earth I swore I'd never return to, wearing of all things, my dag gone bedroom slippers. Either there really is a God, or I need to watch out for you, because you done slipped something into my food."

Joshua released a hearty laugh.

"Trust me, Joshua Keys, it ain't my ankle that I'm worried about right now."

Joshua stooped down so that he was eye level with her. "What are you worried about?"

Bella shrugged. "My ego I guess."

Joshua removed the pillow that propped up her leg. "I think your ego will be just fine." He stood up and extended his hand to her. "Will you join me?"

"What, you mean go up there? With you?"

"I know it's a lot to ask of you on your first day, but so many people want to meet you."

Bella gave her silent assent and took Joshua's hand. When they reached the line and took their place next to the senior pastor and his wife, Bella put on a happy face. Like it or not, her Joshua was a pastor now.

Every now and again, Joshua looked over at Bella and asked, "How you doing, your feet still feel okay?" or "You good?" Countless members approached Bella and told her what a great man Joshua was. How blessed they were to have her. How they couldn't wait for the ministry that was in her belly to come forth. There was something in her belly alright, but it definitely wasn't a ministry. They hugged her, kissed her, a couple of people even cried over her. People she'd never laid eyes on before told her how much they loved her, that for five long years they'd been fasting and praying for her, and that God was going to give back to her what the locust and the cankerworm had eaten away and stolen. And the funny thing was, Bella was actually starting to feel kind of warm and fuzzy about all of it.

One very sincere woman came up to Bella and said, "You have chosen a name for yourself that means bitter herb, but God's going to make you laugh in the days to come."

Bella smiled graciously and thanked the woman, but thought, *Okay, lady, we'll see if I'll be laughing nine months from now when I have this baby and my husband puts me out.*

"Bella," Joshua said, breaking into her thoughts. "This is Anna Parks. She's the woman I told you about."

Anna had a warm smile, and when she hugged Bella she smelled heavenly, like cinnamon and peaches. "I'm so looking forward to having you join our group this Tuesday, Mrs. Keys."

And because this Anna Parks person felt so safe, Bella's response to her was, "Please, call me, Bella." Out of the corner of her eye, Bella saw Joshua's secretary, Selena, flinch. She couldn't have timed it better if she tried. *Double score!*

"Psss, Rose!"

Bella looked over and saw the former residents of the Dunbar Street apartments standing off to the side. Bella waved excitedly at them.

"Go ahead," Joshua said, "You've endured this long enough, go talk to your friends."

"You sure?" Bella said, eyeing Selena, who was waiting in line to talk to Joshua next.

"Yeah, we'll be done here soon. Go ahead."

"Look at you, Rosemary, don't you look like a fine lady!" Lola said.

"I must admit, Rose, you do clean up nicely," Walter said.

"You didn't tell me you guys were coming," Bella said, hugging Maggie.

"We weren't until Joshua called this morning and invited us. He thought we'd enjoy the service." Maggie bumped Bella's arm knowingly, "He also thought it would make you feel better to see some faces you already knew."

Maggie held Bella away from her and surveyed her dress. "I'm loving this dress, Rose! My gosh, you look like a movie star!"

❧ ❧

"Pastor Joshua, you have a beautiful family!" One parishioner said as she clasped his hand between hers. "And your wife is so lovely."

"Yes, she is," Joshua agreed, watching Bella with her friends from her old neighborhood. Just as he'd thought, she'd finally relaxed when her friends had appeared. It was good to see her laughing and happy. He noticed that like so many other sexually broken women, Bella was a natural with men, but a little more uncomfortable and reserved with other women. But Maggie, who was just a few years older than Bella, was proving to be a great friend. Joshua thought about Jabari and how eager he was to go with the other kids in the youth ministry. Then he whispered a silent prayer of thanks, because it looked like Jabari and Bella were both gonna fit in just fine.

CHAPTER 57

J oshua, Dee and I would love to have you, Bella, and Jabari over for dinner tonight," Keith, one of the assistant pastors on staff at New Horizons, was saying just as Micah Ford and his wife Pamela walked up.

"Keith, are you and Dee trying to steal our dinner guests?" Micah asked.

"Hey, why do you guys get to have dibs on them first?" Dee said.

"Well, the last time I checked, I was still the senior pastor at New Horizons," Micah said. Pamela laughed.

"Why don't we just have a cook-out? That way we all get to hang out with Bella and Jabari. Oh, yeah, and of course you too, Josh," Pamela added.

"We appreciate the offer, but it's been a long day. I think I better get Bella and Jabari home."

"We understand, Joshua. Bella, forgive us. We don't mean to be pushy, we're just so excited that you're finally home," the woman called Dee said, hugging Bella tightly.

"Yeah, Bella, feel free to tell us to back off if we get to be too overwhelming for you," Keith said.

There it was again, that word. Home. Bella found herself wishing that she could turn back the hands of time and change her actions, so that this really could be home, permanently. As usual, Joshua knew her inside and out. He knew that she had endured all she could for one day. As he led her and Jabari out of the church, Bella thanked him silently with her eyes. Jabari chatted non-stop once they'd climbed into the car, about the youth department and the friends he had made that morning.

Joshua reached over and patted her hand as he turned onto the freeway, "You did good, Bella, real good."
And in that one sentiment so many words passed.

CHAPTER 58

As soon as they arrived home, Bella made a beeline to the guest room. She removed the dress she'd worn to church and changed into a cute little tank top and a comfortable pair of hip hugging blue jean shorts. Since she'd returned home to Houston and had access to her closet again, *better wear it now or never at all* had become her motto. When Bella walked into the master closet to hang up her clothes, she saw Joshua hanging up his suit. The scowl on his handsome face told her that he was somewhere else in his head; not angry, just deep in thought.

He had slipped into one of the many pairs of official NBA basketball shorts he owned and a Rocket t-shirt. And for the briefest of moments, watching him stand there in uniform, scowling, Bella allowed herself to go back in time. She was here with *him* and they were in *their* master closet. She wasn't sleeping in the guest room across the hall. She was in *his* bed where *she* belonged. *They* were fine. He was Bad Boy Joshua Keys—*her* Joshua and *they* were fine.

But he was hanging up the clothes he had worn to church that morning and it was something about the way his silver cufflinks reflected against the master closet's recessed lighting that compelled her to remember. He looked the same. He smelled the same. His touch from the first and only time they'd made love since she'd returned still burned her skin, but this man was not the same Joshua. Joshua noticed her standing in the doorway so she smiled. "Fancy meeting you in here."

"Yeah, fancy that." His eyes roamed lazily, appraisingly, over every inch of her frame as she passed by him on her way to the dress rack at the far end of the closet. Bella smiled coyly to herself. At least that hadn't changed.

"You hungry yet?"

"Starving," Bella said, returning to stand in front of him. "That cook-out is starting to sound pretty good after all."

"I ordered Chinese, it should be here shortly."

"Great."

"I know today was a lot to take in, so, thank you."

Bella sat down on the large ottoman that flanked the floor of the closet. "I was wondering when we were gonna talk about that."

Joshua avoided her eyes. "Do you have any questions for me?"

"Just one."

Her silence forced him to look at her.

"Why didn't you tell me?"

Joshua released a hard sigh and sat down on the floor in front of her, pulling his knees to his chest. "Honestly?"

Bella nodded.

"I didn't know how. I know how you feel about church and ministers in general. I didn't know how to tell you that I'd become one of them."

"I guess the Rev was right about one thing."

Joshua stared up at her with an unreadable expression. "What's that?"

"He always did say you were called to preach."

"Bella, I'm not him, I'd never—"

"I know. When I think about what happened to me, I don't think about all preachers being like that. Just him."

Joshua nodded. "All that time I wasn't just angry with him. I was angry with God. When he spoke, I felt the power of God. In my mind I couldn't reconcile that. Why God would allow a man like Leblanc to carry His power. I kept waiting for God to do something biblical to him, when He didn't. I told myself I didn't want to serve a God like that. But

I've been hearing His voice since I was a child. And then you left this last time and I thought I would lose my mind."

Bella stared down at her hands until his next words forced her to look into his eyes.

"During the darkest days of my life, God was there. He kept my mind and my soul. This whole ministry thing wasn't a decision I made lightly, but it has been a natural progression for me. I've made my peace with it and I hope you can too."

"The Levitical Order and the Zadok priests," Bella said softly.

Joshua stared at Bella quizzically. "What did you just say?"

Bella cleared her throat and continued her voice gaining strength. "God made a distinction between the Levites and the Zadok priests. The Levites led the people into sin and corruption instead of teaching them how to live right before God, so God pronounced judgment upon them. 'You will take care of my house. You'll lead my people into my presence, but you will never be able to come near me again. Only the Zadok priest who kept my statutes will be able to do that.'"

Bella had closed her eyes as she spoke, when she opened them, she found Joshua staring at her in stunned disbelief. "That's in the Bible. I didn't make that up."

"Naw, yeah, I know."

"You're just surprised that I know it, right? You talk about knowing God when you were a child. Well, once upon a time, Joshua, I knew Him too. I couldn't make sense of my daddy's gift either. Then one day, I got so mad, I demanded an answer."

"From God?"

"Yeah."

"So… He took you to the book of Ezekiel?"

Bella rolled her eyes. "Please, by then I was so angry with God I wouldn't have picked up a Bible to save my life. I asked and He told me."

Joshua stared up at her with a goofy grin.

"What?"

"I honestly never even thought to look at that passage like that. You sure you're not a preacher?"

"There was a time when I actually thought that I would be a preacher. That ship sailed a long time ago, though."

"How long ago?"

"Put it like this, the last message I preached was to my dolls and teddy bears."

"You just freed me from something I'd been struggling with for a long time…and just like that night at my parent's house, you weren't even trying."

"What are you talking about?"

"Nothing, just thinking out loud. That's got to be its own kind of hell for Leblanc, I mean. Having known God's presence then not having it at all."

"It's a fate worse than death." And before Joshua could say anything else, she pushed herself up off the ottoman and changed the subject. "This fits you. I can tell. On that bus I kept thinking I'm leaving one hurricane and walking right into the next. But I see peace in you, Joshua Keys. I'm happy for you."

Joshua stood. He cupped his hand to his ear and stepped closer to her. "What was that? I didn't quite catch that last statement; can you repeat that for me?"

"I said I'm happy for you. It's a good thing we're splitting up, though."

"Yeah, why is that?"

"Because I can't decide which is worse. Being married to a charismatic pastor—which I already know you are. Or being married to a famous jock." Bella held out her hands like she was weighing the options, "Famous jock, crazy fans. Charismatic pastor, late night counseling sessions."

"I assume you mean with the opposite sex?"

"Of course, that's how they get you." Bella batted her eyes playfully and pretended to swoon. She fell back down on the ottoman, laying her hand on her forehead. "Pastor Keys, I just need a few minutes of your time so you can pray my strength in the Lord.' Next thing you know, the panties are coming off."

Joshua shook his head. "That ain't happening at my church."

"What's so special about your church?"

"First of all, men counsel men and women counsel women. In fact, most of the pastors and their wives counsel together in pairs. Keeps down on unnecessary mess."

"Well, we'd really be in trouble then, wouldn't we? Could you just imagine the advice I'd give some of those church biddies?"

Joshua grinned down at her. "I don't know about that. Their husband's might appreciate it. Seriously, I want you to throw out everything you used to know about church. Give these people a chance. They already love you."

"They don't even know me."

Joshua extended his hand to her. She grabbed it and he pulled her up so that she was standing beside him. "They know that you're my wife and that you're a part of me."

"What happens when I'm not your wife anymore? Will these good god-fearing people still love me?"

The doorbell chimed loudly.

Jabari shouted up the stairs. "Dad, food's here!"

"Hold on a sec, Bella." Joshua stuck his head out into the hallway and shouted down the stairs. "There's some money on the counter in the kitchen, Jabari. Pay the man. Your mom and I will be down in a minute."

"Okay!" Jabari called back.

Bella looked up expectantly at Joshua when he returned.

He smiled sheepishly at her. "I'm sorry, could you repeat the question please?"

"When it's over between me and you, will they still love me?"

Joshua walked over to her and stood close. So close she could smell the alluring scent of his aftershave. Bella held her breath as he reached down and tucked a tendril of her hair behind her earlobe.

"My prayer is that you'll be a daughter of Zion by then, and who we once were won't matter anymore."

CHAPTER 59

For the next couple of days, the Keys family seemed to settle into a comfortable sort of rhythm. Joshua and Bella managed to maintain a certain level of civility towards one another, even occasionally going so far as to laugh at each other's jokes. They took their meals together, and every night, at Jabari's insistence, they did some sort of family related activity together, whether it was watching a movie or playing a board game. One night, Jabari had the three of them holed up in his bedroom playing video games. Except for the fact that Joshua and Bella didn't sleep in the same bed, the Keys were pretty much a normal family in every other sense of the word. It was this level of normalcy that was starting to make Joshua think that no matter how strange this living situation might be, maybe somehow, in the mind of God, He had some way to make it work. So far, miraculously, they'd already been able to jump all kinds of hurdles; hurdles that under normal situations would have made Bella run. Hurdles like Selena's stopping by unexpectedly and insinuating to Bella that while she was away, she and Joshua had been having an affair. Joshua's announcement to Bella that everyone who lived under his roof would attend church every Sunday without fail, and the biggest blow of all, Bella finding out that while she was away, Joshua had become the one thing she had hated most: a pastor. Because they had jumped all of these hurdles, Joshua was not prepared for Bella's reaction when he stopped by classroom B to pick her up after his Foundational Truths class on Tuesday.

After class, Joshua didn't linger. He answered a few questions, packed up his Bible and papers, and quickly headed over to the youth room to pick up Jabari. Anna Parks was just praying her small group out when Joshua and Jabari arrived to pick Bella up. After the prayer, Bella made a few polite goodbyes, shook a few of the women's hands, and walked straight past Joshua without so much as a word. Bella was mad. That much Joshua could tell. Other than answering a few of Jabari's questions in the affirmative, Bella remained silent for the entire drive home. Jabari, as usual, talked non-stop. Tonight about the youth group and the friends he had made that evening.

"What about you, Bella, did you make any new friends this evening?"

Her response to his query… arctic silence. She kept her eyes straight ahead and her expression like stone. After that first initial attempt, Joshua tried to feel her out by throwing a few more general, less pointed questions her way.

"Are you feeling well?"

"Yes."

"Is your ankle hurting you?"

"No."

"Did everything go well tonight?"

"Fine."

Joshua pulled into the garage and looked over at Bella.

She opened her car door wordlessly and moved quickly into the house.

Joshua looked through the rearview mirror at his son. "Jabari, I want you to hit the showers and get to bed. You've got a big day tomorrow."

"Alright, Dad," Jabari said.

Joshua noted that Jabari seemed blissfully unaware of any tension between him and his mother. Thank God for that. After everything Jabari had been through, the last thing he needed was to be concerned about problems between he and Bella.

Jabari reached over the seat and wrapped his arms around Joshua's neck. Joshua extended his arms behind him and embraced Jabari.

"I love you, man."

"I love you too, Dad," Jabari said as he scurried out of the car.

Joshua waited for the house door to slam shut, then he leaned his head back against the headrest and closed his eyes. *Father, if you want me to represent you the right way, you're gonna have to help me.*

He didn't even know how to have a decent argument with this woman. She was a master at provoking him. Anything that had to do with Bella at all was a provocation for him. Granted, back in the day, it didn't take much, one wrong look, one wrong comment, on or off the court about Bella—always about Bella—and BAM, compliments of Bad Boy Joshua Keys, some cat would have a fist in his face.

"Josh, next time, save yourself the money, save us both the drama, and just hit me instead," she had told him this as they were leaving his attorney's office in Atlanta. They had just settled out of court for one of his many lawsuits. She had flung these words at him as they were exiting the elevator. Her words stopped him cold in his tracks. He watched her walk out of the building and step into the car waiting to take them to the airport. Joshua climbed into the limo and sat across from Bella.

"So that's what you think? I'mma start hitting you, abusing you?"

Bella turned her body away from him and looked out the window, "Whatever, Joshua."

"I hit that guy because I was defending your honor. Doesn't that count for anything with you?"

Bella held up her hand, signaling that she didn't want to hear it.

"He approached me, asked me for my autograph, and then told me he knew my wife in a biblical way. What was I supposed to do?"

"How about walking away?"

"I did. Right after I beat the hell out of him."

"You didn't hit that man for me, Joshua. You hit him for yourself. You hit him because deep down inside, you believed that what he said about me was true."

Joshua smiled at her coldly then, "Well, is it?"

Joshua sighed heavily at the memory. Back then, he and Bella were both experts at using the past for swords, exploiting each other's weakness like daggers. They didn't fight like two people in love, but like mortal enemies, wounding and cutting each other with painful words. When they had both struck their final blows, they'd come to their senses suddenly, apologizing to each other profusely. They'd tear each other's clothes off and make love to each other passionately. Joshua was resolute; they were not about to go back down that road again, no matter what Bella did to provoke him. That's why he'd nearly run out the house the day she had confronted him about Selena. He just simply wasn't prepared.

Conversations with Bella had a way of going from hot to cold in a matter of seconds. He thought back to her monosyllabic answers tonight in the car. The old Joshua would have never tolerated that. He would have forced her to talk to him. But just lately, since Bella had come back into his life, Joshua had to keep reminding himself that he wasn't that old man anymore, and that he'd better be careful, tread lightly, because even if he wasn't the same person he used to be, Bella was. Everything about her was the same; from the way she looked, to the way she smelled, to the feelings she invoked inside of him.

They were all undeniably the same. If Joshua wasn't careful, she might just be able to resurrect that old man. Joshua went into the house and got ready to face the music.

CHAPTER 60

Joshua found Bella in the kitchen, rinsing dishes. "Need any help?"

Bella's back stiffened at the sound of his voice. "No."

"So far that's one yes, one fine, and two noes since we got home. You want to tell me what's going on?"

Bella turned and looked at him, anger flashing in her eyes. She placed her hands on her hip ceremonially, rolled her neck towards him, and declared loudly, "No."

Joshua shrugged. "Okay, I'll be in my office when you want to talk."

Bella's eyes narrowed. "Wait, that's it?"

"Till you're ready to tell me what's on your mind, yeah, that is it."

"Who are you? Where's the old Joshua? The one who was willing to go the distance with me? To fight with me? The one who was willing to help me, not stick me in some group."

"So, this is about the group."

"No, this is about you!"

"Okay, so it's not about the group. It's about me," Joshua restated calmly.

"That's right. You. I hate this new you. This self-righteous, holier than thou you."

"Does my faith offend you, Bella?"

"NO! It's your self-righteousness that offends me! Your pretentious, egotistical self-righteousness!"

"And it just occurred to you to tell me all of this about myself today?" Joshua stepped out into the hallway for a moment, listening for sounds of Jabari. He lifted the door kick and closed the push door that led into the living room. "I realize you're upset right now, but nobody needs to hear our business but you and me."

Bella slammed the dishwasher door closed and glared up at him. "You see that? You don't even fight the same anymore."

"I've never wanted Jabari to hear us arguing. You know that."

"That's not what I'm talking about."

"What are you talking about?"

"Where's the old Joshua?"

Joshua resisted the urge to smile. *Hopefully in the grave, never to resurface again.* "I still fight, Bella. I just learned how to stop fighting people."

"What does that mean, Joshua? Because if you're not fighting people, who the heck are you fighting?"

Another thought popped into Joshua's head. *Spiritual wickedness in high places.* A thought that, under the circumstances, would be best kept to himself.

"It's like now, you believe that you're right in this situation and that I'm wrong. But you won't even fight for what you believe in anymore."

Joshua walked across the kitchen and stood directly in front of her. "Actually, I'm still trying to determine what our situation is, Bella. You haven't told me why you're angry at me yet."

Bella averted her eyes to the floor. "I told you it's you."

Joshua lifted her chin up toward him. *Lord, does this woman even know how sexy she is when she is angry?* He resisted the urge to kiss her, instead he let his fingers brush lightly across her lips. "Yeah, I know. That's what your mouth is saying, but we both know you don't want the old Joshua back, don't we? How did you put it last Sunday? You thought you were running from one hurricane right into another one? And I also happen to know that tonight before we left the house, you were happy with me."

Bella smirked at him. "Really?"

"Mum hum, you were smiling at me. You even tried to seduce me by filling my stomach with the incredible concoctions coming from your cooking pots. So, if I had to take a guess, I'd say that whatever you're angry about has little to do with me or my self-righteousness."

Bella rolled her eyes.

"I think you're angry about something that happened at your meeting, and that you're deflecting those feelings onto me. So, let me ask you again. Would you like to talk about it?"

Bella turned her back towards him. She folded herself into a hug and tapped her foot agitatedly against the floor. When she turned back around to face him, her eyes were filled with angry tears that she wiped away quickly. "You put me in this group with these…these…people!"

The look of raw rejection and pain coming from her eyes almost burned Joshua's walls of resistance completely down. What he wanted to do, what he so desperately wanted to do right now, was to wrap her inside his arms, but Bella was like a drug for him, and he knew if he held on to her right now at this moment, he'd carry her up those stairs tonight and he would never let her go. Then what would happen to the vow he made to the Lord? If he didn't lead her to the Savior, who would pay her redemption price?

This is too much temptation for one man to bear, Father, please be my guide.

Instead of holding her like he wanted to, Joshua leaned up against the sink next to her, allowing their elbows to slightly touch. In that one touch he tried to communicate to her all the good intentions and love he had for her inside his heart. "I told you, Bella Rose, I prayed about this. This is the best group for you."

"A bunch of crazy women! A cutter, an alkie, and a crackhead!"

"Former cutter. Former alkie. Former crackhead," Joshua stated quietly.

"I don't care!"

"I do," Joshua said firmly. "None of these women are living those lifestyles anymore. Whatever they did, they did because they didn't love themselves. The Apostle Paul calls these the worst kinds of sins. Sins against the body. Their lives are a testimony to what God can do. And, ba--"

He almost called her baby. "Bella, if you would just open yourself up to the process, you might learn a lot from them. You might find that you have more in common with them then you think."

Bella pushed away from him quickly. She stood flat footed in front of him with her hands on her hips. "I've never smoked crack a day in my life! I don't cut myself to feel better, and I sure as hell don't sleep with strangers to get money to support my drinking habit!"

Joshua walked towards her closing the distance between them. "No, just to feed your son, right?"

Bella turned quickly on her heels and tried to storm out of the room.

Joshua caught her by the elbow and with his next words, he forced her to turn around. "And to keep a roof over your head, even though you had a husband who loved you, never beat you, and never took advantage of you, waiting for you at home. It's easy for any of us to justify the jacked-up stuff that we do, Bella. But there comes a time when no matter how bitter the pill is, we have to swallow the truth."

Bella looked down at his fingers pressing into her skin. "Yeah, well, you seem to be real good at shoving my reality down my throat, but I don't see you swallowing no truth."

He released her. "I've had to eat my share."

Bella's humorless laugh echoed across the kitchen. "Oh really, like what?"

"Like the fact that no matter how bad I want to, I can't save you. I can't stop the pain. I can't heal your hurt. I'm not God and I can't stand in the way of what he wants to do for you."

Fire blazed in her eyes, "I don't care what you say to me, Joshua Keys. You can preach to me all night long if you want to, until you turn blue in the face, but I am not going back to that group!"

"You will. The group is non-negotiable, Bella. And this time, you will keep your word to me."

With that, Joshua turned and stalked out of the kitchen.

CHAPTER 61

Joshua knocked twice on Bella's bedroom door before entering the room. Bella looked up and saw him carrying a tray of saltine crackers and mint tea. She rolled over and drew the cover up over her head. How beautiful this sentiment would be if this were actually his child she was pregnant with. Didn't he know his kindness was killing her?

Joshua set the tray down on the nightstand. "You okay?"

It was a loaded question. He was asking how she was feeling physically this morning, yes, but he was also referring to their little argument from last night. Actually, it wasn't really even an argument; it was more like a dismissal. Once he had spoken his mind calmly about the issue, he had walked out of the kitchen just as cool and collected as he pleased. No yelling, no punching walls or breaking things, or any other displays of over the top emotions. The only one who hadn't been in control of their emotions had been her. Even when she tried to bait him into a fight, he wouldn't bite. This was certainly not the Joshua she had known, and it was even more proof to her that things were over between them. He wasn't willing to fight with her or for her anymore. He didn't love her and the finality of their love made her heart ache.

"I'm fine," Bella managed to murmur from underneath the covers.

"That's good, because the doctor's office called. You missed your appointment last week."

Bella felt the economy mattress dip slightly as Joshua sat down on the edge of the bed next to her. He slowly pulled the covers from over her face. "When I asked you how everything went at your appointment, you told me everything went fine."

Bella took a quick inventory of his eyes, no anger there, no judgment, only concern, and God no, anything but that, pity.

"I already know I'm pregnant, okay? I don't need some doctor telling me what I already know," Bella snapped. She rolled over and looked at the wall. Mostly so he wouldn't see the tears swimming in her eyes.

Joshua sighed. "Bella, you still need to take care of yourself and the life that's growing inside your womb. I've rescheduled your appointment for this afternoon."

He rested his hand softly on her head and began to stroke her hair. The touch felt soothing like a prayer, massaging the massive ache that was forming in her heart away.

It was soothing, until Bella noted with resentment, that there wasn't the slightest bit of sensuality in his touch.

"No matter how bad you want it to, this isn't going away."

"I know," she said quietly.

She felt the bed release as Joshua stood up.

"I'm a go get Jabari registered for school today. I should be back within the hour, be ready by noon."

CHAPTER 62

Per his request, Bella was ready by noon, and when Joshua returned home from registering Jabari, just like he'd said, he took Bella to her doctor's appointment. Joshua walked Bella up to the registration desk, gave the receptionist his insurance card, and verified that she was his wife and also covered under his insurance. He filled out his portion of the new patient information form, but when the nurse called Bella's name, Joshua remained rooted in his seat in the receptionist area. Bella looked down at him expectantly, wishing, no—more like hoping— him to come inside.

Joshua averted his eyes. "This is as far as I go," he murmured.

He pretended to ignore her then, scanning the waiting room for interesting reading material. Out of the corner of his eye, he saw Bella hesitate, and the tears of disappointment fall. But unlike the night before, Bella's tears inspired no compassion within Joshua. All they did was make him angry. They rode home in complete silence. Joshua didn't even get out of the car. He just dropped Bella off at the front door and kept on going. He knew he should have at least told her that he was going to pick Jabari up from school, but he was still too angry to speak. At this point, silence was golden. If he opened his mouth now, no telling what would come out.

"What's up?" Joshua said when he pulled up to the school and Jabari got into his truck. Jabari nodded a greeting to his dad and the two of them drove away. Yeah, Bella had made him angry. Truth be told, he was still angry. And not merely annoyed, this anger felt like the moment of fresh discovery. The nerve of her to have the unmitigated gall to actually be hurt; to be disappointed. Bella had no idea what disappointment was. Disappointment was finding yourself ten years later in the same predicament. In a hospital waiting room with a wife whose womb was filled with another man's seed. The fact that he had even walked into that place with her today was nothing short of a miracle. Joshua had been so angry during her first pregnancy, so on the verge of losing it every single day, that he could barely stand to be in Bella's presence, much less drive her to and from those doctor's appointments. Even when she got so big that she couldn't fit behind the wheel of her little two seater. Even then, despite her insistent entreaties that if he really loved her and had truly forgiven her, Joshua still couldn't bring himself to be there in the doctor's office. He just couldn't do it. Not to hear the heartbeat or to rejoice over the strength of the baby's kicks, not to see an image that would bear no resemblance to his own on the ultrasound monitor. What he could, and did do for her, was hire a private car to take her to and from her doctor's appointments. Bella cried every time she went. All the way to the appointment and all the way back, just like she had done in the car today.

On the day Jabari was born, Joshua did get it together enough to be in the birthing room with her; to hold her hand and talk her through. Despite his attitude for the previous nine months, he did love her and had forgiven her. And although he didn't understand it, the voice that had been leading him his whole life was right there beside him, talking him through. Telling him to just put one foot in front of the other one. To trust Him for the moment, not the entire hour, and that if Joshua would just keep going, somehow, some way, he would make it through. In the birthing room, Joshua had cut the umbilical cord, and, in that moment, it didn't matter how this child had gotten here, or what dreams had been shattered in the process, Joshua would adopt this child, name him, and claim him. He would love him, and whether or not things between him and Bella were mended or stayed broken, Jabari would forever more be his own.

Jabari. Joshua had been so caught up in thoughts of Bella and the past he hadn't noticed the unusual silence coming from the passenger side of his truck. Joshua glanced over at Jabari. "How was school today?"

"Alright," Jabari muttered.

Joshua carefully surveyed his son. Jabari was slouched down in the leather seat. The Princeton Prep blazer that Jabari had proudly adorned this morning, the one he had been modeling all week for his mother, now hung sloppily from his slight frame. Jabari's brown eyes stared blankly ahead of him, taking in nothing and everything all at once. He was sporting hard the same blasé, come-what-may attitude that Joshua had seen on the faces of so many black youths. It was the same attitude Joshua had worn like a shield himself for many years, on and off the basketball court. The attitude that said *It doesn't matter what you say or do to me, 'cause I don't give a—*. Nah, this was definitely not the same kid he had left the house with this morning. Not his happy-go-lucky son.

Joshua decided right then and there, that this particular curse would not be visited upon his child. Joshua pulled over to the shoulder of the road abruptly. He put the truck in park. When he turned off the radio, Jabari's head snapped up for the first time. "Why are we stopping?"

"Talk to me," Joshua commanded.

"About what?"

After the afternoon he'd endured with Bella, Jabari's attitude was like a flame near a gas leak, so Joshua fought to keep his own foul mood in check. He blew out a breath and cleared his mind of all thoughts of Bella. "Jabari, did you have a bad day today? Did somebody step to you wrong? What?"

Jabari shrugged. "Why it gotta be anything. How come it can't be nothing?"

"""

"'Cause you rolled up in my ride with just a little bit too much testosterone for it to be nothing. And you know I know. So talk."

Jabari fiddled with his backpack strap and stared down at his feet. As Joshua stared at his son, he felt patience enter his heart.

"Look, you're usually talking my head off in the car, and I like that; right about now, I'm missing it. And at least two of those whack songs by that weak artist you like so much have come on the radio, and you haven't tried to get your groove on to either one. And as horrible as both you and he sound, I kind of miss that too."

A small smile turned up the corners of Jabari's lips. "Man, you know Papa Diggy is the bomb."

"Whatever."

"Dad, they gave me these tests today and I didn't hardly know any of the answers."

Joshua nodded. The headmistress had called Joshua earlier that day. Jabari had scored in the lower percentiles, but according to her, not low enough to be held back a grade level. The headmistress went on to describe Jabari to be a bright and inquisitive child, who, with proper tutoring, she felt could get up to grade level in no time. Mike, who had also enrolled Marcus into Princeton Prep's High School program, had received a similar call. Neither boys test scores had been anywhere near what they had hoped, but coming out of the New Orleans school district, no one was really surprised. Princeton Prep was one of the highest ranked schools in the nation. The school took their standing seriously, and money alone wasn't enough to gain the most influential families entry. They were famous for dismissing children of the wealthy who couldn't pass admittance exams and for kicking out kids who once admitted, didn't perform up to the Princeton Prep standard. In the first place, it was unheard of that Princeton had agreed to allow both Jabari and Marcus admittance without the usual series of interviews, especially after the semester had already started. It had helped that the headmistress was a huge Rocket's fan who had remembered the dynamic duo Joshua and Mike had been in their ball playing days. Despite the boys' test scores, the headmistress wasn't the least bit apprehensive. In fact, the woman's downright cheeriness made Joshua wonder if his brother hadn't thrown a couple of courtside season tickets her way. *Hey, whatever it takes.* Neither he nor his brother were opposed to using their connections to make sure Jabari and Marcus got the best education money could buy.

"Jabari, Princeton Prep is two years ahead of most Houston schools. Three years ahead of New Orleans schools. It's only natural that you'd have to play a little catch up."

"I know, Dad. But it's like this. I was prepared to be the new kid, and I was prepared to be one of the only black kids. But I wasn't prepared to be the new, black, and dumb kid."

"So, since you think you can't cut it academically, you decided to go for new, black, dumb, and gangsta. Show those white folks where you really from. Huh?"

Jabari shot Joshua a look of surprise and then quickly recovered. "I'm your son, so that means I'm not a punk."

Joshua shook his head, "Jabari, I feel you. I've been there, but this ain't you."

"Dad, you are Bad Boy Joshua Keys. You have no idea whatsoever what it's like to be me."

"That's what you think, but when I first came to the NBA, I was the slow kid."

Jabari pursed his lips together. "Yeah right."

"I'm not kidding, man, your dad, Bad Boy Joshua Keys."

"Dad, you were, like, the number one draft pick in the nation. You were, like, the coldest player ever. The Rockets retired your jersey."

"I'm telling you, I thought I knew. But when I hit training camp, that's when I realized why they called it the pros." Joshua shook his head, "Man, the skill and the stamina my teammates had was incredible. I couldn't hang."

"What'd you do?"

"I exercised constantly. I hired a trainer and I drilled every day on my own. In the morning before practice and every evening after practice, until I got up to par; until I got better than everybody else. Cause, I'm a tell you something else about your dad, I hate losing and I can tell that you do too."

Jabari nodded his head in agreement.

"Did I ever tell you why I named you Jabari?"

"No."

"I chose your name because Jabari means brave. When you were born, man, I was so scared."

"How come?"

"A whole bunch of reasons, man. I was scared I wouldn't love you right. Scared I wouldn't be the kind of father you needed me to be. You were so tiny and my hands were so big, I was scared I would break you. I named you Jabari to remind me that I needed to be brave, and because I wanted you to grow up one day to be a brave man too. You lived up to that name when you helped your mom and the rest of those people get out of New Orleans during Katrina. And right now, I need you to be who you really are, and not who you think I am. Cause being real that takes bravery too. Okay?"

"Okay, Dad."

Joshua reached over and caressed Jabari's neck. "I have faith in you, I know what you can do. And just so you know, I already knew about the test scores. The headmistress called me today."

"Aw, man, they gon kick me out now for sure!"

"Actually, she said she thought you'd be a wonderful asset to Princeton Prep, and that she could tell from the oral exam that you were very smart and inquisitive. With a little extra help, she's confident that you'll be up to grade level in no time. Your uncle found private tutors for you and Marcus today."

Jabari grinned. "You mean to tell me you let me squirm through that whole inquisition and you and Uncle Mike already had a game plan in play?"

"Jabari, if you would have come right out and told me what your problem was, you wouldn't have had to squirm through anything."

"So, what's the plan?"

"Plan is simple, son. You will work harder than you have in a very long time. Harder than you ever have in your life. You're going to study every day and exercise that brain muscle."

Jabari sighed. "Alright, Dad, I'm cool with that. Can we go home now?"

"Not yet. Not until you promise me something."

Jabari's eyes searched Joshua's face. "Sure, anything."

Joshua raised his eyebrow and smirked at his son. "Anything?"

"Yeah, Dad, for real, what you need?"

"I need for you to remember this conversation when you turn sixteen."

The cynicism flew right over Jabari's head. "Is that it?"

"No, that's not it. I don't ever want you to be afraid to tell me anything, ever. I don't care how bad you think it is. I don't care how mad you think I'll get. I don't care if it's about some girl you've been messing around with and you think—

"Whoa, Dad, I'm only eleven, okay? Really not ready to go there."

"My point is, Jabari, one day you will be ready to go there. So let's squash this now, before it even gets started between us. I'm your dad. You can always talk to me. I don't want you turning to anybody else if you're in trouble. Alright?"

"Yeah, Dad, alright."

"Can you promise me that?"

"Yeah, I promise."

Joshua held out his fist and gave Jabari a pound. He put the car in drive and pulled back into the street.

"Dad, can I tell you something now?"

"Go ahead, shoot."

"I was scared to tell you about the test scores."

"Why?"

"Well, me and mom have been gone for a long time, and it's kind of like you have to get to know me all over again. It's one thing for the kids at school to think I'm dumb, but I didn't want you thinking that way about me."

"You're not dumb, Jabari," Joshua said firmly. "Even if you were, you'd still be my son. It would concern me if my only living heir was an idiot, but I'd get over it. I might have to leave my money to the church, though."

Jabari broke out into a grin. "Ha ha, very funny."

"That was pretty funny, wasn't it? About as funny as you trying to live thug life up at that school." Joshua's eyes roved over Jabari's junky attire. "Fix your clothes."

"Okay, okay, I promise it won't happen again! Dad, tell me about my tutor. Is she fine or what?"

"What happened to, 'Dad, I'm only eleven and I'm not ready for all of that?'"

"Yeah, but a brother still likes to have a little eye candy."

"She's got blue hair and she's eighty. How's that for eye candy?"

"Aw, Dad, for real?"

Joshua chuckled. "I don't know, man. You have to ask your uncle. He's the one who interviewed her."

"How you gonna play a brother to the left like that?"

"You better focus on your school work and not play yourself. I don't care what she looks like, Jabari," Joshua said, suddenly serious again, "As long as she teaches you what you need to know."

"Alright, alright, true dat. Hey, Dad, one good thing did happen at school today," Jabari said, obviously back to his old self again.

"Yeah, what's that?"

"Marcus spoke to me in the hallway today. All the middle school girls were like, 'Jabari, you know him?' Man, when I was in New Orleans, Marcus wouldn't have ever spoken to me in public, much less stop and give me dap like he did in the hallway today."

"The two of you have been through a lot. When you've weathered a storm together, that creates a bond that can't be easily broken," Joshua said, his mind returning briefly to Bella.

"You mean like you and unc, like brothers?"

"Yeah, son, like brothers."

WINTER, 1999

CHAPTER 63

Bella sat at the breakfast bar, her eyes glued to the docked phone and answering machine. She heard Joshua enter and could feel the heat of his eyes on her back. He sauntered past her, opened the fridge and grabbed a carton of orange juice and then, because she was sitting there and only because she was sitting there, he also grabbed a glass from the cabinet shelf and poured himself some juice like a normal person.

"Where's Jabari?"

Bella watched Joshua's dark eyes come to life at the mention of their son.

"Preschool," Bella said. There was a duh-where-else-would-he-be in her tone that caused Joshua to glance for the first time at the clock over the stove. It was well after noon and he had just woken up. Of course she had an attitude.

"I know," Joshua said, suddenly contrite, "It's just that usually when I have an away game, you let him miss school the next day. I haven't seen him in four days."

"When you didn't come home last night, I thought you'd be in no condition to deal with a rambunctious three-year-old the next morning. So, I sent him to school."

Joshua stared at her for a moment and then lifted the carton of juice to his lips, all pretense of civility gone. He took a long gulp and then wiped his mouth with the back of his hand. "You're punishing me for not coming home from the airport like a good little boy. I stopped off and had a few drinks with my team. Get over it."

"Like I said, I didn't know what condition you'd be in this morning. And since your little girlfriend has already called here three times today, looks like I made the right decision."

"My what?"

"You heard me."

"You're trippin', Bella. I don't know what you're talking about." Joshua turned to walk out the kitchen.

Bella pressed the play button on the answering machine and a female's voice filled the kitchen.

"Hi Joshua, it's me, Amanda, the dancer from Montre's. I just wanted to tell you that last night was amazing for me, and even though you were pretty trashed, I think it was pretty amazing for you too." The woman's laughter filled the room.

Joshua swore loudly and in two quick strides, he was at the phone pushing the end button on the machine.

Bella tilted her head up to meet Joshua's gaze, "What? Don't you want to hear all about your amazing night?" She reached her hand across the counter to press the play button again. "My favorite part was hearing about how another woman climaxed just from the mere sound of your voice."

Joshua's hand stopped hers mid-air. "It was a strip club. I had a lap dance. That's it. Now I'm sorry this followed me home but—"

"You're sorry this followed you home?"

Joshua rubbed his hands over his eyes and sighed in frustration. "What do you want me to say, Bella?"

Bella shook her head and chuckled softly. She got up from her seat at the counter and walked out of the kitchen. Joshua followed her into the living room.

"Why are we still doing this, Josh? You obviously don't love me anymore. Is all of this really for Jabari?"

Joshua grabbed the phone off the coffee table and held it out to her. "Mike never left my side the whole night. He'll verify everything I just said."

"Mike can't tell me the one thing that I really want to know."

"What's that, Bella?"

"Did you climax?"

Joshua looked as if he didn't understand the question.

"I know she did, apparently more than once, must have been one hell of a lap dance. What about you?"

"And if I say yes, what does that mean to you, Bella?" Joshua asked quietly. "That I'm in love with this woman? Oh, I get it. You've deluded yourself into thinking that because you've never been able to have one with anyone else besides me, that you must love me. Are you really that screwed up? Is your mind so twisted that you equate an orgasm with love? That's not love, Bella, it's just a physiological response."

One that requires trust! Bella wanted to scream, but the odd mixture of pity and disgust she saw in his eyes made the words cling to the inside of her throat. Bella blinked her eyes hard, feeling tears dangerously bubbling towards the surface.

"Yeah, I did. I don't drink unless I wanna get drunk and I don't pay for a lap dance unless I want to get off." Joshua dropped the phone down onto the coffee table with a thud and walked out of the living room.

CHAPTER 64

This man does not love you. He doesn't love you. These words steeled her, gave her the strength and the courage to run. It was all she could think about as she loaded first her bag and then Jabari's into the trunk of her car before dawn the next morning. The plan was to wait until Joshua left for practice, until she could be sure he'd be gone all day. Then she'd be gone.

But he had hesitated that morning, lingering a bit as if he knew this was good-bye. Playing with Jabari, trying to make small talk with her. Like they had anything to talk about these days. He had misread her silence. He had thought that his words the other day had hurt her, that they'd done irreparable damage. Little did he know; the damage had been done a long time ago. The day Jabari had been born and the love he had in his heart for her was transferred to her child. She had slept with many men before, that he could forgive, but bringing home a child, even one that he was madly in love with, was the one mistake Joshua Keys had not been able to forgive. It wasn't that Bella felt she deserved to be loved. She knew she had no right to demand anything from him. It was more like she needed to be. And being so close, sleeping in the same bed with the one who had become her sun and her moon and not having him shine down on her skin that impossibly beautiful smile, was more than she could bear. She had no choice. She had to run. Joshua stood in their kitchen that morning making more concessions than he had in a very long time. Talking of taking them out to dinner when he got home from practice that evening. Asking her if she minded if his folks kept Jabari while the two of them went away for the weekend.

"I was thinking we could, you know, go away somewhere, just to talk." It was like he was grasping at straws, like he had read her mind and knew. And Bella knew that if she mishandled this moment, if she didn't respond correctly, enthusiastically, he would know. So she pasted a smile on her lips. It wasn't that hard, she really did want to be with him, more than he knew. She could pretend to be excited about this, even if it would never happen.

"In the middle of the season?" she asked, careful to flavor the question with just the right amount of both hope and doubt.

Joshua shrugged that beautiful smile of his. "I really need this, Bella. Don't you?"

His candor took her by surprise and Bella found herself having to work harder now to keep up the charade. *He doesn't love you, he doesn't love you, he doesn't love you.* She told herself once again. *He's doing this for Jabari, not for you.* The raw pain behind that understanding hit her hard, and that's when the tears came.

Joshua released a hard sigh and pulled her into his strong embrace. He kissed the top of her head softly, and without a backward glance, he was out the door. One last kiss. One last embrace she could savor forever. Bella took one last look around the place she had called home for the last seven years. She strapped Jabari into his car seat and they were gone.

CHAPTER 65

Joshua caught up with her two days later in Chicago. Bella was trying to balance her grocery bags, the key card, and one terribly grumpy three-year-old who kept flailing his body down onto the floor. Jabari hadn't slept well, not being in his own house and his own bed. When she was making her get away plan, Bella had failed to consider that.

"Jabari, stand up."

"No! I want my daddy!" he screamed, twisting and turning his little body until he retched himself free out of Bella's grasp. He took off running down the hall towards the large main doors.

"Stop him!" Bella screamed, but no one seemed to hear her voice. The hotel was on a main thoroughfare and the doors, Bella knew, led straight into traffic. "Jabari, no! No!" she screamed, dropping the bags and running after him.

Jabari ran towards the large automatic doors, screaming for his daddy at the top of his lungs. The large doors flung open and Jabari ran through them at breakneck speed.

Bella ran blindly towards the doors, her heart pounding inside her throat. The last sound she heard was an awful noise of tires streaking against the pavement and the deafening clang of colliding metal. Her legs gave out from underneath her and her mind went blank.

By the time the automatic doors opened again, Bella was unconscious. She never saw Joshua Keys walk into the hotel lobby holding his child.

CHAPTER 66

When Bella awoke, the first thing she saw was the ornately detailed soaring ceiling. That and the softness of the bed she was lying on told her she was not in the lobby anymore. But this wasn't her hotel room either. Someone had seriously upgraded her accommodations. Panic began to pump through her veins. Had hotel management decided to give her a better room because her son had been killed? Bella began to hyperventilate.

"Easy," said the all too familiar voice from the corner of the room.

Bella squeezed her eyes shut and turned her face to the wall, resigned to the truth. He was gone. That's why Joshua was here. Someone had called him. A loud fit of sobs broke free from her chest.

Quickly, Joshua was beside her, scooping her into his arms and rocking her like a baby. That's when she heard the sound. Jabari's laughter. A sweet, overjoyed giggle.

"Again, Uncle Mike, again!" Jabari screamed in ecstasy.

Bella struggled trying to free herself from Joshua's arms. "Jabari!"

"He's with Mike."

Bella heard a woman's voice.

Joshua read the question on her face. "And Tonya." Joshua spoke to the unspoken question in her eyes. "She hopped a plane the moment she heard you and Jabari were missing."

"He was so quick, he took off running and I then I heard the crash and I thought…." Bella's voice wavered, and the tears fell from her eyes.

Joshua handed her a tissue.

"I thought management had upgraded my room because—and then I woke up and saw you, so I figured it must be true, because they'd called you. I had lost him."

Joshua sighed and pulled her head into his chest. And another round of sobbing began.

Suddenly Bella sat up and tried to compose herself. "I'm sorry. He's fine. I should stop all this crying."

Joshua grinned at her sadly. "Don't be sorry. Do me a favor and cry a little bit for me too."

Bella looked at him, not understanding.

"I know what it's like to blink and have your world disappear in an instant. At least you know now that your world is still intact. The jury is still out on mine. Can you imagine what it feels like to be me right now?"

Bella shook her head. "No."

Joshua took her hand gingerly in his. "Bella, these last two days without you have been the hardest days of my life."

"It's been pretty hard on Jabari too," she offered.

The question in his eyes was clear. *Hard on Jabari, but not you?*

Bella looked away from his penetrating gaze.

"You asked me the other day if all of this, us, was for Jabari. Bella, this has always, always been about you. Jabari's my son. No matter what, that'll always be true. Some days seeing his smile is the only thing that gets me through. But, Bella, baby, don't you know what you mean to me?" He pushed her gently down onto the bed. "Don't you know that you are my air?" He was on top of her, his hands caressing her head now, and Bella felt all her resolve slipping away underneath his touch. "I'm not complicated. I can live without a lot of things, but I can't live without air. Bella, please," he whispered. "Please, baby, don't do that to me again. Please don't take away my air."

CHAPTER 67

On the second day after his arrival, Joshua took Bella out for a quiet evening stroll, but after the couple was accosted by a series of the Windy City residents all vying for Joshua's autograph, Joshua decided that excursions outside of the hotel for the two of them should be few and far between. It had been agreed by the brothers, though, that since neither Bella nor Tonya carried with them the extra burden of fame, the two of them would be fine hanging out in the city together alone.

Tonya had relished the idea of a girl's day in Chicago. She had envisioned the two of them perusing the wares of street vendors and hailing taxi cabs on Michigan Avenue, but Michael had abruptly killed that fantasy when he announced at breakfast that morning that he had reserved a private car.

Okay, so even she had to admit riding in a limo was far better than hailing cabs on Michigan Avenue, but when the bodyguard he had also hired showed up at their penthouse suite that morning, Tonya dug her heels in and flat out refused to budge. Mike asked the man to wait outside and closed the door.

"Blackbird—"

"No. I am fully capable of guarding my own body."

"No doubt. Still, I would feel better about the two of you being alone in an unfamiliar city if my guy were to accompany you."

"Michael, this day isn't supposed to be about you, so why am I dealing with your incessant need to control everything?" Tonya could tell by the way his jaw muscle tighten that her last statement had gotten his ire up, but he kept his voice modulated so as not to disturb Jabari, who was watching cartoons in the bedroom across the hall, or Joshua and Bella, who were saying their goodbyes in the adjacent parlor a few feet away.

"It's not supposed to be about you either, remember? This is supposed to be about you spending the QT time you keep complaining you never have with Bella. And for the record, nobody's trying to control you. There's a big difference between protecting and controlling. Your problem is you can't tell the difference."

"Oh, I can't tell the difference?"

"Tonya, just stop with all the I-am–woman-hear- me-roar-crap and go downstairs and get in the car."

"No, I won't. You have literally sucked all the fun out of girl's day."

꒰ ꒱

"That has got to be the most amazing thing I have ever seen."

"What's that?" Joshua asked. He wrapped his arms tighter around Bella, who was sitting in his lap.

"Mike and Tonya. They are whisper arguing. Are they back together? Cause I swear this feels just like old times."

Joshua penned her with his gaze. "Are we?"

"I'd say we're about half way there."

"Only half way?"

Bella snaked her arms under his shirt. "I'm gonna need a whole lot more love and personal attention."

"This all-expense paid spa day with your bestie doesn't count?"

"It's a start. Especially if she actually attends." Bella sighed. "Josh, I'm with Tonya on this one. We should nix the idea of a bodyguard altogether. The two of us together will be fine."

"Naw, we don't know this city like that. That's not gon happen."

"I'd much rather have you there to protect me."

"You'd prefer me to Tonya?"

Bella frowned up at him. "I prefer you to everybody."

Joshua threw his head back and laughed. "Woman, you lie. You are dying to spend the day with your friend." He pushed a loose curl behind her ear. "I don't blame you. I want you to have a good time."

"Okay, I'll admit, Tonya is much better at girl talk than you are."

"And you don't have to worry about her punching anybody on your date."

"I'm not so sure about that. I thought she was going to clock Mike a minute ago when he made that I-am-woman-hear-me roar crack."

"Bella, are you really listening to their conversation?"

"Yeah, aren't you?"

"No. I got all the drama I can handle right here."

"Josh, look, they're kissing," Bella whispered, excitedly.

He pulled her attention back to him by planting a trail of soft kisses at the base of her neck. "I think you should mind your own business."

⚘ ⚘

Bella waited patiently for the waiter to set their plates down and leave before asking her question. The one she had been dying to ask from the very first moment Tonya had showed up four days ago with Joshua and Mike in Chicago.

So far, Bella and Tonya had experienced massages and pedicures at a premier spa. They'd had their hair done at a local upscale boutique and had enjoyed a shopping spree compliments of the brothers on Michigan Avenue.

True to Michael's word, the bodyguard had ridden up front with the driver and had been nearly invisible to them for the whole day. The only time Bella or Tonya remembered him at all was when he emerged, seemingly out of the shadows, to

217

relieve the two of them of their packages. Right now, was the first time Bella could say that the two of them had really been alone the entire day. Since Michael and Joshua were both such high-profile celebrities, Bella wouldn't dare speak about them in front of strangers.

"Can I get you ladies anything else?"

"No, we're good. Thank you," Bella said, rushing the waiter away. Bella bowed her head politely as Tonya blessed their food. Then she waited a respectable two minutes for Tonya to taste her food before she launched headlong into her interrogation.

"So, you and Mike?"

"What about us?"

"I saw him kiss you before we left today."

"That was nothing. Just a peck."

"Naw, the forehead thing Mike gave me on the way out the door that was a peck. The two of you were swapping spit."

"We both agreed that we are here on official Godmommy and Goddaddy business. That's all. This is about you and Jabari."

Bella stared at her friend.

"Really. Sorry to burst your bubble. I can tell you've been wanting to ask me about it all day, but there's nothing more to it."

Tonya was smiling far too brightly for Bella's taste. Bella watched Tonya cut into her salmon and take slow, deliberate bites.

"Tonya, last night during the movie, your head was in his lap. He was playing in your hair. It was like no time had passed at all between you two."

Tonya shrugged. "What can I say? Some old habits are very hard to break. Try not to read too much into it, Bella. I'm certainly not going to."

"So you don't love him anymore?"

Tonya paused for a moment, as if truly weighing the question. "I think we will always love each other. But I'm doing what I feel led to do, and apparently Michael is too. Trust me, I read the magazines. He's moved on."

Bella thought about the string of beautiful women her brother-in-law had dated over the past few years and decided to leave well enough alone. "Are you seeing anyone else?"

"There is this one guy. I met him on my last mission trip. Ted. He's a pastor. He lives in New York. He kind of asked me to marry him."

Bella's mouth fell open. "And when were you going to get around to telling me this?"

Tonya shook her head. "I didn't tell you because we aren't anywhere near ready for anything like that. He knows it too. I just think he wants to make his intentions clear."

"Tonya, spill it. Tell me everything, is he gorgeous?"

"He's attractive. He has a nice physique, but he's kind of short."

"How short? Short like you can't wear heels on a date short?"

"No, not that short. He's 5'6."

Bella laughed. "Tonya, that is not short."

Tonya frowned. "You don't think so?"

"I mean, it may feel short to you having previously dated an NBA god, but trust me, 5'6 is average height.

Bella paused for a moment before she asked her next question. "Do you love him?"

"He loves children and he has a heart for missions. What more could I want? So far he's starting to look like everything God told me he had in store for me."

"Only he's not Michael," Bella finished quietly. "Tonya, I don't know anything about this guy, but I do know that you've trusted God this long. I don't think you should just settle for the first minister who comes your way. Maybe—"

"Bella, before you go any further, Ted asked me to move to New York. He wants me to help him start a ministry focused around homeless children. I got accepted into graduate school out there, so I'm going."

"Does Mike know?"

"He knows about the grad school part, but nothing about the Ted part, so please —"

"I wouldn't. Not to Joshua or anyone else, for that matter."

"I'm not trying to hide anything from him. It's just that when we're together, we don't discuss other people. Dems the rules."

Bella watched the tears form in Tonya's eyes. "Tonya, I…I don't know what to say."

"How about telling me that we'll always be sisters whether I marry your brother-in-law or not."

Bella found herself wiping away her own tears. "Are you kidding me? As far as I'm concerned, you're the only sister I've got. Which is why I've always wondered about something."

"What's that?"

"How come you've never asked me about Jabari's father?" Tonya wiped the last remnants of her tears from her eyes and smiled at Bella. "Bella, I've known Jabari's daddy all my life, what else do I need to know?"

"You know what I mean. I figured Mike told you."

"He did and I figured you'd tell me when and if you were ready."

"I'm ready."

"Then I'm listening."

"He was my World History professor."

"Was this for money?"

"No money ever changed hands. I just needed to feel numb for a while…whenever Joshua touches me, I feel so alive."

Tonya reached across the table and grabbed Bella's hand. "Why is that such a bad thing?"

"It's not. Not in the moment, at least. In the moment it feels like the best thing in the world. I feel reborn. But when he's not there, not holding me, I just feel. Every single thing I've ever wanted to forget and I just want to be numb again."

"Oh, Bella, why are you trying so hard to run away from love?"

"I don't know, Tonya. Why are you?"

CHAPTER 68

For the next four days, Jabari refused to let Joshua out of his sight. If Joshua wanted to get any type of morning workout in, he had to sneak out and do it before the toddler awoke. But even then, he and Mike would return to find Tonya and Bella trying to calm the inconsolable three-year-old.

"He's just feeling a little separation anxiety, Josh," Tonya had assured him.

So Joshua gave up his morning workout and hung back at the hotel, watching cartoons with Jabari. Bella couldn't pry the child away for anything, not even a bath. Jabari refused to go to breakfast downstairs in the hotel with Tonya and Bella, so every morning Joshua ordered room service for the two of them instead. But when it was time for Jabari to fly back to Houston with Mike and Tonya, he threw the biggest fit of all. Jabari gripped Joshua's leg, howling like a wounded animal.

"Hey, where's Daddy's brave little guy?"

"I'm right here!" Jabari screamed.

When Bella tried to pry him a loose, Jabari bit her hard on the hand and ran into the bathroom and slammed the door.

"Jabari!"

Joshua stopped her. "Let me handle it, alright?" Joshua knocked on the bathroom door. "Jabari, it's Daddy. Can I come in?"

"Am I gonna get a whipping?"

"Naw, man, I'm not gonna whip you. I just want to talk to you." Joshua waited for the soft click of the bathroom lock before opening the door and walking inside the bathroom. He took a seat on the floor against the giant jacuzzi tub next to the three-year-old.

"What's up, little man? Tell me why you're so upset."

"I wanna stay with you."

"I know, but I'm driving Mommy's car back to Houston and that's a really long car ride for you. It's almost too long for me. I wish I was flying on the plane too."

"You do?"

"It's much quicker and a lot more fun."

"What's fun about it?"

"Well, there is food and movies. You get to meet a lot of interesting people in first class. And you don't have to wait for a rest stop to go pee."

Jabari considered this. "Then come on the airplane with us."

"Can't. I need to drive Mommy's car home. But because you are flying home, you get to hang out with Grandma Mel, Grandpa Jack, and Uncle Mike for a few days."

Jabari's face lit up like a Christmas tree. "And Auntie Tonya too!"

"Yes. But just until Mommy and I get back. You'll see us in three days. Count with me."

Jabari held out three stubby little fingers. "One, two, three."

Joshua leaned over and kissed his son. "I love you, buddy."

"I love you too, Daddy."

"You ready to apologize to mommy?"

Jabari pouted. "For what?"

Joshua raised an eyebrow at his son. "For what? Jabari man, you can't bite your mother."

"Why not?"

"Because it's not nice to bite anybody, but especially not your mother."

"But why not?"

"Because she's your mom and because she's a girl."

Jabari frowned. "Mommy's a girl?"

"Of course she's a girl. And should guys ever hurt girls?"

Jabari shook his head. "No never."

"Right now, Mommy's bigger than you and stronger than you, but it won't always be like that. One day you'll be bigger and stronger than her. So, I want you to treat her like she's weaker than you. You feel me?"

Jabari nodded. "When I get really, really mad, I bite."

"I get it, man. When I get really, really mad, I punch."

"Is punching okay?" Jabari asked hopefully.

"No, Jabari, punching is not okay."

"What if it's a guy and not a girl?"

"Still not okay."

"Tobias at school punched Margie in the stomach because she tore his airplane. That made him really mad."

Joshua sighed and blew out a breath. "That's the thing, sometimes people are gonna make you mad, but you gotta use your words and walk away. What do you say, little man, you willing to practice that with me?"

Jabari held out his hand to Joshua. "We gonna use our words, Daddy, and walk away."

CHAPTER 69

Joshua sat in a chair in the corner of the master bedroom of the penthouse suite studying his sleeping wife. The phone in his pants pocket vibrated. He walked out of the bedroom into the large office across the hall to answer it.

"What up, Steve. It's after midnight. Why are you still up?"

Steve sighed deeply, the way his manager often did when he was upset. Joshua could almost picture him running his hand over his bald head and pacing back and forth in front of his large office window.

"I don't know, Joshua. Maybe it's because my star player is still in Chicago. I can't tell you how incredibly shocked I was to discover that only one Rocket was on that plane headed for Dallas this morning."

"I'm driving Bella's car back. It'll give us time to talk."

"You're driving Bella's car back because you need time to talk. Well, that's just great. Great."

"You sound like a parrot, Steve. You going deaf or something?"

"Look, Josh, I don't mean to sound insensitive about all of this. But I don't need to tell you that during the middle of the season is the worst time for Bella to be having an emotional meltdown. Management has given you a lot of leeway. But I need you on a plane back here yesterday. Forget the car, alright? I'll have one of my assistants fly down there and pick it up for you. I'll buy you a new one if you want me to. Bella can pick the color. But I need you on that plane first thing tomorrow morning. The Rockets are playing the Heat and they need the dynamic duo out there on the court."

"Steve, relax. The game isn't for another three days. I'll be there."

"Joshua—"

"I said I'll be there!"

Joshua looked up when the door to the office opened and Bella padded into the room wearing only her negligee and bare feet.

"I'll hit you back later. I gotta go." Joshua pushed the end button on the call. "Did I wake you?"

Bella shook her head. "Was that Steve?"

Joshua hoisted her up on top of the desk in front of him. He drew her close and buried his head into her stomach. He felt himself relax as Bella's fingers combed through his tight curls.

"Joshua, I wasn't trying to eavesdrop, but I think Steve's right. As much as I love having your undivided attention like this, you need to get back. I don't want you getting into any more trouble because of me. I was thinking that if your mom and dad agreed to keep Jabari for a few days, I could fly out with you to Miami."

Joshua looked up at her. "You up for that?"

"Being where you are? Oh, yeah."

"You haven't been to one of my games in years."

"I think it'll be fine if you can promise me one thing. No fighting."

"You got it. No fighting."

"Josh, I'm serious. No matter what?"

"I promise."

"I don't care what anybody says to you about me—"

Joshua scooped her up off the desk and carried her back into the master bedroom. "Bella, I made a promise to my son today. There's not going to be any fighting."

CHAPTER 70

Believe it or not Steve, yours is not the first voice in the morning that I want to wake up to."

"I'm sorry, Joshua. I tried to wait till a decent hour, but we have a situation. I got a call from Amanda Striker's attorney. That name ring a bell to you? She's a dancer at a club you've been known to frequent once in a while called Montre's."

"No."

"Well, that's unfortunate. I was hoping you could shed a little light on this for me, since she's claiming that you are the father of her unborn child. She's also threatening to go straight to the press if she can't have a sit down with Bella."

"You mean she wants a sit down with me."

"No, I mean Bella."

Joshua looked over at Bella sleeping peacefully in their bed. He slowly eased out of bed and walked into the master bathroom.

"Then call her bluff, tell her to go on record."

"Joshua, we should at least find out who this woman is. What type of information she may have on you. Before—"

"I don't screw around on my wife, Steve. She doesn't have anything."

"Hey, for the record, I believe you, kid. But here's the thing. I did a little fact checking into this situation myself, and at least three different waitresses at Montre's can remember at least one instance where you asked for this Amanda by name. Now, that's not exactly proof of an affair, but it sure will sell a lot of newspapers. We have had four—count them, Joshua— four glorious months of negativity free press. If you had a squeaky clean record, I'd say fight it. I'd lead the band wagon and put this chick through the ringer myself. But you're no choir boy, my friend. You are Bad Boy Joshua Keys. America's rebel-without-a-cause. A scrimmage or two on the court, people expect that, but not this. Not infidelity. You pay me very well to protect your money, and I'm telling you that your image cannot recover from something like this. We need to squash this, Joshua. Quiet and quick."

"Let me call you back."

"Joshua, take it from a man that's been married for almost twenty years. The best approach is always honesty."

Joshua walked back into the master bedroom and climbed back into the bed, only to see that Bella was no longer sleeping.

"I woke you."

"Only when you got up. I heard you talking to Steve on the phone." She peered into his eyes. "Is everything alright?"

Joshua laced his fingers through her hand. "Things have been good between us lately, right? I mean, you feel like I'm listening. That I'm 100% in, giving you what you need?"

"Joshua what's wrong. What did Steve want?"

Joshua stared at her.

"Okay. Let me back up and answer you. Yes, I feel like for the first time in a long time, I'm not just a charity case for you. You're all in."

Joshua nodded. "A woman name Amanda Striker is claiming that I am the father of her child."

Bella's eyes narrowed. "The chick who called three months ago from the club?"

"I don't know. Maybe. Steve's worried that my career can't handle this type of scandal. What I'm most concerned about right now is my marriage."

"Is it true?"

"No."

"Because I would understand. It would still hurt, but I would understand."

He lifted her chin so that she was staring directly into his eyes. "No more lies between us, remember? Even when it hurts, we always tell each other the truth."

Bella nodded. "She must have a price. What is it?"

"She says she wants to have a sit down with you."

"Call Steve and tell him to set it up." Bella slipped from the bed and walked into the bathroom.

CHAPTER 71

I saw you on Sports Center once, you looked like a real classy chick. I thought that if we could talk woman to woman, the two of us could work something out, privately."

"I appreciate that," Bella said smiling at the woman, a smile that didn't quite reach her eyes.

The woman nodded. "I know this must be difficult for you. So, thanks. For understanding, I mean. A part of me really hates doing this. Regardless of how brief our affair was, Joshua was the best lover I've ever had."

"I know exactly what you mean," Bella said as she and Joshua shared a private look that was hot enough to make the walls blush. Bella turned her attention back to the woman then, who seemed to be somewhat thrown off kilter by the couple's solidarity. "What does it look like?"

"W-What does what look like?"

"My husband's penis."

Color crept into all the white faces around the table, including Amanda's. Steve's assistant choked on his water. Mike's deep chocolate face remained impassive, as did Joshua's golden honey colored one. Both brothers remained unfazed. As if Bella had just inquired about the weather or the time of day.

"What kind of question is that?" Amanda's attorney finally managed to sputter out.

"Surely if you've had my husband as many times as you say, in as many positions as you claim, then describing it shouldn't be a problem. You had to have gotten a good look at it."

Steve paged through the report in front of him. "Joshua Keys is unbelievable. Best lover I've ever had. Yadda,

yadda, yadda. Hits all the right spots. Oh, here it is. Unforgettable. Given your client's statement, I'd say Mrs. Keys' question, albeit unorthodox, is still quite reasonable."

Steve had wanted to bring in the suits for this one. Bella vetoed that move, saying that the presence of Joshua's extensive legal team would send the wrong message.

"This woman's been around the block a few times. Don't forget she has two other children by NBA players. I say if we fight, we let the legal team duke it out with her," Steve countered.

"Bella's right, Josh," Mike said. "We can't come locked and loaded on this. We do that and we make her think she's won."

Steve looked at Joshua. "It's your call."

"I'm not willing to buy my way out of something I didn't do."

"The media will crucify you. Again."

Joshua shrugged. "What else is new?"

Steve ran his hand nervously over his bald head. "Yes, yes. I know you don't care. That's my job, right? I care."

"Steve, when I finish with Ms. Striker, she won't be going to the press," Bella said.

"So that's it then, we're gonna fight this?"

"It was one dance in a club, man, that's it," Mike said. "Hell yeah, we gon fight it."

"I-I can't tell you what it looks like!"

"Why not?" Bella asked calmly.

"I don't know, I forgot, alright?" Amanda turned to her attorney, "I thought you said she was ready to work a deal!"

"I did a little research of my own." Bella looked at Steve, who motioned for his assistant to dim the lights. An image appeared on the projector screen in front of them.

"Where did you get those? That is an invasion of privacy! Those are my kids!"

"Yep, them your babies alright. I see you all up in them." Bella advanced the slide. The next slide featured two photos side by side. A photo of a well-known NBA player next to a photo of Amanda's oldest child. "But, Amanda, come on, you and I both know this is not his baby." Bella advanced the slide again. Another NBA player's photo appeared on the screen beside the second child. "And this ain't his baby either. We both also happen to know that these two men are huge whores who can't remember who they've slept with from one night to the next. They didn't want to go through the hassle of the court proceedings, so they just decided to pay you. And I get it. You need a daddy for baby number three growing inside of you. You gave my husband a lap dance, looked into those big, dreamy, brown eyes of his and decided it should be him. But he's not the one and neither am I."

Amanda stood abruptly from the table. "I don't have to sit here and listen to this."

"Actually, you do. You need to sit down and listen very carefully."

Amanda fixed Bella with a hard gaze and then slumped back down in her seat.

"I know how hard it is making ends meet swingin' from a pole these days. So I'm going to a do my best not to mess with your game. But if you ever try blackmailing me again, trust and believe I will destroy you."

"Objection! She just threatened my client!"

"I want a written retraction in one hour," Bella continued. "If I don't have it in exactly one hour, I will insist on a paternity test. And when it comes back negative, as we both know it will, I will see you in criminal court. I will take your house, your car, your child support, and that little white dog in the photo too. It won't be personal either. From one working girl to another, it'll be all about business." Bella locked eyes with Amanda's attorney. "I just offered your client a way out. If she knows what's good for her, she'll take it." Bella turned her attention back to the now very visibly distraught woman. "Amanda, when someone offers you a gift, what do you say?"

Silence permeated the entire table.

"You say thank you. Thank you, Bella, for not exposing me to these two fools who are paying me child support," Bella coached.

The woman sat across the table from Bella, trembling. Silent tears rolled down her face.

"Say it now or whatever deal we have here is off the table."

"Thank. You."

Bella nodded. "You're free to go."

Amanda jumped up from the table and nearly ran from the conference room.

"Don't forget we'll need that written statement, notarized, within the hour, Chuck," Steve called to the attorney's departing back.

Mike leaned back in his chair and spoke to Joshua. "I think Steve lost the belt today."

Joshua pulled Bella up from her chair beside him and onto his lap. "Steve definitely lost the belt."

"Hey. What are you guys talking about? I handled mine. I made it rain."

"Naw playa, Bella made it rain," Mike said smiling at Bella.

Steve nodded. "Okay, okay. I guess I can agree with you on that. You did good, Bella. Real good."

"So good I'mma have to get you some personalized plates to go with your new whip," Joshua said.

Bella's eyes brighten, "I'm getting a new whip? What kind?"

"Baby, with the money you just saved us in legal fees, you can have any kind of car you wanna drive."

"What would my plates say?"

Joshua grinned down at her, "Bad Girl Bella Keys. What else?"

PRESENT, 2005

Walter stood in the full length mirror and surveyed himself for about the 100th time. Maggie stood behind him dusting invisible lint balls off his suit.

"I'm so glad you're meeting with Joshua today. I've been praying for him and Rose, that they can get over the past and really make a go at it this time."

Walter grunted and straightened his tie.

"Here, let me." Maggie slipped in front of him and with competent hands she adjusted his tie perfectly.

Walter stared down at her. There was a touch of gray now at her temples, but the same heavenly face. She was just as beautiful as the day he married her, even more so to Walter, now that they had weathered the storm together.

"What you smiling at, man?"

"You, with your fine self." Walter lowered his head and kissed his wife softly.

All of his hopes and dreams he tried to impart to her with that one kiss. If things went his way today, just for once, he'd be able to treat her like the queen she was. He'd be able to buy her fine clothes and fine furniture, like the things that had been donated to them.

Maggie stood on her tiptoes and kissed him back, matching his fervor with a passion all her own.

"Don't get nothing started, woman," Walter growled. "You know they're sending a car for me. You'll have me standing at attention for the rest of the day. What kind of job you think I'mma get if I walk in there like that?"

Maggie laughed. "Walter, you're so crazy."

"You make me that way."

He touched her elbow, once smooth, now scabbed over from when Charles Terry had pushed her to the ground.

Walter cursed the dead man under his breath. His Maggie had been through enough. If God hadn't dealt with him, Walter surely would have killed him.

"Walter, I've been talking to Rose, taking her under my wing, and I was kind of hoping that today, if the opportunity arose, you could maybe do the same for Joshua."

Walter stared at his wife. "Maggie, whatever idea you got, get it out of your head right now. I am not getting into that man's personal business. I'm going over there to talk to him about a job, that's it."

"I think Joshua is a good man."

You damn right he's a good man! We sitting up in this apartment, ain't we?"

Maggie ignored him and pressed on. "On the way out here, Rose shared with me about her past. Walter, the things that child went through at the hands of her own daddy, it's enough to make anybody run. That kind of abuse makes you not know the difference between a good man and a bad one. I know."

Walter's face softened. Even though she had been healed from the abuse she had suffered as a child, the fact that she still remembered the pain always made Walter feel helpless.

"Baby, listen to me, that man don't know us from Adam, alright? What I look like, trying to climb up inside his head?"

"It's just that I gotta soft spot in my heart for her, you know? Because of what happened to me. God knows I wasn't always easy to love. We've had our ups and downs, right? Even in a good marriage it ain't easy."

"No, but you were worth it, and we made it work."

"Well I think Rose is worth it too."

"Aw, Maggie!"

"Aw, Maggie nothing! Now, Walter, you're always around here blustering about how grateful you are to Joshua

Keys for helping you, saving you. You should return the favor and save him right back!"

"Now how in the world am I supposed to do that, Maggie? I ain't in no position to give him nothing! What do you expect me to do?"

"Say something to him, Walter! Give him a reason to fight for his family."

With that, Maggie turned and walked out of the bedroom.

CHAPTER 73

Joshua greeted Walter in the waiting area with a hand shake and a hug. "Thank you for agreeing to meet with me today, Walter."

"Hey man, thank you for sending a limo to pick me up."

"Can we get you anything? Coffee, soda, some tea?"

"I already offered," Selena said quickly. "Mr. Trendale said he didn't want anything."

"Yeah, she already offered. I'm fine, I don't need nothing."

"You sure? Because it's no problem."

"Yeah, man. I'm cool."

"Alright, let's go on back and talk then. Selena, hold my calls, and tell Mike to just come on in."

Joshua led Walter into his office. "Mike will be joining us shortly. He's coming from another meeting this morning."

"That's cool." Walter looked around the office admiringly, his eyes settling on the large leather seating area by the fireplace. He let out a low whistle through his teeth. "Man, these are some really nice digs. I knew you were living large, but nothing like this. This office is bigger than our whole apartment back in New Orleans."

"After my wife and son moved out, I kind of threw myself into building Home Court Advantage. I spend a lot of time here, so I need this place to be comfortable."

Walter nodded. He let his gaze settle on the large floor to ceiling windows behind Joshua's desk and the extraordinary view of the Houston skyline, side-stepping a potentially tender conversation. "So, who you think gon take the championship this year? You think your old squad got a chance with you and your brother gone?"

Joshua grinned. "I might not wear the uniform anymore, but it's Rockets all the way, baby, you know this!"

Walter slapped Joshua's hand in appreciation.

"Yeah, after you left, I gave up any chance that New Orleans would ever be a contender and after Katrina—"

Joshua put his hand on Walter's back. "Don't worry man, they'll rise from the ashes again."

Walter chuckled. "This is unbelievable. I don't mean to sound star struck or nothing, people probably say this to you all the time, but honest to God, man, I'm your biggest fan. To be standing in your office now, talking sports like this; man, this is blowing my mind!"

Joshua chuckled. "Trust me, man, the feeling is mutual. You got my family out of New Orleans alive. When I think about what their fate could have been, a million dollars doesn't seem nearly enough. That's why I've decided to increase the reward."

"Hold up, man. I know that's why you called me over here today. I also know that's more money then somebody like me will ever see in my whole lifetime, but I can't take your money."

Joshua sat back on the couch and stared at the man beside him.

"We 'preciate ya'll treating us like we some heroes and thangs, but we ain't no heroes, Josh. We were just people with our backs up against the wall. We did what we had to do and we got the hell up outta New Orleans, man. We ain't do it for the money. We did it because it was the decent thing to do, cause we were neighbors. I ain't never been no praying man myself, I leave all the praying to Maggie, but I was a praying man that day. If anybody deserves the reward, it's Marcus. He's the one who got the bus and drove us out of New Orleans."

"Okay, I respect that, but Jabari tells me you saved his mother's life. That puts me in your debt."

"I hate to talk about a dead man, but that Charles Terry was a nasty son of a gun. He took advantage of a lot of young girls in that apartment complex. He grabbed your wife, man. He knew he was dying. I've seen that look in a man's eyes before. He knew it and he figured he might as well take someone else with him. He lived that way, tried to die that way too. I saw him grab her, man, and well, I couldn't let that happen. Rose—I mean, Bella—is a good woman. She and Jabari have been like family to us since they got to the Ward. My wife adopted them. Family don't take reward money for helping family."

"How can I repay you?"

"Man, all I need is to be able to provide for my family."

"Consider coming to work for Home Court Advantage. I know New Orleans is home, but I hope you fine Houston suitable enough to stay."

"I ain't seen much of the city, but my wife and kids like it just fine. That's good enough for me. We're simple folks. Truth is, we living a whole lot better here than we ever did in the Ward."

"That's good to hear, because Bella and I both would really like for you to stay. Bella's really taken to your wife, and that says a whole lot about the type of people you are. She's never had many friends."

"Hey, man, you had me at job."

Mike knocked on the door and walked in. Mike extended his hand to Walter. "Walter, it's good to see you again." Walter rose to shake his hand.

"Mr. Dutton, good to see you!"

"Man, please, call me Mike."

"Alright, Mike, cool."

Mike sat down on the couch and extended one long arm over the back of it.

"Walter won't take the reward money," Joshua said.

"You sure 'bout that, man? That's a nice piece of change to put away for the kids' college fund. College ain't cheap these days," Mike said.

"Man, like I told Josh here, the only thing I need is to be able to take care of mine, you hear? Like a man."

Mike nodded. "Tell me about yourself, Walter. What did you do before you left New Orleans?"

"Well, I served fifteen years in the military as a Marine, served until I got a back injury and they couldn't really use me anymore."

"A Marine, that takes a lot of discipline and strength of character. Much respect, man."

"Thanks, man, but I'm 45, and that's a young man's game. Ever since I got out, I've had to support my family the best way I can. Ain't too many jobs out here for brothers these days. I've worked as a shade tree mechanic, a construction worker, an electrician, and a fix-it-man. You name it. I can do almost anything with my hands. I ain't no stranger to hard work. So whatever y'all have for me would be fine. Y'all got to have something that needs fixing around here, a work crew I could join or something."

"Philip was certainly impressed with you, he said you knew your way around a power tool." Mike looked at Joshua. "You thinking what I'm thinking, man?"

"Safe Harbor?"

"Yep," Mike grinned. "Philip would be glad to get that off his plate."

"Hey, anything you brothers can throw my way, I'm game."

"We need a Facilities Director for Safe Harbor," Joshua said, looking at Walter.

"Director?" Walter sat back stunned. "That sounds pretty important. Would I have to wear a suit?"

Mike studied Walter, weighing his words carefully. "I would, but that's me. Everybody don't like dressing up and I can respect that. We give our management team a lot of flexibility, so we would leave that entirely up to you."

"Mike, I ain't got a problem dressing up. It's just that since the service, I ain't never had a job that I had to dress up for. I miss that," Walter said earnestly.

"You'd be directly supervising a team of about twenty or so maintenance workers, making sure our properties are up to code and everything is neat and orderly, things like that. If you're in the field with your crew, you might want to be comfortable, but for meetings, VIP tours, that sort of thing, you might want to dress the part. If you like, I can hook you up with my tailor," Joshua said.

"Oh yeah, that would be sweet. That is, if I can afford it. I can tell those threads you wearing ain't cheap."

"The job comes with a clothing allowance," Mike said.

"Y'all do all of that?"

"Well, yeah, for our facilities director, sure. I mean, all the other directors are in the office all day, but your job, like Josh said, requires you to be in the field sometimes. Can't have you getting your gear all greased up."

Joshua sent his brother a knowing smile. Mike would find a way to give the reward money to Walter, one way or another.

"We'd start you off at $125,000 a year, excellent benefits, vacation, stock options, and since we'd want the Facilities Director for Safe Harbor to live in that community, we'd also like to build you a house there as well."

Walter looked back and forth between Mike and Joshua.

"Wait a minute, did he just say what I think he said?"

"Is that alright with you?" Joshua grinned, pleased with his brother's generosity.

"Yeah, I mean, naw! Y'all ain't got to do that, a job is enough. Hell, $125,000 a year, that's more than I've ever made in my whole life. The apartment you already gave us is more than fine. We don't need a house."

Mike shook his head. "Walter, turning down a million dollars is one thing, but this is a house designed to your specs. I think you better discuss that one with your wife first, bro."

Walter chuckled. "My Maggie is a God fearing woman, but she'd whip me for sure if she found out you guys offered me a house and I turned it down."

"Walter, we need you to understand that the house, and the cars—"

"That's right, two," Mike interjected, "one for you, one for Maggie."

"These aren't in addition to the job, they are included in your benefit package," Joshua finished, he and Mike together making it up as they went along, just like they did on the court in their ball playing days.

"The house, of course, helps us, because of the type of investors we're trying to attract. We need a home in Safe Harbor that can be kind of like a showpiece," Mike said.

"What, you talking off the chain?"

"I'm thinking off the hizzy, but not too off the chain, otherwise Stan our numbers guy would have a complete coronary."

Joshua smiled at the thought. "We're thinking something spacious, suitable for entertaining various VIP clients and possible investors that would visit Safe Harbor. Something you could host a large social gathering in if need be, with a small guesthouse off the back for overnight guests. Something that would be welcoming but still gives your family the sense of privacy needed so that you don't always feel like you're taking your work home."

"Are you kidding? Maggie loves that stuff. I'm not exaggerating to make us look better either. Ask Rose what everybody in the old neighborhood called her.

Mike looked at Joshua. "Rose?"

"Bella," Joshua said.

Mike took out his Blackberry. "She at home?"

"She was when I left this morning."

"Hey, Bella baby, what's up? Yeah, what you cooking? You know I love your cooking, girl. I tell you what, I've got a meeting later on tonight, but put a plate up for me and I'll swing by. I'm sitting in a meeting right now with Josh and Walter. Walter says to ask you what y'all used to call Maggie back in New Orleans." Mike released a long hearty laugh. "Alright, thanks, baby."

Mike hung up the phone. "The Martha Stewart of the Ghetto."

"See, what I tell you!"

Joshua laughed. "You can't get a better recommendation than that. So let's have Maggie sit down with the designers and see what they can come up with."

Walter shook his head, "I don't know what to say. This is more than I ever thought or dared to even imagine."

"You can say, 'Yes, I accept the position,'" Mike said.

"Yes! Man, like I told your brother before you got here, y'all had me at job!"

Mike and Joshua both stood and shook Walter's hand. "Welcome to Home Court Advantage, Walter."

CHAPTER 74

Bella glanced quizzically over at Joshua as they drove through the large outer gates leading into the Safe Harbor Community. "I thought we were going home?"

"I know you haven't had a chance to talk with Maggie in a while, and I have some business I need to take care of with Walter. I hope you don't mind. We don't have to stay long if you're not feeling up to it."

Bella grinned. "I don't mind at all. I feel great."

Jabari pulled his iPod earplugs from his ears. "Look, it's Uncle Mike's car!"

Bella looked over at the silver Lamborghini with the personalized Man of Steel hubcaps. There was no mistaking whose car it was. There was only one like it in Houston and it belonged to Michael Dutton, the Man of Steel himself.

"Funny, I thought I saw Mike driving the Porche this morning."

"You did. Mike is letting Marcus push the Steelmobile for a while. It's better than having to drop him off everyplace."

"Sweet!" Jabari sang.

"Do you think that's wise?" Bella asked.

Joshua shrugged. "I don't see why not, he's a good kid."

"He's a great kid, but he is a teenager, Josh. How can he not be tempted to speed in a car like that?"

"The boy did have enough sense to hotwire a school bus and drive you safely out of New Orleans. I think he can manage to stay under the speed limit."

"Yeah, Mom, that's like an unfair stereotype. All guys don't speed in sports cars."

Joshua stuck his hand out over the seat for Jabari. Jabari slapped him five. "That's what I'm talkin' bout!" Joshua said.

Bella rolled her eyes playfully at them both. Joshua pulled up in front of Hope House and killed the engine. As soon as the car came to a complete stop, Jabari jumped out and ran up the front stairs and disappeared. Joshua walked around to the passenger side and opened Bella's door.

"I'm sure Mike gave Marcus the rules before he handed him the keys, but if it'll make you feel better about it, I'll have a talk with him before we leave."

"Thank you. It would," Bella said.

"Y'all just in time. Come on in and sit down so we can eat. Maggie's cooked a huge Sunday dinner," Walter said as they walked through the door. All the former Dunbar Street Apartment residents, including Ms. Sally who had been released from the hospital some days ago, were already at the table. Bella felt right at home in the presence of such familiar, loving faces.

After dinner, a movie was put on for Maggie and Walter's twins and Marcus and Jabari went to play some hoops. Lola, Pearl, and Belinda cleaned up the kitchen while Ms. Sally went down for her afternoon nap. Walter and Joshua went off somewhere to talk business, and Maggie and Bella stole away to the twins' bedroom for some long overdue girl talk.

"In a few more months, we won't have to come in here to talk, we'll be able to have tea like proper ladies in my very own parlor!" Both women jumped up and down squealing like schoolgirls.

"Show me everything: floor plans, paint chips, fabric swatches!" Bella said.

"Because, girl, you know I got it all right here, don't you?" Maggie said, pulling out a large fabric covered box from under one of the girl's beds. For the next hour the two women talked of nothing else besides the new house.

"Oh, Rose, what Joshua and Michael are doing for us, it's like a dream I didn't even know I had coming true," Maggie said.

"If anyone deserves this, Maggie, it's you. I'm so happy for you," Bella said.

Maggie bumped her shoulder playfully against Bella's. "I'm pretty happy for you too. You and Joshua look real good together. You look happy. And when he says your name—Bella Rose—it sounds like music."

Sadness clouded Bella's face, "It's just for show. It's over between us, Maggie. I'm pregnant."

Bella spoke to the unspoken question on Maggie's face. "I-I was pregnant before I left New Orleans. About a month ago, things got tight. I couldn't make rent. When Terry suggested an alternative payment, I thought what do I have to lose? It's just sex, right? I was so broke I couldn't afford a condom. I let him take care of that, and, well, this is what it got me."

"Oh, Rose honey, I'm so sorry! You not the first young girl in that building he offered that so-called arrangement to. When a woman's desperate and trying to provide for her child, she'll do just about anything. The good thing is you told the truth. Joshua's not brand new to your past. That's gotta count that you told him the truth, Rose."

Bella shook her head. "I didn't tell him. He found out after our first night together. The next morning, he made me breakfast. I love omelets with red onions, but I just couldn't have them when I was pregnant with Jabari. When I smelled the onions, I got sick and…he knew. Maggie, the look in his eyes, he was so hurt, so betrayed. It was like déjà vu."

Maggie stroked her friend's hair. "The two of you slept together, didn't you?"

Bella began to weep. "I'm sorry, I don't know if it's the baby or what I'm feeling right now. But it's like I want to break out in tears every day," Bella said.

"It's probably a combination of both." Maggie handed Bella the box of tissue on the night table. Bella blew her nose and collected herself.

"You're under a lot of pressure right now, Rose. Your life has changed significantly in the last two weeks. But this is not unto death, I say try not to worry about this."

Bella cocked her head and stared at her friend.

"I'm serious, lady. God will handle it. He answered one prayer you prayed already, didn't he?"

"What prayer?"

"On the bus, remember?"

Bella thought back for a moment.

"God please let us make it out of here. And don't let nobody die. See, we all alive, ain't we? He's still on the throne and in the prayer answering business. Joshua is a good man, Rose. I don't care what you say, he's not the type of man who does anything for show."

Bella told Maggie how Joshua had acted when his secretary stopped by. "It's over, Maggie. He told me that I can stay until this baby is born, but after that I have to get a place of my own."

"Nine months is a mighty long time from now. Who knows, God may change his heart. How is Jabari taking the news about being a big brother?"

"I haven't told him."

"Rose, you can't keep living a life of secrets. They'll come back to haunt you. You got to tell him before he finds out some other way."

"Jabari's all I have, Maggie. I can't lose him and Joshua too."

Another round of sobbing started and Maggie held her until her crying subsided.

"What does Joshua say about all of this?"

"We've never discussed it. Jabari not being his birth child is a sore subject."

"Don't make the decision alone. Talk to Joshua. Secrets have a way of catching up with you."

CHAPTER 75

Bella looked up from the magazine she was reading to see Joshua standing in the doorway of her room. "Mind if I come in?"

Bella didn't answer. She just scooted over and made room for him on the bed. Joshua sat down and the bed groaned under his weight. "We should probably get you some more furniture in here. A desk or something."

"What's up, Josh?"

"Actually, I was going to ask you the same thing. You've been awfully quiet since we left the Trendales. Everything okay?"

"Why do you ask?"

"Because when you left the room with Maggie, I could tell that you had been crying."

"Maggie thinks that I should tell Jabari about the baby."

Joshua fingered the pages of the magazine. He didn't look at her and Bella couldn't bring herself at the moment to look at him. She could feel his sadness, though. And she could just kick herself for it. She hadn't thought about how her sharing this news with Maggie would be yet another betrayal of him.

"You told Maggie about the baby."

"Besides you, she's the only friend I have here, Joshua."

"I know."

"Joshua, things…things didn't quite work out the way I planned. I was supposed to find you this time. I was supposed to get my life together, become someone I could be proud of, and then I was going to come home and find you."

Joshua studied the floor, still refusing to make contact with her eyes.

"This last time I left, I went to the bank and I withdrew $5000. I came back home, called a cab, and bought two one way tickets to New Orleans. I found an apartment in a nice little neighborhood, paid my rent up for three months, put a $1000 down payment on a little car, and then I took three hundred dollars cash and paid for a community college course in jewelry making. After my course, I got a cart and went into business for myself. And I thought, 'This is it. I made it out. I'll never have to hook again.' But then my rent money ran out and I wasn't making enough selling jewelry to afford our apartment and buy food. I came home from the market one day and found Jabari standing outside our apartment, crying. When I saw the tears in his eyes, I vowed that I would never let us be homeless again. We drove around the city all night until we found a vacancy in the Dunbar Street Apartments. Two months ago, was the first time in a long time that I couldn't make my rent. I went to my mother, but she wouldn't give me the money. She said I could always come back home, but I would never bring Jabari into that house. Not ever. So, when I couldn't make my rent this time… I guess I want you to know it wasn't for love, Joshua. It was, but not the kind people might think. I had to take care of my son." Bella sighed deeply. "Maggie is right. I need to learn how to be honest. When I was a little kid, I was such a stickler for the truth. The truth is, I suspected I was pregnant before I left New Orleans."

With this bit of revelation, Joshua finally looked into her eyes.

"But I wasn't trying to trick you. I swear I wasn't. I never expected us to sleep together on that first night. I wasn't even trying to find you. You found me."

Joshua smiled a smile that didn't quite reach his eyes. "I always do."

"That first morning when you went downstairs to make breakfast, I told myself that I would drive to the drugstore and buy a test. If I was pregnant, I'd get an abortion and live happily ever after with you. I convinced myself I could live with that. But you did find out and I'm glad. Not about hurting you. I hate more than anything that I did that, but I'm glad that you found out because I don't think I could have lived with myself if I aborted this child." Bella rested her hand lightly on her womb. "This wasn't for love, Joshua, it was for survival. Whatever I did out there was for survival."

❦ ❦

Bella's words rang over and over again in Joshua's head as he lay before the Lord in his prayer closet that evening and wept. The weight of Bella's admission had forced him to his knees, but the reality of the condition of his life had him prostrate before God on his face. *Whatever I did out there was for survival. Not love, but survival.*

It broke his heart to think of his family out on the streets moving from pillar to post. Then there was the thing he could barely stomach to think about. The thing that caused the most anguish in his soul. He had been given an assignment to find her before something disastrous happened and he had failed. If he would have found her just one month sooner, she wouldn't be pregnant.

"If you wanted me to take her back, why didn't you awaken me a month earlier?" Joshua cried out to the walls. "Holy Spirit, if your timing is so perfect, why'd you let her come back to me this way again? You knew I wouldn't be able to accept this. Why'd you let me fail?"

Joshua felt a familiar shift in the atmosphere as the King of Glory stepped into time and space and entered the room. In a mere instant all the heaviness in his heart, the crushing heaviness that knocked him to his knees in the first

253

place, suddenly took flight like a bird and absconded from the room. Joshua felt peace flood his soul. It was like the fingers of God had slipped inside of him and were gently massaging the massive ache, squeezing the pain from his very heart. That's when he heard the voice of the Lord speak.

You did not fail, and I cannot fail. This dark night is but a season. You will know joy when the daybreaks again. I give life. Children are an inheritance from Me. Like arrows in the hand of a mighty warrior, so are the children born in one's youth. Happy is the man whose quiver is full. Name this child, Joshua. Claim her as your own. She will be yours in every way.

CHAPTER 76

I n Broken Vessels, we count the testimony stage as an important part of our healing process," Sister Anna Parks was saying. The word of God tells us that we overcome by the blood of the Lamb and the word of our testimony. Let's receive our very own dear sister, Thelma Carter, as she comes." The women all around the circle stood and clapped as Thelma Carter approached the podium. Bella followed suit and did the same. In her short time interacting with the people in the group, Bella had been somewhat hostile towards Thelma. The woman had sought her out quite a few times, asking Bella out for coffee or lunch. Frankly, Bella couldn't figure out what Thelma was doing in the group in the first place. She was a beautiful, young and stylish woman. She didn't have the hard edges that the other women in the circle had. Women who had gone through pain. Bella could deal with these women; they made her feel like her situation wasn't so bad off. What she couldn't deal with was Miss Picture Prefect Thelma Carter. Thelma wore a wedding ring. She figured that Thelma's husband was probably one of those spiritual dignitaries that sat up in the pulpit on Sunday mornings. The same pulpit that Joshua used to sit in every Sunday morning, up until the day her and Jabari had returned. Bella squirmed in her seat, maybe she was giving this Thelma person too hard a time. Maybe the woman wasn't a plant to say, "See, this is what the perfect minister's wife is supposed to look like." Maybe Thelma had her share of pain and God had done what Bella hadn't dared asked Him to do for her. Maybe He changed Thelma and removed from her the very smell of smoke.

Bella sat there, repenting in her mind. Then she began to open her heart enough to hear the woman who seemed to have all the pieces to her puzzle intact. Bella was totally unprepared for what happened next.

CHAPTER 77

Joshua had just split his Foundational Truths class up into their small discussion groups when the head pastor of New Horizons Christian Training Center, Bishop Micah Ford, stopped by. He stood quietly in the doorway of the classroom until Joshua noticed him. Joshua waved and walked towards the older man.

"I'm sorry, Joshua, I didn't mean to interrupt."

"No, actually this is the perfect time. What can I do for you?"

"Do you think the class could finish up on their own tonight? I'd like to speak to you for a moment in my office."

"Not a problem. I'll be right there." Pastor Ford walked out of the classroom and Joshua got Mike's attention in the back of the room.

"What's up? I saw Pastor Ford talking to you. Everything cool?"

"Can you pray the class out tonight?"

Mike looked at his brother sternly and shook his finger at him. "I know what you're tryin' to do, Josh, but it's not gon work. There's only one preacher in this family."

Joshua threw his hands up in surrender. Making his face as innocent as possible, he managed to hold back a smile. "Hey, bro, I'm not tryin' to do anything. Pastor wants to talk to me. You saw him standing in the doorway."

"Yeah, alright. But this is the first and the last time," Mike said.

"Fair enough, thanks." Joshua hugged his brother, gathered his things, and walked out the door. A few minutes later, Joshua knocked on the open door of the older man's office. Pastor Ford rose to greet him.

"Joshua, come on in and close the door behind you, son."

Joshua took a seat in one of the office chairs.

"I don't want to alarm you, but Bella left her group early tonight."

"What? Where did she go?"

"She was feeling poorly, so I asked Sister Carmichael to drive her home."

"Why didn't someone come get me?"

"Bella was very adamant about not disturbing you while you were teaching. Sister Parks did, however, come and get me. When I arrived, Bella was a little disoriented and very upset. She wanted to call a cab, but I was able to get her to calm down a bit, pray with her, and get her to accept the ride from Sister Carmichael."

Joshua sat back in his chair and pondered all of this for a minute, "She was fine on the way over this evening. Did she say why she was upset?"

"She said it was female problems. She complained of a stomachache and a headache. Sister Parks did mention that Bella seemed perfectly well until one of the group members, Thelma Carter, began to give her testimony."

Joshua tried to put the name with the face.

"You may remember sister Thelma's husband, Danny Carter, better. Danny passed away three years ago from the AIDS virus."

Of course he remembered Danny. Danny's testimony, his unwavering commitment to God, and his family while facing death, was what drew Joshua back in. After hearing Danny's testimony, Joshua decided to stop feeling sorry for himself and answer God's call. Hearing Danny's testimony had been powerful, and life changing, for Joshua. He had no idea what effect Thelma's testimony could have on Bella.

Joshua stood up. "I need to get home."

"Of course, is there anything you need me to do?"

"Jabari's on a field trip with the youth group tonight. They won't be back until eight; if you could let my brother know about this and send Jabari home with him, that would be great."

"Of course," Pastor Ford stood. He shook Joshua's hand and gave him a fatherly pat on the back.

"I know you and Bella have had challenges in the past and a long uphill battle in front of you. But I'm praying for you."

"Thank you."

"Take it easy, Joshua, and give Bella my love."

CHAPTER 78

B ella! Bella!" Joshua called as he walked through the house that evening. Joshua looked everywhere with no signs of Bella. Finally, he heard the sound of muffled crying coming from one of the third-floor bathrooms. Joshua took the stairs two at a time. He tried the door and found it locked.

"Bella, open the door. It's me, Joshua."

"Go away!"

"Not until you open the door and I see that you're okay."

There were no more words on Bella's end, just the sound of her muffled sobs.

"Bella, open the door or I'm coming in." Joshua did a quick survey of the door. He pulled a credit card from his wallet and forced open the lock. When Joshua stepped inside the bathroom, he saw Bella balled up on the floor beside the commode.

"God, I'm sorry! So, so sorry! I'm sorry, Joshua!" Bella wailed.

Joshua got down on his hands and knees and wrapped her in his arms.

"She g-g-g-gave her husband AIDS! He-he-he d-d-died," Bella gagged. "Oh God! I'm going to die."

"No, you're going to make it through this."

"I don't deserve to live. Oh, God. I'm gonna lose my baby!" Bella stuck her head in the toilet and began to violently wretch into it.

Joshua held her hair back and prayed softly as she released her insides into the toilet bowl. Joshua spoke softly but firmly in her ear. "Bella I'm fine, you're fine, and Jabari is fine." Joshua laid a calming hand on her womb. "This baby will be healthy and happy. And when she gets here, she'll be loved. You got that?"

"Okay," Bella whined.

"You are not going to lose anybody. Now take a deep breath for me."

Bella inhaled.

"That's it, breathe."

"I'm sorry, Joshua. All those m-m-m-men. If anything ever happened to you, I would d-d-d-die."

"Nothing happened to me or you, for that matter. Nothing that God can't fix. I thank God for that. I've forgiven you. It's time you forgave yourself too."

"I d-d-don't even know h-h-how to d-d-do that."

Joshua stroked her head and smiled. "You know what I think, Bella Rose?" Bella lifted her head off the toilet seat and stared up at him.

"I think it's time to say goodbye to things that have been with you for a long time. I think if you do that, you'll be able to do the next step, which is to forgive yourself."

"Things l-l-like w-w-what?"

"Things like bitterness. Shame. Regret."

Bella shook her head violently. "I d-d-don't know how to do that."

"How about I walk you through it?"

CHAPTER 79

The next morning, Bella woke up in the master bed to the sounds of Joshua snoring softly in the chair beside her. She hadn't felt this much peace in years. If she ever doubted the truth of Joshua's conversion, last night had proved to her that it was true. Joshua had prayed over her with such authority. He commanded things to unlink themselves and go and they did. She could not remember a day when bitterness and un-forgiveness did not occupy a part of her heart. She didn't know what it was like to live one day without regret. *This is what it feels like. This is what it feels like to be free.* She felt like a ten-ton weight had been lifted off her chest.

"I hope that smile means you're feeling better this morning."

Bella touched her face. Apparently, she was feeling so good, she didn't even know she was smiling. "Words can't even describe the peace I feel right now. I haven't felt this good in years, thanks to you."

"Thanks be to God. He did the work, all I did was hold your hand," Joshua said.

"You did a lot more than hold my hand. You called some things up and out of me, and they went. I'd heard about people with deliverance ministries, but I always thought that stuff was fake until now. I feel like a million bucks."

Bella glanced over at the clock. "Jabari's going to be late for school if one of us doesn't get a move on it."

"Jabari went home with Mike and Marcus last night. Mike will get him there on time." The phone rang. Joshua looked at the caller ID. Mike's number came up on the screen. "That's him now," Joshua said, pushing talk on the receiver.

"Hey, Dad. This is me, Jabari. Are you guys alright?"

"Yeah, man, we're fine. Your mom wasn't feeling so hot yesterday, so she left Bible Study early, but she's fine now. Wanna talk to her?"

"I kind of want to hear both your voices at the same time, if that's alright with you."

"No problem, buddy, let me put you on speaker phone." Joshua held his hand over the receiver and spoke to Bella. "He wants to hear both of us at the same time."

A look of concern flew over Bella's face. "Oh God, I traumatized him." Bella reached franticly for the phone.

"Relax, he's fine."

"Hey, baby," Bella said, speaking into the speaker base. "You okay? We didn't scare you, did we?"

"No. I'mma go to school from here this morning. Uncle Mike bought me clothes for when I need to crash here. I've got uniforms, regular clothes, church clothes, play clothes, pajamas, everything. I never even have to pack a bag if I wanna spend the night."

"That's great. I'll see you when you get home from school," Bella said.

"Tell your uncle he doesn't have to bring you home today, Jabari. I'll pick you up myself," Joshua said.

"Hum, well, actually, I was wondering if Marcus could pick me up in the morning and drop me off at school from now on. We're going to the same place, and Marcus said he didn't mind since our house was on the way. Please, Dad? Please! I know, Mom, that you had some reservations, but, Dad, you saw Marcus driving the other day and you said he was a really good driver."

Bella shot Joshua a can-you-believe-this-boy look.

Joshua responded with an I-told-you-he-wasn't-traumatized look.

"Jabari, I don't mind as long as your mom doesn't mind."

"I guess it's okay," Bella agreed grudgingly.

"Thanks, Mom, thanks Dad! You're the greatest parents ever."

"Yeah, yeah, yeah," Joshua said.

"Just remember that the next time you ask us something and the answer is no," Bella added.

"I will. This is possibly the coolest day of my life! Oh, Marcus is out front. I gotta go."

"Bye, Jabari."

Joshua clicked end on the phone call. He stood up and stretched. "Want some breakfast?"

"Actually, I have to get going. I forgot I had a doctor's appointment. I'm supposed to be there within the hour." Joshua pulled his cellphone out his back pocket. "I scheduled all your appointments in my phone, you don't have anything scheduled for today."

"Dr. Cadwell's office called yesterday, he wanted to go over the results of some lab test with me. Nothing serious, I'll probably have to take some iron tablets again. I didn't tell you because I know you were going back to work today. It's no big deal, I can manage by myself."

Joshua picked up his phone and dialed his office. "Selena. Hey, it's Josh. Cancel my morning. I'll be in this afternoon."

"Joshua, you didn't have to do that."

Joshua kissed the top of her head. "I wanted to. I'mma hop in the shower right quick. You've got less than an hour to get to this appointment, so you might want to do the same. I'll meet you downstairs in twenty minutes."

CHAPTER 80

Joshua was sitting in the waiting room reading the paper when Bella's doctor approached him. "Mr. Keys, I'm Dr. Cadwell, I'm the OBGYN handling your wife's case. Can we talk for a moment?"

"Certainly." Joshua got up and followed the balding, gray haired man into the office.

"I just sent Bella down to the lab to get some blood drawn. I thought that would give us a moment to talk privately."

Joshua leaned forward in the metal chair, concern etched across his face. "Are Bella and the baby okay?"

"For the moment, yes, but her blood pressure is a lot higher than I'd like for it to be."

"Anything you can do for that?"

"Not much, I'm afraid, except write her a prescription for a little more rest. But there is something you can do."

"Anything," Joshua said without hesitation.

"If you want your wife to deliver a healthy, full term baby, Mr. Keys, you've got to do more than drive her to these appointments and wait for her in the lobby. She needs your emotional support. She needs you in here with her holding her hand. This is a stressful time for a woman." Bella walked through the door and Dr. Cadwell shifted gears quickly.

"Here she is now. The mama-to-be. I'm going to leave the room and give you a moment to undress and put on one of our lovely fashion-less paper gowns. And, Dad, when I come back, you'll get a chance to hear baby's heartbeat for the first time. Won't that be a treat?"

CHAPTER 81

Joshua pushed the overhead control button and drove his truck into the garage. He looked over at Bella anxiously. "You're sure you're okay with this? Because I don't have to go in today."

For what seemed like the millionth time to Bella, she said, "I'm fine." Joshua had been treating her like she was a piece of glass ever since they'd left the doctor's office today.

"And if you need anything, anything at all, call my cell. If I don't pick up, call the office. Selena will know how to reach me."

"Seriously, Joshua, I will be fine."

Joshua and Bella walked into the house and found the ladies from Bella's accountability group camped out in their living room. The women all stood in unison when Joshua and Bella walked through the door.

"Anna called to check on you this morning and the housekeeper said something about you being at the hospital," a woman named Jilly said.

"Anna couldn't tell us much more than that, so we all called into work today and came to see about you," Renee said.

"Pastor Josh, please don't get mad at your cleaning lady. We were so afraid that something had happen to Sister Bella that we practically barged our way in here," Anna said.

"No worries, you all are welcome anytime."

"Bella, we wanted to apologize. We just feel awful about the way things went in group last night. We all do, especially Thelma. That's the only reason why she isn't here. She wanted me to give you this though." Renee held out a bouquet of roses for Bella,

"They are beautiful," Bella breathed.

"A peace offering from Thelma's garden. She cut them fresh for you this morning. I watched her, she wore gloves, and she didn't prick herself in anyway. So you don't have to worry about that," Jilly said.

"Why would I worry?" Bella asked.

"Thelma figured, well we all figured, you left out the way you did because of your child, the one in your womb. You are pregnant, right?" Jilly said.

Bella shot Joshua a look. He shrugged his shoulders as if to say, *you know I didn't tell nobody nothing.*

"Thelma thought that somehow you thought she might contaminate your baby," Anna said gently.

"Oh, God no! Nothing like that. I mean, I am with child, but, no, I would never think anything as ignorant as that. *I'm an ex-prostitute myself. What kind of business would I have looking down on somebody with AIDS?* "I had a doctor's appointment this morning, just a prenatal check-up. And as for yesterday, I guess…well, to be perfectly honest, Thelma's story just hit a little too close to home."

The women nodded in silent understanding. There was an awkward moment of silence until Renee spoke.

"Can I just say, for once, that it's nice to meet a rich sister who is real."

Bella grinned. *Lord, these poor women, if they only knew how real.*

Joshua cleared his throat. "Bella, I'mma go get ready for work."

"We should get going then," Anna said.

"No, please stay. Today's my first day back at the office. I'd feel a lot better knowing Bella had some company while I was there," Joshua said.

"Well, we did take off work. Bella, what do you say? We brought movies and unhealthy snacks," Renee said.

Bella laughed. "I love both!"

"You look like a chick flick kinda girl," Jilly said.

"Oh, yes!" Bella moaned. "And there's not a soul in this house willing to watch them with me."

Joshua grunted. "You got that right. Bella, why don't you and your friends have your chick flick-a-thon in the home theatre?"

"You don't mind?" Bella asked.

"Of course not, just don't overdo it on those unhealthy snacks. I'll have Mrs. C prepare you ladies some light appetizers and a healthy lunch."

Bella smiled up at Joshua. "Sounds good to me. But I need to call Thelma first. This girl's day just wouldn't be the same without her."

CHAPTER 82

Joshua and Selena sat together by the fireplace in Joshua's office. Selena scribbled notes as Joshua spoke. "I need you to send out a heads up to the department managers. I'm going to be spending less time around the office, so I'm going to need everyone to step up and pull their weight, especially on this Pacific Heights Project."

Selena frowned. "Does that mean we won't be working anymore late nights together."

"I'm afraid not."

"Dang, I hope this doesn't mean I have to start moonlighting. I was making a killing in overtime."

Joshua laughed. "You'll still get your overtime. Somebody's gotta do my share of the work. I just won't be around to micromanage you. Now that Bella and Jabari are home, Home Court has to take a back seat. My family is my number one priority."

"I guess I'll have to settle for working lunch dates with you then."

"Yep." Joshua stood and stretched his leg muscles.

"How about now? We could go out, or I could order in?"

Joshua looked down at his watch. "My bad, Selena. You must be starving, go take your lunch."

"You haven't eaten anything either, and you said you really wanted to have those projections finished by five. The way I see it, the only way that's going to happen is if we work through lunch. I've got my tablet and recorder, I can travel."

Joshua thought for a moment then decided. "Let's order in."

"Any special request?"

"Nah, whatever you choose is fine."

⚶ ⚶

Selena was at her desk looking through her menu stash when Bella walked up. Bella breezed past Selena's desk and headed straight for Joshua's door.

"Wait, you can't go in there."

Bella turned around. "Why not?"

"He's in a meeting."

"Okay, well, then I guess you should do your job and let him know that I'm here."

"I can't." Selena pasted a fake smile on her face and pointed to the lit red call light on her phone. "It's a phone meeting and it would be unprofessional for me to barge in and interrupt. And after that we have a lunch date, so I'm afraid you'll have to come back another day."

Just before Bella could cut the fool, Joshua stuck his head out of the door. "Selena—" He stopped short when he saw Bella, her hands folded akimbo looking very displeased.

"Bill, let me....I'll call you back," Joshua said. He clicked the receiver off and walked over to Selena's desk. "This is a pleasant surprise," he said, smiling just a tad bit too brightly for Bella's liking.

"Really?" Bella said dryly.

"Of course," Joshua said, leaning down and planting a soft kiss at the nape of her neck. To Selena he said, "When Bella stops by, you don't have to call first, just send her back." Joshua led Bella into the office and closed the door behind them.

Bella looked around the spacious office; it had Joshua's style written all over it. Her eyes took in the cozy seating arrangement around the fireplace and the empty coffee mug with the red lipstick stain on it. *Did that heifer leave this in here on purpose? Is she trying to mark her territory?* Bella stared at the coffee mug and felt herself growing hot.

Joshua's warm greeting in the reception area had soothed her for a moment, but now imagining Selena in here with Joshua was making Bella crazy. Bella's gaze landed back on Joshua. He was watching her like she was a time bomb about to explode. "I was in the building, meeting with Carol and Maggie about paint swatches."

"You love that kind of stuff, that must have been fun," Joshua said, smiling that overly bright smile again. It was either an attempt to hide guilt or to coax her out of her obvious funk. Bella hadn't quite figured which one.

"It was. I thought I'd stop by and say hi, you know, keep the fun going. I didn't know I'd be stopped by the Gestapo. Next time I guess I should call first."

"This is new for everyone, Bella," Joshua said quietly. "She's just doing her job."

Bella nodded and rose to leave.

"Have you eaten yet?" Joshua asked quickly.

Bella shrugged. "I can fix something at the house."

"I'd really like it if you would stay and have lunch with me."

Selena rose when she saw the door to Joshua's office open and he and Bella walk out. "Joshua, I ordered Paninis. They're on the way."

"I have to take a rain check on that, Selena."

"But what about the projections?"

"They'll hold."

Bella couldn't resist looking back over her shoulder and smiling as Joshua led her out of the office door.

CHAPTER 83

I hate her! She ruined everything!" Selena paced back and forth in Leslie's living room as she recounted for her cousin how Bella had stepped to her today at the office.

"If she keeps playin' with me like this, I'm gonna have to cut that whore and then I'll lose my job for sure."

Leslie swirled around in her computer chair. "Funny you should use that particular word choice."

"What?"

"Whore."

"Look what I found." Leslie stood and motioned for Selena to take her seat at the computer. Selena sat and began scanning through page after page of the gossip website about Bella and Joshua. *Rosemary Leblanc is a prostitute. Joshua Keys is married to a prostitute.* Unbelievable. That's why Bella was able to peep her game so quickly. She was from the streets. Literally. "Leslie, girl, you really did it this time. You hit the jackpot. Now all we have to do is figure out how we can cash in on this mug."

"You could always threaten her with what you know. Force her to leave. Ain't that what y'all call it in the corporate world a 'forceful takeover?'"

"I don't think that's gonna work. She's not the type to scare easily."

"Try dangling a fine piece of meat in front of her teeth. Once a whore, always a whore. She might not scare easy, but I bet she'll bite."

Selena rolled her eyes and vetoed her cousin again. "She's married to Joshua Keys. Anybody I could find to dangle in front of her would be dog meat compared to him."

"So how you gonna get your man?"

"I'm gonna bide my time. Like the old folks in the church say, I'm gonna hold my peace and be still."

CHAPTER 84

When Joshua got home, the aromas were calling him from the garage. He made a beeline straight into the kitchen. It was a wonder that they weren't all overweight, Bella was such an excellent cook, especially when it came to Louisiana cuisine. Before, when she was cooking for him, he was a star player in the NBA. He had games and daily practice to combat the extra pounds. Now that he was no longer in the league, he had to be super diligent about his workout. Joshua had seen his share of retired ball players get saggy around the waist, and he had decided, right after retirement, that would not be him. When Bella walked in, Joshua was leaning over the stove tasting the stewed concoction in her pots.

"Hey, no tasting."

"Sorry. Couldn't help it, you know how I love this. It was calling me. This is that stuff that—" Joshua snapped his fingers trying to remember the name.

"Etouffee."

"Yeah, ah-today.'

"No, Joshua listen: ah-too-fay."

"Yeah, yeah, I know. It's great."

"Not too spicy?"

"You kidding? It's perfect." Color rushed into her cheeks at his compliment. "Where's Jabari? Let's eat."

"Oh, we're not eating together, remember? I'm hosting my small group. The etouffee is for them."

Joshua's face fell. "You're taking this to the church?"

"Actually, we're going to meet here for dinner and Bible study. Our group felt like it would be more intimate to meet in each other's homes. I told you about that. Remember?"

"Yeah, I guess I do remember you mentioning something like that."

"I'm sorry, I should have reminded you."

"Naw, it's cool. It's not like this is going to be an every week thing, right?"

"Well, we won't be meeting here every week. I just happen to be first in the rotation. Joshua, I'm sorry. I should have asked your permission before I volunteered to have our group meet here."

"Don't be silly, you don't have to ask my permission to do anything. It's your house."

Her house. The words sounded strange coming from his mouth, but it was true. This was the house Bella had wanted. She had decorated every inch of it. Everything from the colors to the wall paper in the dining room, which they never used, to the paint in the upstairs bedrooms, it was all her style.

"I know, but for the last few years this has been your space. You've gotten out of practice sharing it."

"I like having you and Jabari in our space. It fits, always has. I'm just disappointed that you made the ah-today and I won't be getting any."

"Etouffee."

"That and the fact that we won't be riding to church together anymore."

"You still have Jabari. I'm sure he'll talk your head off all the way there and back. You'll never even know I'm not in the car. Besides, we'll still be riding together on Sundays, at least until I get my own place, anyways."

Joshua nodded.

"And as for the etouffee, I know it's your favorite, Josh, so I set some aside for you and Jabari. It's in the microwave."

Joshua's eyes lit up like a kid on Christmas morning when he saw the two saran-covered plates of food.

"Thanks." He leaned down and kissed her cheek softly. An awkward moment passed between the two of them before Joshua maneuvered around her and grabbed the two plates and a pitcher of tea out of the refrigerator.

"Jabari home yet?"

"He's upstairs doing his homework."

Joshua headed for the stairs.

"Joshua, you guys can eat at the kitchen table."

"That's okay, we'll stay out of your way."

"Don't you need cups?" she called to his back.

"Naw, it's cool, we'll improvise."

CHAPTER 85

Once the Broken Vessels small group started meeting inside of each other's homes, a sort of natural gelling began to occur between the women. Outside of the walls of the church, the natural barriers each woman put up began to fall away. If they had a good ole fashion cry and they left the meeting with red eyes, nobody had to worry about explaining herself to another good intentioned member of the body of Christ. They were making progress and becoming stronger than ever before. As for Bella, she enjoyed entertaining the women from the group at her house. She loved their realness. She could truly say that these women weren't a group of strangers Joshua had forced her to meet with anymore. They were her friends. This is why Bella had decided she wanted to do something special for the women for the upcoming holiday season. She had been going over the designs in her head all week. Now, if she could just get Joshua on board, everything would be perfect.

Bella moved around the kitchen preparing everything for Joshua's arrival. She wanted everything to be perfect and in place when he got home, because she had something important to ask him. She needed him to be in a receptive mood. Bella had been gone for five years, but she'd easily fallen into her old patterns of communication with Joshua.

Before, when she wanted to ask Joshua something that she was almost certain he wouldn't agree to, she would always cook him a good home cooked meal. He loved her cooking and a hot meal on the table always seemed to make

Joshua more agreeable. But these days Joshua was always agreeable. It was like living with a new person entirely. So Bella really didn't know what to expect when she made her request tonight, but she would cover all her bases. Joshua arrived home from the office and found the table set for one. He did a quick survey of the pretty tablecloth that adorned the table, the flowers, and the good dishware. "Wow, smells great in here."

"Thanks. Jabari called and asked to spend the night at Mike's. Since it's a Friday, I didn't have a problem with it."

Joshua nodded. "Aren't you eating?"

"I had a late lunch with Thelma. I can't eat another bite right now. I'll eat later."

Joshua's face turned up into a crooked half smile. "So all of this is for me?"

Bella nodded. Joshua took off his suit coat jacket and laid it on the back of the kitchen chair. He sat down and took the warm towel Bella offered him to wipe his hands. Joshua grabbed Bella's hand, bowed his head, and began to pray.

"Dear Lord, thank you for this food, and thank you for Bella and the care she took in preparing this meal. Bless it and sanctify it in Jesus' name. Amen."

He opened his eyes and released her hand. Joshua opened the pretty little cloth napkin she had laid out for him and set it on his knee. "You've been going to lunch quite a bit lately. How are you paying for that?"

Bella startled at the question and then quickly recovered. It certainly wasn't like he didn't have reason to suspect her. To ask her anything, but that was the past and she was a completely different person, now she would never . . . Bella looked into Joshua's eyes and saw no accusation there, just a question. So she relaxed. "I have friends who work. They know I don't, so they treat me."

"You've been getting pretty close to the ladies in your group." Another statement that was more of a question.

"It was kind of weird at first, but with Maggie, and now the women from the group, for the first time in my life I feel like I'm wealthy in the friend department." Bella looked down for the first time, realizing he hadn't even touched his food.

"That's one of the gifts that Christ affords us when we come into communion with other believers," Joshua said.

She nodded, still perplexed by the uneaten food. The old Joshua would have come in and got right down to business, eating the food on his plate. He wouldn't have looked up once, except to ask for a refill. She could have asked him for anything she wanted then, because he was in nirvana. Bella did not know how to handle or relate to this new man. Joshua smiled, seeming to sense her confusion and disappointment.

"So, you want to ask me whatever it is that you want so I can eat?"

"Huh?"

"Every time you want something that you think I'm going to say no to, I get the king treatment. You don't have to do that."

"Do what?" Bella said, quickly recovering and looking as innocent as possible.

"Manipulate the situation."

"I didn't know that's what I was doing. I was under the impression that I gave you the king treatment every day."

Joshua smirked. "Just ask, Bella, so I can eat."

"Oh, well in that case, I was thinking that the holiday season is approaching and that I would like to do something special for the ladies in my group. Only problem is I don't have any cash. I was hoping you could loan me the money to buy a few Christmas gifts."

"What'd you have in mind?"

Bella held her breath, because the thing about it was, Joshua was always really generous when it came to her, just not so generous when it came to other people.

"I was thinking jewelry. See, I'd like to use different precious—well, mostly semi-precious—stones for each of the women. Anna's always talking about how we are precious gemstones to God. I got to thinking that I could make necklaces with stones that represent each woman's personality. Like Thelma, when I think of her, I think of amethyst. And Renee, whenever I think of her, I think of tiger's eye. I'd like to make Anna an emerald necklace. Look, I can show you better than I could tell you."

Bella grabbed her sketchbook off the counter and offered it to Joshua. He silently flipped through design after design of each necklace she had created for the women, studying them intently. Bella moved to the refrigerator and removed a pitcher of freshly chilled tea.

"So, what do you think?"

"This is really impressive," Joshua said, admiring her work.

"Thanks."

"And expensive."

Bella took the sketchbook back from him. "Not terribly, every thing's cheaper when you make it yourself. Plus, I can get the stones at wholesale prices because of my seller's permit."

Joshua nodded. "Good thinking."

"So, does that mean you'll loan me the money?"

"No."

Bella's face fell.

"You can pay for this little project of yours out of your rainy-day fund."

Bella swallowed. "My rainy-day fund?"

The account he had opened in her name the second time she ran. The money he had given her so that she wouldn't be doing God knows what with God knows who if she felt like she needed to go. So she could be safe.

"You don't plan on going anywhere anytime soon, do you?"

"No, of course not, it's just...I didn't know that money was still...there."

"We had a deal, remember? As long as you felt you needed it, it would always be there. Last I checked, there was a little over twenty thousand dollars in that account. If this project of yours is going to cost more than that, well...then you might want to rethink your little gift idea." Joshua picked up his fork and started eating then.

Bella just stood there holding the pitcher of iced tea in shock.

"May I?" Joshua motioned to the iced tea.

Bella poured him a glass and sat down beside him at the table.

"I'm glad you're making new friends, Bella, but you don't have to depend on the kindness of others. What's mine is yours and I make more than enough to take care of you. If you want to keep these new friends of yours, try footing the bill sometime."

"So...you want me to use the rainy-day fund for lunch dates?"

"No. I pay for food, shelter, and clothing. Use your credit cards for any of that."

"And you don't mind me treating my friends?"

Joshua shrugged. "You ain't gotta floss. You don't have to pick up the bill every time. Nobody likes a showoff. But then, nobody wants to be friends with a moocher either. It's a delicate balance. You feel me?"

"Huh… yeah, I think so," Bella said.
"Good. Are we done?"
"Yeah."
He pointed to his unfinished plate. "Can I?"
"Of course."

CHAPTER 86

Joshua rapped once on the bedroom door and walked into Bella's room carrying her morning breakfast tray of mint tea and crackers.

Bella rolled over and groaned. "Is it Thanksgiving already?"

"It's almost noon. What's the matter? You usually love the holidays."

"Yeah, when I'm not spending them at some spiritual dignitary's house."

"We went to dinner with Micah and Pamela last month. You had a good time. Remember?"

"That was on neutral ground. This is her house and the others will be there. She seemed nice, but I don't want to get over there in front of all those other minister wives and be clowned."

"Why do you think they would clown you?"

"I don't know, cause I'm five months pregnant with somebody else's baby." Bella had meant the words to come out sarcastic, but with the tears building in her throat, all she could manage was pitiful.

Joshua ignored her current unglued state. "When you think of pastor's wives, you think of what? Your mother, right?"

"Yeah."

Joshua nodded. "I did too at first. But, Bella, these women are the exact opposite of that."

"Opposite how?"

"They remind me more of you."

"Me?"

"All the best things about you." Joshua sat on the edge of the bed. "We have to be there in an hour. So can I pray for you?"

Bella nodded her head.

CHAPTER 87

All the way over to the Ford's house, Bella threw question after question at Joshua about who was going to be there. So far, he had confirmed that Anna and her husband Paul would not be there. *Bummer.* "What about Mike? Will Mike be there?"

"Mike's going to my parents. Mom says he's bringing a girl."

"Wow. You think it's serious?"

"I doubt it. He hasn't been serious about anybody since Tonya."

Bella's face lit up at the mention of her old friend. "Josh, how is she?"

"Moved on and engaged to some pastor in New York. It's a real sore subject with Mike, so don't bring it up around him, okay?"

"No, I won't," Bella said, reading the sudden pained expression on Joshua's face. Bella loved the closeness Joshua experienced with his brother. They couldn't be closer if they'd shared the same womb. She knew that Tonya's engagement to a pastor had to be a sore subject with Mike, since Tonya had turned down his marriage proposal years ago because at the time he'd asked, Mike didn't know the Lord.

"Mike's saved now, right?"

"Yeah."

"Maybe there's still a chance. Maybe if Tonya knew that the thing she'd been hoping and praying for—"

"Tonya wants to marry a minister. Mike ain't trying to be that."

Bella had been there the night that Mike had proposed. Tonya had wept bitterly in her arms after she had turned Mike down. Actually, what Bella remembered Tonya saying was that God had called her to marry a minister, not that she wanted to marry one. Tonya desperately believed that Mike was indeed that man, but the Spirit had told her that she could not take his hand until he answered the call. Tonya, like Maggie, was one of the best examples of a Christian Bella had ever known. Bella looked over at Joshua's stone face and decided that now wasn't the best time to split hairs about it.

"I know he might not think of himself in that way, Josh, but the work you guys do through Home Court is definitely ministry."

The silence coming from the driver's side of the vehicle told Bella it was time to change subjects. Bella sighed. "I wish Mike was coming today, he would have been a nice comfort."

"Stop worrying, I told you it'll be fine. The minute you're ready to bounce, just give me the signal."

"The signal?"

"You do remember it don't you?"

"I—of course. I'm just surprised that you do."

"There's not much I can forget about us, Bella." Bella felt her face go flush. She turned her head away, pretending to look out the window.

"Did you wish Mel and Jack a Happy Thanksgiving for me this morning?" Bella asked.

"Shoot, I forgot. Jabari?" Joshua looked through the rearview mirror at Jabari, who was lost in his hand-held video game. Jabari's head snapped up upon hearing his name.

"Huh?"

"Call your grandparents." Joshua dug inside his blazer pocket for his cellphone. He threw it over the backseat to Jabari, who caught it.

"What am I supposed to say?" Jabari said.

"Wish them a Happy Thanksgiving, man."

"Hey, Grandma Mel, yeah, it's me, Jabari. Happy Thanksgiving! Why am I calling from my dad's cellphone? Because we're in the car. Yep, he's driving. Mom's right here."

"Happy Thanksgiving, Mel and Jack," Bella called over the seat. "Love you both."

"They said they love you too, Mom," Jabari said. "We're on our way to dinner at Pastor Ford's house. Oh, okay. Dad? Grandpa Jack says, 'Happy Thanksgiving'."

"Happy Thanksgiving to you too, Dad," Joshua said.

"Grandma Mel says, 'Happy Thanksgiving and to keep your eyes on the road.' Yeah, he said it back, the Happy Thanksgiving part. Tell you when we come to a red light? Oh, okay. We're at a red light now, Grandpa." Jabari announced. "Dad, Grandpa Jack says to tell you to give Mom a kiss."

Bella's heart began to race and Joshua leaned in dutifully and placed a soft kiss on Bella's lips.

"Did he slip her the tongue? Ugh, I don't know, Grandpa. That's gross!" Jabari said.

"Dad, Grandma wants to know when she's going to see us again."

"Tell her we'll be home for Christmas."

CHAPTER 88

As they stood on the front porch of the Pastor's house, sounds of music floated outside, and it wasn't Gospel music either. Bella was pleasantly surprised, to hear the voices of some of her favorite R&B artists playing. "Is that secular music I hear?"

Joshua rang the doorbell. "I told you to throw out everything you thought you knew."

Pamela Ford answered her own door. "Hello, hello, come on in." She hugged Joshua, Bella, and then Jabari. "Jabari, I hope you're a gamer, because Pastor Ford and some of the others have a video game tournament going on downstairs. He's found an old black and white in the attic. The losers have to play on the small television."

Joshua shook his head. "Not the young guns versus the old guns again."

Pamela laughed. "You know it. They've been waiting on you. I think the old guys are taking a beating."

Jabari's eyes lit up. "You mean I get to play against my dad?"

"You think you can handle that, sport?"

"Oh, I am so there. It'll be nice to finally beat you in something for a change."

Pamela and Bella both laughed. "Jabari, I see you're going to fit in just fine. Just follow your dad downstairs. He knows the way." Pamela stepped aside so the two males could pass by. When Joshua hesitated, she looped her arm through

Bella's. "Bella, why don't you come on into the kitchen with us?"

Bella looked at Pamela when Joshua and Jabari disappeared. "The Pastor plays video games?"

Pamela rolled her eyes, "Girl, it's one of his favorite pastimes. He claims it's how he stays connected to the youth in the church. But, honey, I am no fool. I married a big ole kid."

Pamela looked down at Bella's heels. "Those are some bad shoes, woman, but they cannot be comfortable. Let me get you some slippers."

Bella surveyed Pamela Ford as she rummaged through the hall closet for a pair of extra house slippers. Bella noticed that the first lady was always flawlessly put together, just like her mother. But unlike her mother, Pamela did not exude the air of church royalty. At a dinner party like this one, Sylvia Leblanc would never have answered her own door. She would have had one of her flunkies from the church do that. Her mother would also find a way to make a grand entrance. And, most importantly, as the host of her own party, Bella's mother would be dressed to kill. Although Joshua had warned her to be comfortable, Bella had insisted on arming herself with an outfit that seemed more befitting a church folk situation. When Joshua realized that Bella was determined to dress up, he threw a stylish sports coat over his clothes so the two of them looked like a well-dressed pair. Just as Joshua had predicted, Pamela was dressed comfortably in a silk lounging suit. Her shoulder length hair was pulled back in a ponytail, and even without make-up, her milk chocolate skin was beautiful.

Pamela turned and handed Bella the slippers and Bella felt herself relax. After Bella had changed into the house shoes, Pamela looped her arm through Bella's again and the two women walked towards the kitchen. When Bella and Pamela entered the kitchen, Bella was greeted with the smiling eyes of four women in various shades sitting around the island countertop. A petite, blonde haired, pixie faced woman named, Deanna. A sharp Asian sister who introduced herself as, Kim Lee, a tall mocha colored sister who introduced herself as, Sharon, and a lovely Latina woman by the name of Carmen. The Latina sister won Bella's heart right away. She stood up and spun around for Bella to see.

"Look, Bella, we're twins. I remember what it was like the first time I came to one of these. I figured you'd dress up for this, so I dressed up too."

"I didn't know what to expect at one of these my first time either. I showed up in a kimono." Kim Lee rolled her eyes, remembering.

"What are you talking about? You looked great, Kim, you were working that kimono to death," Carmen said.

The other women nodded their heads in agreement. That's when Bella knew she had been worried for nothing. There were no spiteful, jealous women here.

"Joshua told me to dress casual," Bella admitted.

"Hum hum, but you knew you were coming to a church affair with some bougie church people, so you figured you better come correct, right?" Sharon said.

Bella laughed. "Yeah."

"Well you came correct, alright. Bella, you look amazing in that dress," Deanna said.

"Yes, she does, doesn't she?" Pam set a mug of hot tea down at the open seat around the counter. "We always drink our favorites, and Josh told us that mint is yours," she explained.

Bella saw that the other women were drinking tea as well. "Thanks."

"Bella, we've actually been eagerly awaiting your arrival. As you can see, we have our own little pastors' wives club at New Horizon and right now, I'm in the middle of sort of a mini ministry related crisis. We were discussing it before you came and well, we all just feel like maybe you could give a unique perspective on it," Deanna said.

Bella set her mug of tea down. She knew she'd have to have this conversation sooner or later. She just didn't expect to have it so soon. "Yeah, about the ministry part. I won't be able to help you. Joshua's the minister in our family, not me."

All of the women broke into laughter like she had said the funniest thing ever.

"Bella, I assure you every one of us said the same thing when our husbands became pastors at New Horizons," Kim Lee said.

"We all felt the same way you do. It's a club," Carmen said.

Pam raised her hand. "I'm the president."

"Trust me, you have expertise when it comes to this one. You've been married to a famous ball player for years. I'm sure you've learned the difference between women who are misguided and those who are desperate. That's what I'm trying to figure out right now. Whether the woman in question is misguided or desperate," Deanna said.

Bella sat back in her chair and relaxed. "Well, why didn't you say so? I can tell you everything you want to know about the desperate and the misguided."

๖๙ ๖๙

As soon as the youth pastor, Dave, saw Joshua and Jabari enter the room, he defected to the Young Guns team.

"Dave?" Micah said, a betrayed look on his face.

"Traitor," Keith scoffed.

"Hey, I'm their pastor, alright? My sheep need my guidance. Besides, I'm tired of losing."

Joshua took off his jacket and laid it on the couch. "Well, you'd better get used to it, cause now I got to beat you like you stole something."

Micah clapped his hands in jubilation. Dave looked warily over at Jabari. "I hope you got skills like your dad, man."

"Man, I'm way better than my dad. He don't know nothing about this. This here is a young man's game," Jabari boasted. Jabari moved through the room slapping Dave's son, Teak, then Keith Jr. and both of Carlos' boys, Manny and Angel, high fives.

Keith Sr, smirked. "You sure know how to talk smack like your dad."

"I can do more than that," Jabari said.

Joshua grinned but said nothing.

Dave slapped Jabari on the shoulder. "Your dad is going to be leading the other team, so we're going to make you captain. This is serious, Jabari, you think you can handle it?"

"Yeah, yeah, sure, sure."

"Not too much pressure facing off against your old man, is there?"

Jabari put a reassuring hand on Dave's shoulder. "Come on, Pastor Dave, the key word here is old."

Everybody hooted with laughter. Still, Joshua said nothing and just grinned.

"I just need to know one thing. What are we playing?"

"Basketball, of course. It's the only chance any of us have of beating your dad."

❧ ❧

"There's a recently widowed woman in our church," Deanna began. "And so you don't think we're all a bunch of raging gossips on your first day among us, I'll keep her name out of it. I mean she might not be after Keith at all, she could just be...."

"Misguided?" Bella finished for her.

"Yeah."

❧ ❧

Just as Joshua had predicted downstairs, the Old Guns were beating the Young Guns badly. Joshua and Jabari sat side by side on the couch, staring at the big screen television with fingers gripped fiercely on the remote controls. Joshua had just scored the game point when he spoke. "Jabari, remember the morning after you came back from New Orleans and your uncle and I took you and Marcus to play some hoops? Remember how I told you that your uncle was gon take you to school?"

"Yeah."

"Well, son, I'm getting ready to take you to church."

All the boys groaned. Jabari's eyes darted quickly to his teammates, not understanding his father's meaning.

Dave slapped his hand against his forehead and yelled, "Josh, come on! Not on his first day!"

Keith Sr. and Darren slapped each other high fives, and Micah and Carlos pumped their fists excitedly in the air and shouted, "Come on, baby, take him to church!"

In one death defying move, Joshua's player leapt high into the air and dunked the ball so hard into the net that shards of fiberglass exploded all over the screen. Joshua's player remained suspended in the air, holding on to the rim as the words, "game over" flashed in large neon lights across the TV screen. Jabari stared at the screen in shocked amazement.

Jabari's face wrinkled in confusion. "How?"

Joshua looked at his son. "That's the wrong question. What you should be asking right now is 'why?' The answer is very simple, son. No servant is greater than his master."

"Well!" Micah sang.

"The student isn't greater than the teacher. And since you, my young pupil, still have a lot to learn, you need to take your little squad to the backroom. You can play on the little TV for a while."

"Yeah, sons!" Carlos said.

Angel and Manny rolled their eyes at their dad.

Micah jumped up and grabbed a bag off the table. He handed each of the boys one of the black controllers. "Back to the basics, boys." The boys looked at the objects with confusion.

"What is this?" Jabari asked, examining the large, clunky object that Pastor Ford had placed in his hand from all angles.

"That is a joystick. You're going to need it to play Centipede on the Atari 2600 back there," Micah said.

Keith Jr. looked to his father for help. "Dad, seriously?"

Angel and Manny both groaned.

"Yeah, and if you show any promise, we might let you move up to Pacman," Keith Sr. said. The men looked on in delight as their children trudged into the back room.

Teak laid a reassuring hand on Jabari's shoulder as they walked to the back. "Don't sweat it, man, I looked in all the cheat books. I still can't figure out how he does it."

Joshua got up from his seat on the couch.

"Hey, Josh, where you going? I'm about to beat this joker real quick and hand you the controller," Carlos said.

"I'mma head upstairs for a moment and grab something to drink," Joshua said.

Micah jumped up from his seat on the lazy boy and walked over to the kitchen area. "What you need, Josh?" Micah said, opening the fridge wide to show that it was fully stocked.

"He wants a bottle of Bella," Dave sang out.

"Cool it, Dave, before we send you back to the little boy's room," Joshua said.

"She's fine, Josh," Carlos said, never looking up from his game.

"Seriously, man, leave them alone," Darren said.

"Yeah, you're just gonna mess around and get cussed out," Keith said.

Micah raised his eyebrow at Keith. "I know you are not talking about my sweet, virtuous woman?"

"Nope, I'm talking about mine. You're causing problems in my home, Josh. Do you know how long I've had to listen to Dee complaining about you hogging Bella and Jabari all to yourself?"

"Bella hasn't had the best experiences in the world with church people, she's been a little nervous about meeting everyone. I may have delayed our getting together a bit."

"Four months," Darren said.

Joshua shrugged. "Okay, so a lot. It's been good having my family home, but it ain't exactly easy. Bella and I still have a lot to contend with."

Darren and Carlos both looked at each other when they heard the note of seriousness in Joshua's voice. Carlos pressed the pause button on the game.

"Like what?" Carlos asked.

"Like the fact that while she was gone, I'd become the one thing in the world she hated most."

Darren scratched his head. "What, you mean a pastor?"

"Yeah."

All of the men took this in.

"So you see why I couldn't bring her around a gaggle of pastors and their wives, right?"

"Yeah, man, we get it. And we want you to know, we're praying for you and Bella," Dave said.

Carlos nodded. "Man, I'm just glad y'all decided to come today. I overheard Carmen on the phone the other night. If y'all didn't show, the wives were planning some straight up espionage stuff. They were talking about paying your housekeeper to disconnect your security camera and straight up bum rushing your place."

Joshua smirked. "Thanks for the heads up, Carlos."

Darren tossed a pillow at his head. "Yeah, what gives, Carlos?"

"You know I love you like a brother, man. I really do. But Carmen caught me eavesdropping. She said that if I breathed a word of this to any of you guys, there would be no sex in my house for two weeks."

All the men groaned.

"Well, Pam and I had the pleasure of dining with Bella, Joshua, and Jabari last month," Micah said. "We all had a great time. I don't think you have anything to worry about, Joshua. Bella's going to fit in just fine."

❧ ❧

"So, she's widowed and she has a son who is seventeen. Dad died in a tragic accident last spring. The mom has been reaching out to Keith to help her with her son. She calls him at all hours of the night. But I mean, to be fair, the kid is doing pretty poorly right now. Keith has gotten up out of bed at one and two o'clock in the morning to go searching for him. But now she's depending on him for other stuff. And I know it sounds unchristian of me to say, but this is starting to get on my nerves. Helping her refinance her house is one thing. I get it, okay? She's a single mom and Keith is a banker. But she's calling on my fricking husband to do chores around her house. Keith doesn't even do chores around my house."

"What kind of chores?" Kim Lee asked.

"Anything from fixing a leaky sink to mowing the grass. Last Sunday she walked up to us after church and asked Keith to come by her house and install a ceiling fan."

"What did Keith say?"

"Never done it before, but what the heck, I'll give it a whirl," Deanna said, imitating her husband's voice. "He always takes Keith Jr. with him when he goes, but I guess it bothers me that the two of them have history."

Bella's head popped up from her teacup. "What kind of history?"

"They grew up in the same town. Keith says she's never had any interest in him. But come on, have you seen my husband? Keith is fine."

"No, sweetie, that's *f—ine*," Sharon said, putting the proper emphasis where it belonged.

Bella smiled. As far as white boys go, Keith was pretty hot. And with that dimpled smile and sexy Southern drawl, he reminded her of the actor Matthew McConaughey. She could see how any number of women would be trying to push up on him. Especially since his wife couldn't tell the difference between a skank and a schoolmarm.

"Her husband grew up in the same town too. Keith says that the woman and her husband were childhood sweethearts. He thinks I'm crazy for even suggesting that she could want anything more than friendship."

"What do you think?" Pam asked.

"I don't know what to think. A huge part of me says he's the ordained minister in the family, not me. Maybe he understands people better than I do. But then there's another part of me that says this doesn't feel right, you know?"

"Does she call your house phone or his cell?" Bella asked.

"Most always his cell."

Kim Lee frowned. "You never told us that."

"We didn't have Bella here before," Pam said, smiling up from her mug of tea. "She's asking the right questions."

"Bella, do you really think it makes a difference which phone she calls on?" Deanna asked.

Bella looked at the pretty woman with the button nose, and pixie face sitting before her. *Was girlfriend really this clueless? Yeah*, Bella decided, *she was*. Instead of telling her the obvious, Bella decided it would be best to simply lead this horse to water. "The few times she calls the house phone, who answers," Bella asked gently.

Deanna rolled her eyes. "Please, I do. Keith never answers the house phone."

"Does she take time and chat with you? Ask about you and your son when you pick up?"

"No, she's very short with me. Just wants to talk to Keith."

Bella remained quiet for a moment, allowing the revelation to sink in.

Deanna's grey eyes sparkled with indignation. "She's not misguided at all, she wants my man." Panic showed in Deanna's eyes. "Bella, what do I do?"

Bella shook her head. "I think this is where my consultation services need to end. I'm what you ladies would call a backslider. Trust me, you don't want to do what I would do."

Besides, old Joshua might approve of her advice, but Bella was pretty sure that new Joshua would kill her. He wasn't even in the room right now and Bella could feel his disapproval. *You told a pastor's wife to do what?*

"I need to do something. Her son just got kicked out of public school and now she wants Keith to drive with her three hours north to drop him off at a military school next week. Keith told me he was planning to take Keith Jr., but that she'd said there wouldn't be much room in the car because they'd have to haul all of his stuff."

I'll bet, Bella thought.

"Why does she have to go? Can't you and Keith drop him off?" Sharon said.

"Or better yet, Keith and Dave." This kid is a youth in our church. This would fall under Dave's ministry. Dave is crazy about each and every one of those kids. I'm sure he wouldn't mind," Kim Lee said.

Pam nodded. "That certainly handles one part of it. But Dee, you still need to have an honest conversation with Keith about what you are sensing concerning this woman and how you feel about him doing projects around her house."

Carmen sucked her teeth. "I wish Carlos would call himself fixing anything around anybody else's house. And I've got scripture to back it up. Charity begins at home."

"You have to talk to this woman too," Kim Lee said.

"I wouldn't even know what to say to her," Deanna whined.

"You can let her know that you're a Christian, yes, but that you are no punk. You can see right through her, and your husband isn't the mark that she's made him out to be," Kim Lee said.

Bella smiled admiringly at Kim Lee. Kim Lee was no punk.

"Then you're going to give her one of our Helping Hands volunteer brochures and tell her that your husband is no longer available to service any of her needs," Sharon said.

Deanna bit her lip. "Bella, what do you think?"

Bella looked around the room at the women who had in one afternoon become her friends. "Considering what I had in mind, I think this is a much better plan."

Deanna began to cry. "I'm sorry to be bawling like this in front of you, Bella, on your first day, but this has all been so overwhelming. I'm just glad I have you ladies to talk to."

Everyone reassured Deanna that it was perfectly fine to cry. Pam gave Deanna a minute to collect herself before speaking. "Dee, let's get you upstairs and get you cleaned up. The guys will be up in a minute, and you know your husband does not like to see you cry." Pam took Deanna upstairs to wash her face. When Deanna came downstairs, she looked radiant with a fresh application of make-up. Sure enough, the men had come upstairs, laughing, joking, and bragging about their win. Keith took one look into his wife's eyes and realized that something was wrong.

"Sweetheart, have you been crying?"

Deanna shook her head, embarrassed at the sudden attention. "It's nothing. I had a little problem but the girls helped me work through it. We can talk later when we get home."

Keith stood close to Deanna, examining her face like she was a fallen baby bird. His touch was so sensual and private that Bella wished she could manufacture a few tears of her own so that Joshua would hold on to her like that.

Micah met Pam's eyes. "Baby, is everything all right in here?"

"It's fine, honey. I think Dee will feel a whole lot better when she and her husband have a chance to talk."

Deanna pasted a smile on her face. "I'm fine, see. It can wait till we get home."

Micah reached into his pants pocket and pulled out the key to his home office. He threw the key to Keith, who caught it effortlessly. Keith slung his arm around Deanna's shoulder. "Come on, baby doll. Let's take a walk."

CHAPTER 89

On Sunday morning, the tight mouth, white gloved usher lady was waiting to escort them into the aisle as usual. She asked the same question she'd asked every Sunday since Bella's first Sunday there. "Will you be sitting in the pulpit today, Pastor, or will you be sitting with your family?"

"I'll sit with my family today, Ms. Alberta, thank you," Joshua said. Usher lady held out her hand and Bella and Joshua both walked to their seats.

"Alberta? You mean she actually has a name? I thought it was just mean usher lady," Bella murmured to Joshua once they were seated.

"Be nice."

"Uh, Dad, if you don't mind, I'd like to sit with the kids from my youth group today." Bella and Joshua both looked up to see a group of pre–teens in the balcony section eagerly waving to Jabari.

"Go sit with your friends, man, just make sure you pay attention," Joshua said.

"Don't worry, Pastor Dave gives us a pop quiz each week. We have to pay attention."

Bella watched Jabari scurry back up the aisle.

"Bella!"

Bella looked up to see Pamela and the other pastors' wives waving in her direction. Bella waved excitedly at her new friends.

Joshua wrapped his arm protectively around her seat and crooned softly—if they hadn't been at church, Bella would have said seductively—into her ear. "Are you going to leave me too, Bella Rose?"

Bella shook her head. "As long as you want me, Joshua, I'll be right here."

They looked like a happy couple. Like a couple in love. And she decided that this time, right here, right now in public, this was the best part of her life. Once she had hated their public life. Now she decided that it was the best part. In private they would become separate again, like polar opposites. Absolutely no touching at all in private. But in public they were always touching. His hand resting gently on the small of her back, his lips brushing against her ear when he wanted to tell her something privately so no one else could hear. His hand taking hers almost unconsciously during the service. Didn't he know that his touch felt like fire on her skin? That especially in church like this, it made it difficult for her to concentrate? Most days Bella just allowed herself to get lost in his touch. She would totally forget about the sermon altogether. But today was different, she actually wanted to hear the message that Deanna's husband Keith would preach. After her conversation with the ladies at the Fords' house, Bella found herself very interested in what Keith would have to say. Bella liked Deanna, and she had been watching Keith closely since she heard Deanna's story. He had exhibited so much love and care for his wife in the kitchen at the Ford's house. And Deanna had reported back to the women that Keith had been genuinely perplexed about the advances of the other woman. But experience had shown Bella that, in general, when it came to women, men were not as clueless as they appeared to be. And since she had never met a preacher who wasn't crooked, Bella sat in her seat and willed herself to take her mind off of Joshua's touch. She honed her attention to Keith's sermon, looking for signs of culpability. It was a message Bella wasn't prepared for. A message full of hope and new beginnings.

"Before I got married, I won't lie, I was a hound. My wife Deanna there wouldn't give me the time of day. She's beautiful, isn't she?"

The crowd clapped in agreement. Bella found herself clapping for Dee as well.

"That's right. Give her a round of applause. That's the love of my life right there. She was way out of my league." Keith's eyes looked at Deanna with so much love. "But then Christ got a hold of me and He changed me. He forgave me and made me into a new man. One who was worthy to take the hand of His precious daughter. That's what Christ does for us. He takes those of us who are bound and makes us free. I've been with more women than I care to imagine. Christ broke every one of my soul ties, because every time you sleep with a person that is not your ordained mate, you leave a piece of yourself with them, and a part of them becomes a part of you. Pretty soon, if you sleep with enough people, you don't even know who you are anymore. That's how I was. I didn't know who I was. But here's what Christ will do for you folks, He'll set you free. He'll call those pieces you lost back to yourself and he will make you whole again."

"Hallelujah!" a voice in the audience called.

"If you've had relationships that were outside of God's will for your life, I'd like to pray over you and break those soul ties today. You come to the altar. And if you don't want to come to the altar, you can take a knee right where you are and make an altar at your seat. But whatever you do, respond."

"Joshua, I think I'd like to go up to the altar and pray. I'm not ready to make any sort of commitment yet, but I'd like to ask God to break the ungodly ties."

"Alright, let's go," Joshua said without hesitation. He stood with her and walked her down the aisle.

As Bella and Joshua made their way down the aisle, Bella could hear Keith talking about how when Christ forgives, He separates our sins as far as the east is from the west. He throws them into the Sea of Forgetfulness and He doesn't remember them anymore. All the men she had slept with, could God really forget that? She had repented during her time of deliverance with Joshua, she knew God had forgiven her, but could He really forget?

Don't you remember the Sea of Forgetfulness.

A hitch caught in her throat as Bella was transported back to a childhood memory. The very first sermon she had preached. She had preached to a completely captivated audience of her best doll friends and teddy bears. They had all been dressed up in their Sunday best for the occasion and had been seated in the window seat of her bedroom—one long, curving pew. The message title had been the Sea of Forgetfulness.

"When God forgives you, he doesn't remember it anymore." Five-year-old Bella belted into the gigantic sucker she'd won at the State Fair, the one her mama refused to let her eat because she said it was entirely too much candy. Bella had been mad at first, but now it didn't make no never mind at all, because she found a better use for it as her microphone.

Bella stared into the glass eyes of her doll Ms. Suzy. "I know what you're thinking right now, Ms. Suzy and Captain Bill, you're asking yourself how and why? He's God, He made the stars and the ocean, each little grain of sand, how can He ever forget a single thing? I'm going to tell you how today. He's got this really big ole sea up there in heaven called the Sea of Forgetfulness, and every time you do something wrong, and you say sorry and mean it from your heart, He releases a great big, mighty angel, and that angel comes along and takes that ugly little thing right out of your hand and he flings it into the sea of forgetfulness. And that's how come God doesn't see it any more. All you got to do is mean it in your very heart and hold out your hand."

As the memories flooded her soul, Bella wept at the altar. Then she held out her hand, and in that moment, she knew that God could do it. That He would do it. He would forgive and He would forget.

CHAPTER 90

After service, Bella and Joshua stood chatting with the pastors and their wives. "When Joshua is ready to go back to the pulpit, and he'll have to go back sooner or later," Pam whispered, "There will always be a seat waiting for you with us."

Bella hugged her. "I know, Pam, and thank you."

The conversation had turned to Keith, who was still shaking hands and talking to parishioners. Everyone was congratulating Deanna on his sermon when mean usher lady approached the tight circle.

"Pastor Joshua, Pastor Ford would like to see you and your wife in his office before you leave today, please."

"Thank you, Ms. Alberta," Joshua said.

"Relax, Bella, it's just Micah, it's not like you're being called into the principal's office," Dave joked.

Joshua caught sight of the fear in Bella's eyes and steered her away from the group. "I can tell him no. We don't have to do this."

"I don't know why I'm so anxious all of a sudden. He's really nice."

"Going into Pastor Ford's office reminds you of your father's office."

Bella shrugged. "I guess you're right, it does."

Joshua pulled her close and kissed the top of her head. "Ms. Alberta, please give Pastor Ford our regards—"

"No, Joshua, wait. I'm not that same person anymore. I can do this. That was one of the soul ties I broke at the altar this morning. I don't have to be afraid. You'll be right there with me."

Joshua nodded. "Ms. Alberta, please let Pastor Ford know we'll be right there."

"Bella, Joshua, please come in, come in!" When Bella saw the older minister's jovial face, she relaxed.

"After you left our home, my wife talked all night long about that necklace that you were wearing. So, I did a little snooping around and rumor has it that you made it yourself. It occurred to me, Bella, that you are the answer to my prayers. I'd like you to make my wife a necklace and earrings for Christmas. That is if it's okay with the both of you."

"Bella, what do you think?" Joshua asked.

"I'd be happy to, but I'm afraid I don't know Pam well enough to gage her style."

"She loves rubies and pearls." Pastor Ford turned around and opened a safe behind him. He pulled out a velvet purse and handed it to Bella. Bella gasped when she saw the stones. "These are beautiful."

"The pearls belonged to my grandmother. And the rubies I got from a broker."

"Can you tell me what your vision for a ruby and pearl necklace would be?"

"Well, let's see. I could draw it better than I could tell you."

Pastor Ford scrambled for some paper on his desk. He handed Bella a notepad and pen.

Bella studied the jewels in front of her then quickly stenciled the design on the pad. "Pam has a graceful neck like a dancer. I think long drop earrings would look great on her. And for the necklace, I was thinking something like...." Bella turned the paper so Pastor Ford could see it.

Pastor Ford looked up at Joshua. "Wow, she's quite the artist, isn't she?"

Joshua smiled warmly at Bella, causing a flush to rise to her cheeks. "She absolutely amazes me."

"I know it's the holiday season, so I'm prepared to double your fee."

"Oh, no, Pastor Ford, you supplied the jewelry. I wouldn't dream of charging you."

Pastor Ford held up his hand. "You most certainly will charge me. Your time and your skill are of great value. You are preforming a much-needed service for me and my wife. The workman is worthy of his wage. And as David said in the Good Book concerning our Lord, I won't offer something to my beloved that I got for free. So, let's start again, young lady. How much will this cost me?"

Bella looked at Joshua for help.

"Think of it like this, Bella, how much would a jewelry set like this one sell for?" Joshua asked.

"Wholesale or retail?"

"Retail!" both men said in unison.

"Okay, around $5,000."

Pastor Ford pulled his checkbook out of his inside jacket pocket and wrote her a check for ten thousand dollars. Bella looked at the check and gasped. She handed it back to him. "I can't take this."

"Not enough?"

"Too much. I couldn't dream of charging that much for something so…simple."

"Think of it as seed money for your new business."

CHAPTER 91

Bella found Maggie at the construction site of her home going over plans with the contractor. "Maggie, there you are. I have been looking all over for you. I really, really need to talk to you."

Maggie looked at the contractor sitting across the table from her. "I'm sorry, Dan, do you mind?"

"No, of course not, Maggie, take your time."

Bella threw a weak smile over her shoulder at the man as she pulled her friend out of the room. "Sorry, emergency."

Maggie took a seat on the built-in window bench in what would soon be her new living room. "Rose, what in the world is going on?"

"I need you to talk me out of something really stupid."

"You aren't planning on running again, are you? Because you're right, that would be really stupid."

"No, not that. The ten thousand dollars Pastor Ford paid me."

"To start your business?"

Bella nodded. "I think I hear God, the Devil, or somebody telling me to do something crazy with it."

"Rose, sit down, you're scaring me."

Bella took a seat next to Maggie on the window bench.

"Now, what exactly do you think you hear?"

"That I should use that money to buy a Christmas gift for Joshua. Which wouldn't be so bad, but I feel like I'm supposed to trust God and use the whole thing."

Bella pulled out a dog-eared magazine page and showed Maggie a picture of the Rolex watch.

"I thought you said the two of you weren't doing Christmas gifts this year?"

"Exactly! We aren't even doing gifts this year! He set me down and made this long speech about my saving money and how he didn't want me spending any on him. He said I would be out on my own soon and that I needed to start managing my affairs. Now this voice is telling me to do this and he doesn't even want it."

Maggie nodded. "I see, like a seed."

Bella groaned. "Maggie, not you too."

"What? You the one heard it, Rose. I'm just agreeing with you."

"I don't need you to agree. I need you to talk me out of this."

"Now why in the world would I do that?"

"Because that money is supposed to be set aside for my future. In a few more months I'm going to be a divorced mother of two. I've got to think about how I'm going to support myself."

"You scared of rejection, Rose."

"No, I'm scared of being left without a pot or a window."

"You know that ain't gon happen."

"I was going to use that money to have a professional write my business plan."

"You gon pay somebody ten thousand dollars to write a business plan? Child, please."

"I've been talking to Stan, the money guy at Home Court. He said that if you want to get funding from a bank, that's how much a professional one will cost."

"Girl, you better obey God."

"How do I know this is Him and not the same-old-self-sabotaging-me?"

"Have you ever thought this long or hard about sabotaging yourself?"

Bella shook her head. "No, I just jumped."

"You know it's Him because He don't change. The same God you heard when you were a little girl is the same one speaking to you today. He never stopped talking, Rose. You just stopped listening."

CHAPTER 92

Bella stood in the doorway on the morning of Christmas Eve and took in the sheer volume of stuff that blanketed the living room floor. She could only imagine that Joshua was making up for every Christmas he'd ever missed with his son. The spirit of regret reached out his hand beckoning to her, but Bella shook her head and stepped away. Joshua handed Jabari the controller and walked over to her when he saw Bella standing in the doorway. Jabari looked up briefly from his game to shout a Merry Christmas in her direction.

"Merry Christmas," Bella said, her eyes still on all the stuff. "Josh, you know this is way over the top."

He smiled down at her. "That's what you used to say every year. Come on, let me show you your gift, since you're up."

Bella followed Joshua down the corridor to the bank of stairs leading to the third floor. The third floor boasted four more bedrooms, bringing the grand total of the house's sleeping accommodations up to nine. Together they had built a home that they could grow into. But with the exception of Joshua's workout room, which was located on the third floor, the Keys family hardly came up here at all. Most of the rooms on this floor were empty and locked. Joshua stopped at the door directly across from his workout room, reached in his pants pocket and fished out a key, which he handed to Bella. Bella folded her arms across her chest. "I'm not opening it. You made this big old speech about not doing Christmas gifts this year. How we should only focus on Jabari and then you go out and do the opposite of what you said."

"I have money."

"I have money too."

"Not to spend on me, you don't. I want you to put that money up so when you get on your own—"

"I don't start hooking again when I feel the crunch."

"I didn't say that. I don't ever expect you to return to that lifestyle again. I just want you to feel secure. And having your own money—"

"I do have money in my rainy-day fund—"

"Having your own money outside of me has always seemed to make you feel secure. Bella, can we not do this? It's Christmas Eve."

"Are we fighting? Because I thought we were having a reasonable discussion."

A small smile flew across his lips. "Can we not have this reasonable discussion on Christmas Eve? Open the door. Please. Don't ruin this for me, alright? If you don't like it, I promise I'll have everything put back the way it was before."

Bella sighed, then took the key and unlocked the door. She released an audible gasp when she stepped inside the room.

"I thought you might like a room where you could create."

Bella looked around at her new art studio and at all her new toys. "How did you know?"

"Know what?"

"You have all the right tools in here. Everything I could ever want or desire." Bella walked around her new space. Her fingers traveled over top of the line jewelry tools, paints, and canvases. Things she had often drooled over.

"You can thank Carol and Maggie for that. They did all the research."

Bella sat down on the lime green cushy desk chair and laid her palms down on a raspberry colored desk. "And the colors." Bella looked down at the wooden floorboards that had been individually stained in shades of pinks, yellows, creams, and greens. All colors she loved. "Josh, everything is perfect."

"Maggie and Carol said that these were all the colors you were drawn to when the team was designing Maggie's home. They thought you might enjoy them in your creative space."

"I like the sound of that," Bella said spinning around in her chair. "My creative space. I can't believe those two hid this from me. I feel like a real artist in here."

"You are a real artist, Bella Rose. You have tremendous talent. I'm proud of you."

Bella leapt up from her chair and flew into his arms. "Thank you. You couldn't have gotten me a more perfect gift." And without thinking, she kissed him. Not like the chaste kisses they had shared. This one was full of passion and longing and Joshua matched her stride for stride. Then, as if suddenly remembering themselves, they both simultaneously pulled away.

"Sorry."

"Naw. Yeah. It's cool." Joshua stepped back, increasing the distance between them. "I got you something else." He reached into his back pocket and handed her a piece of paper. Bella opened the paper and read. "Metalworking classes at the Art Institute and Design School."

"I figured this would be a whole lot safer than bootleg classes from Stuart."

"Oh, Joshua, you shouldn't have."

He raised an eyebrow playfully at her.

"Okay, I'm glad you did, but you shouldn't have. I wasn't expecting any of this."

Joshua tucked a stray strand of hair behind her ear. "I know. All these things can move with you when you go. We leave for my parents in a few, so I'll let you play for a bit."

CHAPTER 93

Despite holiday traffic, the Keys family still managed to arrive in Dallas in good time. When they drove up onto the Kennedy's property, Bella surveyed the drive for signs of one of Mike's many cars.

"Where's Mike? He's coming, right?"

"He decided to hang back awhile and do the holiday thing with Marcus first before dropping him off at Safe Harbor for the weekend."

"Marcus isn't coming?" Jabari asked, clearly disappointed.

"This is the holiday season, Jabari. I know you enjoy spending time with Marcus, but he does have a family. They'd like to spend some time with him too."

"Who's going to play me in my new game?"

Joshua handed a bag to Jabari from the trunk of the car. "I guess I'd be willing to shut you down a time or two."

"That would be the best Christmas gift of all. Shutting both you and Uncle Mike down."

"You're unc's bringing company this weekend, so don't get your hopes up, alright?"

Bella followed Joshua and Jabari up onto the porch. "You didn't say Mike was bringing company. Who's he bringing?"

Joshua looked at Bella warily for a second. Then the screen door opened, and Bella swore she saw a look of relief on his face.

Jack Kennedy stepped out onto the front porch. "Mel! They're here!"

"Merry Christmas, Dad," Joshua said as he embraced his father.

"Merry Christmas, Happy New Year, and all that jazz. Come on in!" Jack stepped out of the way, so Bella, Jabari, and Joshua could walk through the front door.

Bella was still eyeing Joshua quizzically when Melissa walked into the living room wiping her hands on her apron.

"Merry, merry, merry Christmas!" Melissa said as she embraced Jabari, Bella, and then Joshua. "Oh, Bella, I am so glad you are here. I've been searching like a mad woman for that slap-your-mama cinnamon bun recipe you gave me years ago. I can't find it for the life of me."

"Well, search no more, because the creator of that world's famous recipe is right here. Just tell me where I can put my bag and we can get started," Bella said.

"Leave them. The boys will get the bags. Jabari, you're in your usual spot. Joshie, you and Bella are in your old bedroom."

Bella set her purse down in the pile of luggage that Joshua and Jabari had left by the door. She watched Joshua's face for a reaction. There was no couch in Joshua's childhood bedroom, but if he had a problem with their sleeping arrangements, he never let on.

Joshua caught Bella's hand as she walked past him to follow Melissa into the kitchen. "You didn't tell me you were gonna make your world's famous slap-your-mama cinnamon rolls."

He was smiling his overly bright smile, the one he reserved for when he was in trouble. This reaction gave Bella pause. "And you never told me the name of Mike's date."

"Hey, Joshie, look!"

Joshua and Bella looked up to see Jack looking at them through the lens of a very nice SLR digital camera.

Joshua frowned. "Hey, man. You weren't supposed to open that yet."

"Not at me! Over your head, doofus!"

Bella and Joshua's eyes traveled up to the mistletoe hanging just above their heads in the doorway."

"Go ahead, lay it on her, Joshie."

A thousand butterflies took flight in Bella's stomach as Joshua leaned in and kissed her softly.

CHAPTER 94

Uncle Mike's here!" Jabari called from the living room. Melissa and Bella brushed flour off their hands and made their way into the living room to see Mike.

"Merry Christmas!" Mike lifted first Melissa up off the floor into a giant bear hug and then Bella.

"Merry Christmas, honey!" Melissa said breathlessly. "So, where's Selena."

"Selena? Selena Mason, as in your secretary?" Bella said to Joshua, who refused to meet her eyes

"Yeah, Mom. I'mma get to that in a minute," Mike said.

"Hey, Mikey, say cheese!" Jack said as he snapped a photo.

"Isn't that a Christmas present?"

"Nice isn't it? I looked it up online. Set your brother back about $2,500."

Joshua shook his head. Mike frowned at his father. "How'd you do that? I thought your computer was busted."

"On the new Mac Book Pro you bought me, of course."

"He's like a kid in a candy store. I warned you boys about sending things directly to the house," Melissa said.

"I'm an old man. I could die tonight. I don't believe in delayed gratification."

"So, Mikey, tell us where Selena is," Melissa said.

"Yes, Mike do tell us. Where is Selena?" Bella said, still glaring at Joshua.

Mike sniffed the air. "Yo, Josh, man you smell that? I know I don't smell slap- your- mamas?"

Joshua grinned. "That's Bella, man. You know how she do."

Mike leaned in and kissed Bella's cheek. "Sis, I love your slap-your-mamas."

Bella stepped out of his arms. "Yeah, yeah, I make the best cinnamon rolls ever, but that ain't what we talking about right now."

Melissa took a seat on the couch. "Bella's right, Mikey. Why are you being so evasive? Did something happen with Selena?"

"No, Mom. Nothing happened. Bella, baby, please sit down," Mike said.

"Can't. I need to go check on my rolls," Bella said sullenly.

"I'll check 'em," Jack said.

"Jack Kennedy, you are not the only person in this house, if you so much as touch one of those rolls—"

"I'm just gonna check 'em, Mel, honey. I promise." Jack kissed Bella's cheek and ushered her over to the couch. "Now you sit right there, sweetie, and take a load off those pretty little feet while I go check the food."

Melissa sighed. "Alright, Mikey. We're all ears. Tell us what's going on."

"I dropped her off at the mall. She wanted to pick up a few gifts for the family and I wanted a chance to talk to everyone before she got here," Mike said, studying the two women in front of him. "Here's the thing. Selena doesn't have any family except for one very eccentric, old aunt who raised her. They never celebrated holidays of any kind, so she's never had a Christmas before.

"Cry me a river," Bella muttered under her breath.

Jabari looked up at his uncle "Seriously, never?"

"That's right. Never. So it's up to us to show her how it's done. You think you can help me do that?"

"Oh, for sure, unc," Jabari said, giving Mike a fist bump.

"My guy." Mike looked at his mother then Bella. "I want to make it clear that Selena is here this weekend as my guest. I'm also putting out a special request for my family to be nice to her."

Melissa pulled her hair back into a ponytail. "Of course we'll be nice, honey. We're always nice. Why wouldn't we be?"

Bella, who had been picking her nail, looked up to see Joshua and Mike staring at her.

"What?"

"You think you can do this, Bella? Josh mentioned that in the past you may have felt a little threaten by Selena."

Joshua cleared his throat loudly.

"Uncomfortable. The word Josh used was uncomfortable."

Bella sucked her teeth. "Mike, you don't have to worry about me. Because if you like having her here, I love it." And with that she got up and marched into the kitchen.

CHAPTER 95

After dinner, everyone moved into the living room and congregated around the large Christmas tree.

"Okay, let's see by show of hands who followed the rules this year," Melissa said.

"Somebody fill me in. What are the rules?" Selena asked.

Mike plopped down on the living room couch next to Selena. "Remember, I told you my mom has a fit anytime anybody spends more than five dollars on a Christmas present."

"Selena, we have a twenty-dollar gift limit for Christmas presents. My sons, however, have a very hard time following that rule. Especially this one over here," Melissa said, pointing to Mike.

Jabari raised his hand. "I followed the rule, Grandma Mel."

"Very good, Jabari."

"I did too, with one exception," Bella said.

"Which one?"

"My gift for Joshua."

"I thought we agreed not to do gifts this year," Joshua said.

"I saw her stash it under the tree earlier," Jack said. "It's a pretty nice one, Joshie. Trust me, you're gonna want this one."

"Jack, you didn't."

"I didn't open the box, Mel. I just read it. I just looked up the make and model on the Internet. Set you back quite a penny there, didn't it, sweetheart," Jack said as he snapped a photo of Bella's totally taken aback face.

"Inappropriate, Jack. So inappropriate," Melissa said.

Melissa turned to Bella. "It's fine, honey. Spouses and grandsons don't count this year."

Mike smirked at Melissa. "Since when, Ms. Make-Up-the-Rules-As-You-Go?"

"Mikey, you and your brother have been breaking the rules for years. I make one minor adjustment and you have the audacity to complain."

"I'm just saying, what's the point of a tradition if nobody is going to follow it," Mike said, watching Jack as he aimed his camera at him and Selena and snapped a photo of them.

"You ought to be glad I opened my stuff early. Now I can take pictures of the festivities and load them up to my Facebook page."

"If you're on Facebook, God help us all," Joshua muttered.

"Joshie, your father knows how much we value our privacy in this family. He would never put our pictures on the Internet. Now, another rule we have, Selena, and this one stands, the person giving the gift gets to say whether the person receiving the gift gets to open it tonight or if they have to wait till Christmas morning. Jabari, would you like to hand out the gifts?"

"Yeah, sure thing, Grandma Mel." Jabari made his way over to the Christmas tree.

"Jabari, go ahead and hand me your mother's gift first," Joshua said

"Which one is it?" Jabari asked.

"Look for the bag that says 'Rolex'," Jack said.

Jabari retrieved the bag from under the tree and handed it to his dad. "You have to ask Mom if you can open it right now."

"May I?" Joshua said, nearly burning her with the heat of his gaze.

"Yes, you may," Bella said softly.
Joshua removed the box from the bag and removed the platinum Rolex watch from the box. Bella watched anxiously for his reaction. He turned the timepiece over and over again in his hand, studying the detailing, and then he read the engraved message. "To Joshua, From Bella. Christmas 2005. Purchased with all my love and—"

Joshua stopped suddenly overcome with emotion. "And my honest gain."

Mike nodded his head in approval. Tears filled Melissa's eyes. Even Jack looked choked up.

Joshua looked at her and Bella's heart caught in her throat when she saw the unshed tears in his eyes.

Oh God, please don't let this backfire. Please don't let this hurt him.

"Come here," he said.

Relief flooded through Bella's body as she nearly tripped across the room, running into his arms.

"Now that's the way you kick off Christmas," Jack said.

CHAPTER 96

Jabari threw a present across the room and Joshua caught it with ease. He threw another one across the room and Mike caught it as well.

"You can open mine now. I got you underwear!" Jack said.

Joshua and Mike both tore open the presents. "Tube socks," they both said at the same time.

"Thanks, Dad. Can never have too many of these," Joshua said.

"You're welcome."

"These next two are from Grandma Mel to Dad. And Grandma Mel to Unc."

"This time, Jabari, instead of throwing the presents, why don't you just pass them to your father and uncle," Bella said.

"Oh, okay," Jabari said, handing a present to Joshua and then one to Mike. His tone said that she had clearly taken away all the fun.

"You two know the drill. I want you boys to wait till Christmas morning to open mine," Melissa called.

"This next present is from Grandma Mel to Marcus. Here's another from Grandma Mel to Marcus. And another for Marcus. Dang, my man Marcus ain't even here and he got the hook up!" Jabari said.

"Actually, you can push all those to the side, Jabari. I think everything in that corner right there belongs to Marcus," Melissa said.

"Let me guess, for the purposes of your holiday rule breaking antics, Marcus would fall under the grandson category?" Mike said.

"He got my family out of New Orleans alive. You're damn right he is," Jack said.

Joshua sat on a large cushioned ottoman with Bella between his legs. He nuzzled his chin against the back of her neck.

"You're a fine one to talk, Mikey. Joshie told me about the obscene amount of stuff you bought Marcus for Christmas this year."

"Did he really now?" Bella said, twisting her body around to peer into Joshua's eyes. "Because Joshua certainly cannot talk about anybody overdoing it. It is unbelievable the sheer amount of stuff that is sitting in our living room right now. I wouldn't be surprised if we came home to find the floor caved in."

"First of all, I never said he overdid it. Second of all, I can't be held responsible for what Santa decided to bring to our house."

Mike smirked. "Exactly."

Jack chuckled. "Grab that envelope to the left right there, Jabari. That one's for you," Jack said.

"Can I open it now or do I have to wait till tomorrow?"

"Of course you can open it now," Jack said.

Jabari opened the envelope and silently read the contents of the page. He looked up at his grandfather in disbelief. "You serious?"

"It's right there in black and white. She's all yours."

"Go head and read it, man. Don't keep us in suspense," Joshua said.

"It's my very own horse. Grandpa Jack got me a horse!"

Jabari looked at his mother and father. "Did you two know about this?"

"You think you'd be going anywhere near a horse without your mother's approval?" Joshua asked.

"Thank you, Mom! Thank you, Dad! Thank you, Grandpa Jack! Is she here?"

"She's out in the barn."

"Your grandfather searched the tri-city area for that horse. I have to say, she comes from excellent stock. She'll be very safe. She is a beauty," Melissa said.

Jabari stood up. "I gotta go."

"What about the rest of your gifts?" Mike teased.

"I'll save the rest of my stuff for tomorrow. I gotta go see my horse."

"It's late, Jabari, can't it wait till morning?"

"No, Mom, I gotta see her right now."

"Bella, nobody wants to do the delayed gratification thing," Jack said. "Come on, Jabari. Let's go see about your horse."

CHAPTER 97

Well, we've seemed to have lost our holiday host, so I guess I can fill in for him. Unless someone else wants the job," Melissa said.

"I can do it," Bella said, rising from her seat.

"No, that's my Christmas present, seeing you sitting right there," Melissa said.

"What?"

"You've been on your feet all morning, honey. Just sit back down there with Joshie. I'll hand them to you."

Joshua pulled her back down gently onto the ottoman with him.

Melissa handed Bella a lavender envelope.

Bella frowned as she read the envelope. "This says that this is for Selena from me."

"Thank you. May I open it now?" Selena asked.

"Please do. I'm dying to see what I got you."

Selena opened the envelope. "A $100 gift certificate to the Aveda salon and spa. How very generous of you."

"Heck, yeah it was," Bella muttered.

"Bella got spa certificates for all the Home Court office staff this year. Just our way of saying thank you for all your hard work and support," Joshua said.

"Melissa, that bag over there is mine." Selena pointed to a large gift bag under the tree. "And, Bella, if you don't mind, I'd like to hand them out myself."

Bella shrugged. "Fine with me."

Selena pulled a large, handsomely wrapped rectangular box out of the bag and handed it to Mike. She removed a smaller jewelry sized box and handed it to Joshua. She pulled two more packages out of her bag.

"This one is for Jabari and, Melissa, this one is for you and Jack."

"Thank you, Selena," Melissa said, taking the gift.

Selena reached into the bag one last time and pulled out another item, encased in flimsy plastic. "I'm sorry, Bella, but the store I got your gift from didn't offer gift wrapping."

"You want us to open them now or later?" Mike asked.

Selena bit her lip and smiled coyly at him. "Really, I get to decide?"

"Dem the rules."

"I would like for you all to open your gifts now." Everyone began to tear the paper off their packages. Everyone except Bella, who let hers slide out of her lap and onto the floor. Mike lifted the lid from the box and pulled out a t-shirt, a necktie, and a baseball cap. All of which had the Man of Steel emblem stitched on them from Mike's ball playing days. Joshua let out a hoot and pumped his fist in the air.

Selena beamed proudly. "When you told me you didn't have any Man of Steel gear, I thought this was perfect. I couldn't believe the Man of Steel didn't wear his own stuff."

"Thanks."

"Do you like it?"

Mike put the baseball cap on top of her head and leaned over and kissed her cheek. "Yes, I do."

"And this is a beautiful picture frame, Selena, thank you," Melissa said.

Mike looked over at the frame in Melissa's hand. "I thought you got my mom the other thing," he said quietly.

Selena shook her head. "Nope, I changed my mind. I gave it to Bella instead." She looked down at Bella's gift on the floor. "Aren't you going to open your gift, Bella?"

"Naw, I'm good. I like to keep the wrapping on things I plan to re-gift," Bella said sweetly.

"You might like it. Joshua was very instrumental in helping me pick it out for you," Selena said.

With one hand, Joshua reached down and picked the package up from the floor. With the other he pulled Bella closer to him and whispered into her ear. "I have no idea what she's talking about, but for my brother's sake, could you please just open the stupid gift?"

Bella tore off the flimsy plastic and unfolded a black apron with hot pink block lettering on it.

"I belong in the kitchen," Bella read.

"Joshua is always bragging about your cooking, so I figured an apron would be practical," Selena explained. Selena looked at Joshua eagerly, waiting for him to open her present. He lifted the top off the jewelry box and pulled out a gold man's bracelet.

"I had my gift engraved too. See, it's a Bible verse," Selena said proudly.

Joshua read the verse quietly to himself. Then he laid the bracelet back in the box and rewarded Selena with a friendly smile. "Thank you, Selena, that was very thoughtful of you."

"Read it out loud, Joshie," Melissa said.

"Yeah, read it. We're dying to hear what it says," Bella said.

"Later, alright," Joshua said quietly to Bella. To his mother he said, "Let's just keep this moving, we got a whole bunch of other stuff we still need to get through tonight."

Bella took the box from Joshua's hand. "Don't be a scrooge. We can all certainly make time for one Bible verse, can't we, Pastor Josh?" She stood away from Joshua's reach and felt the heaviness of the bracelet in her hand. She flipped it over and read. "'You brought me to the banquet table and your banner over me is love. You are altogether beautiful, my love, there is no flaw in you.' What the—"

"Bella!" Joshua said sharply.

"Are you serious? Is she serious?"

"Oh, Lordy," Melissa said

"Sit down," Joshua demanded.

"No!"

Joshua pointed his finger in Bella's face. "You're hardheaded, you know that? I knew you wouldn't like this and I told you to let it go. But you had to be slick."

"No, see what you need to be doing is checking your secretary right now. Not me!"

"It's the Bible. I really don't understand why she's so upset," Selena said.

Joshua groaned.

Selena looked to Melissa for help. Melissa looked away.

Selena paused for a moment then started again. "Do you all think I meant something romantic by that? Mike, tell me that's not what you think."

"You may not have meant that, but in Bella's defense, that is the way it appears," Mike said gently.

Bella turned her glacial stare onto Selena. "Thank you!"

"Come on, sis, you know I got you," Mike said.

Selena shook her head. "That's not what I meant at all."

Mike nodded. "Okay then. Break it down for us."

Selena looked up. Her eyes met Joshua's. "I chose that particular passage because you led me to Christ. Your example of a godly lifestyle day in and day out before me is what caused me to come all the way into the kingdom. You brought me to the banquet table of God's love."

Everybody in the room visibly relaxed. Everybody except Bella, who stood there tapping her foot thinking, *this is some bull.*

Relief, then compassion, flooded Joshua's face.

Selena reached for the gift in his hand. "I can just take it back and get something else."

"I'm keeping the gift, Selena, so come over here and give me a hug, girl."

Selena rushed into Joshua's arms. "I really wanted you to like it."

"Yeah, now that you explained it, I do. You had me scared there for a moment. I thought I was gon have to fire you."

Mike chuckled.

Selena's hand flew to her mouth. "Please don't tell me I almost lost my job trying to be all deep and spiritual."

Joshua released her and smiled. "It was either fire you or risk getting fired myself." He stared at Bella, who refused to meet his gaze. "It was an honest mistake, so let's just enjoy the rest of our weekend."

"I think that is a fabulous idea, Joshie," Melissa said.

Selena sat back down on the couch next to Mike.

Bella rolled her eyes and remained standing.

"Bella, come sit back down, please," Joshua said.

"Nope, that's okay. I'm good."

He flashed a lopsided sexy grin in her direction. "Pretty please?"

"Bella, come sit by me," Mike said. He patted the space on the other side of the couch next to him.

Bella stalked past Joshua and sat down beside Mike.

"What do you say, everyone, shall we try to do a few more or shall we call it a night?" Melissa said.

"How bout we open two more gifts. Then call it," Mike said.

"Mom, there should be two more presents under that tree from me," Joshua said.

Melissa searched till she found two small jewelry store gift bags. "It looks like this one is for me. Thank you, Joshie, although I can't imagine for the life of me what Cartier makes for under twenty dollars, and this one is for Bella." Melissa placed the bag lightly in Bella's lap.

Bella stared down at the bag and then shifted her gaze over to Joshua.

"Mom, you can open yours in the morning. I know how you love doing that. Bella, you can open yours right now," Joshua said.

Bella shrugged. "I'm good."

"My gift, my rules. You open it now. And we settle this tonight."

"Please handle this," Mike said.

Joshua grinned at his brother.

"What are you talking about?" Bella said.

"I don't want to go another day without seeing a symbol of our union on your finger."

Confusion clouded Bella's face. "You bought me a wedding ring?"

"Open it and see."

Bella opened the box and stared down at the large, emerald cut diamond. Selena released an audible gasp and Bella covered her face with her hands and sobbed.

Melissa rose from her seat on the floor. "Mikey, Selena, join me in the kitchen for some hot cider. Let's give these two some privacy."

Joshua watched as his mother, brother, and Selena filed out of the room. He walked over and took a seat next to Bella on the couch. Gently, he pried her hands away from her face. "Please tell me why my giving you a wedding ring makes you so unhappy."

"I don't know; could it be because in a few more months you plan on divorcing me?"

Joshua sighed. "You told me that you lost your ring."

"And I did," Bella said defensively.

"And I believed you. That's why I got you another one."

"If you just needed a symbol so people would know we were married, why didn't you just get a cheap gold band, Joshua! Why did you have to go out and get this ring?"

"What's wrong with this ring?"

"Everything! It's too elaborate, it's complicated, it's…beautiful!

"Has there ever been anything simple about our love? You tell me, Bella. When has it not been elaborate and complicated? I don't know about you, but when I look back over our life together, I can tell you it's been all those things, but never cheap." Joshua took her face and pressed it between his large hands. "Bella, loving you has been one of the greatest privileges of my life, but it has come at a very high price."

He released her. "I couldn't put a cheap gold band on your finger even if we planned on being married for just one day."

Joshua took the ring out of the box and slid it onto Bella's ring finger. "I got you this because I wanted to clear up any confusion that you, my secretary, or anyone else may have. Until a judge says otherwise, you are my wife."

CHAPTER 98

Melissa, Selena, and Mike were sitting around the large island counter when Joshua and Bella walked into the kitchen holding hands. Melissa smiled at them from over her coffee mug. Mike stood up and greeted Joshua with a chest bump and hug.

Mike looked down at Bella. "Bella, baby, you like your ring?"

Bella blushed. "Yes, very much so."

"Can we see it?" Selena asked.

Bella held her hand up shyly, so the two women could examine it closely.

"It's beautiful, Bella. Really," Selena said.

"And yet not nearly as beautiful as you," Melissa said. "We've got cider and chocolate waiting on the stove. Which can I get you?"

"Cider, please," Bella said.

"Joshie, call over to the barn and see what's taking your father and Jabari so long. I mean, for goodness sakes, how long can you look at a horse?"

"If I know Jabari, he's waiting for me to come out and check her out too. I'mma run over there real quick," Joshua said.

"I'mma go with you," Mike said.

Joshua looked over at his brother's dress pants and shoes. "You wanna change?"

"Yeah. Let me do that real quick."

"I'll meet you on the porch."

"Don't stay out there all night," Melissa called to their backs.

"We'll be back in twenty minutes tops," Mike said.

CHAPTER 99

"Hey, Josh, can I talk to you for a minute?"

Joshua looked up to see that Selena had followed him out of the kitchen.

"What's up, Selena?"

"I wanted to apologize again for—"

Joshua shook his head. "No. We're good."

"You sure?"

"Definitely, so stop trippin'."

"Well, good, because I kind of have a favor to ask you. Privately."

Joshua held the door opened and motioned for her to join him on the porch. "What's up?"

"Mike wants to take me riding tomorrow. But I haven't been on a horse in a really long time. Not since boarding school."

"You have nothing to worry about, my brother's a really good teacher."

"Yeah, I kind of get that about him. But I can't really impress him if I'm falling on my face. So . . . I was hoping that between now and then you could give me a refresher course so I don't look like a total geek in front of him."

Joshua laughed loudly.

"What?"

"I wish you could see your face right now. You look pretty desperate."

"I guess I am. This is the first guy I've really liked in a very long time."

"What time are you two going riding tomorrow?"

"Late afternoon, right before sunset."

"Meet me in front of the stables tomorrow morning at 7:30 sharp."

"Really?" Selena squealed.

"Jabari will be dying to take his new horse out for a test drive. You might as well come along with us."

CHAPTER 100

Jack, Jabari, Mike, and Joshua sat down on the back porch and removed their shoes. "You boys leave your boots out here, otherwise your mother will go all ape crap on us for tracking that stuff into the house," Jack said.

"Dad, when we go inside, can we please play my new game?"

Joshua removed his Timberlands and knocked the hard dirt out of the treads. "Why don't you get a good night sleep, son. I'll embarrass you in the morning."

Jack and Mike both chuckled.

"Dad, please, just one game!"

"It's late, Jabari. You want to go riding in the morning, remember?"

"Look, Dad, I know you're old and you need your rest, but seriously, this beat down I'm about to give you will be so quick—I promise, you'll be able to get a full night's rest and be ready to take me on the trails in the morning. I'll even let you have my mama."

"Oh, you gon let me have your mama?"

"Yeah, she can rub your back and wipe your little tears away."

Joshua threw his head back and roared with laughter.

Mike put his fist to his mouth. "Yo, Josh, do you hear this kid? Baby Keys talkin much junk, like Mr. T at his back."

"What you talkin' bout, Unc? After I shut my dad down, I'm comin' for you next. Your girl can watch."

Jack howled with laughter.

Joshua looked at Mike in astonishment. "I can't believe he just said that."

"You know, Jabari, since it's the holidays, I was gon give you a break," Mike said.

Joshua raised an eyebrow at his brother, "That's pretty generous of you, bro, letting him win."

"Naw, man, I ain't *that* generous. I'm still gon beat him, but I would have at least let him walk away with some dignity."

"I feel you. Now you saying he's got to cry." Joshua slapped Mike a high five as the four of them walked into the kitchen. "Oh, he's gonna cry. Hard," Mike said.

"Who's crying?" Melissa asked.

"My dad and my uncle are going to be crying in a few when I beat them on my new video game. Mom, you wanna watch? I think Dad may need you for moral support."

"I am not getting involved. I'm going to take a hot shower and read a book. Joshua, don't you make my child cry."

"I'm tellin' you right now, baby, get your mind right, because he's gonna cry."

Mike laughed. Jack took a swallow from the coffee mug Melissa had set in front of him.

"What about you, Ms. Selena, you want to be my cheering section?"

"Sure, Jabari. Why not?"

⸎ ⸎

Melissa found Bella later on that evening asleep in the three-season sunroom.

"Why don't you turn into bed, honey?"

Bella sat up and yawned. "Are the guys still playing the game?"

"Oh, Bella, don't try to wait up for them. They may be playing that silly thing all night."

"I'm actually just going to read a little longer before I turn in."

Melissa started to leave the room, but then she stopped, turned, and sat down on the couch beside her daughter-in-law. "Bella, were you planning on sleeping out here tonight?"

"I'm guessing by now Joshua has told you about the baby."

"Mikey told us."

"We don't share the same bed anymore. Josh has agreed to help me through the birth, but he plans on divorcing me right after the baby is born."

"When's your little one due?"

"In the spring."

Melissa patted her knee. "Well, you mark my words, a whole lot can happen between now and spring."

"I don't mind you sleeping out here, dear. It's one of my favorite places to nap. I'll just close the windows and bring you an extra blanket."

⁂

Joshua said his goodnights to Jabari, Mike, and Selena around midnight. He retired to his childhood bedroom to find the bed undisturbed and empty. From her toiletry bag that was out on the sink in the bathroom, Joshua could see that Bella had showered and gotten ready for bed, but it was clear that she had decided to take up residence somewhere else in the house. Fifteen minutes later, after he had brushed his teeth and readied his own self for bed, Joshua went looking for Bella. He found her nestled in the corner of the couch in the sunroom. He lifted her up, despite her sleepy protest, and carried her back to his bedroom.

CHAPTER 101

Bella awoke twice in the night to the weight of Joshua's body surrounding hers like a hard protective shell and a very full bladder. Each time she had tried to carefully extract her limbs from his without waking him up, and each time she had failed.

"Where you going?" he mumbled.

"I have to pee."

"Hurry back."

When she crawled back into the bed, Joshua cocooned her in his massive arms and fell right back into a deep, sound sleep. Bella, on the other hand, hadn't slept a wink. At least she felt like she hadn't. The reality was that she'd slept pretty darn well. All things considered. Because from the moment he'd carried her back into the room and laid her down on his childhood bed, till the moment the first light of day crept into the sky, she had been filled with a childlike zeal. *I'm in his bed! With him! He came and got me because he wants me here.* Somewhere around 3AM, when the butterflies in her stomach settled and the newness of their sleeping arrangement wore off, Bella tried to reel her thoughts back in. Yes, you're in his bed now, but when you get back home, things are going back to the way they used to be.

Maybe so. But I'm here now. I'm here now. I'm here now, her thoughts danced.

Don't do it, Bella, she warned herself. *Not this time. He cannot become your everything. Your sun. Your moon. Your water. Your air.* It made absolutely no sense for a woman to love a man the way she loved Joshua Keys. It was unhealthy and addictive. She thought about how she had managed to break the cycle once for five whole years, and how in about four more months she would have to do it again. His nearness made it impossible for Bella to sleep, so she decided instead to listen to the sound of his breathing and memorize him. Somehow in the midst of her memorizing, Bella must have actually fallen asleep, because she awoke to find Joshua staring down at her.

Bella blushed. "What?"

"I was just thinking how surprisingly well I slept beside you last night."

She had assumed it would be difficult too, ergo her plans to take up residence somewhere else. "Maybe it's just being home and sleeping in your old bed."

"No, it's definitely you."

"I don't see how you got any sleep at all. You kept waking up whenever I got up to go to the bathroom."

"I haven't felt this rested in years."

"You have me for four more months, maybe you should take advantage and catch up on some rest."

His dark eyes traveled up and down her body and Bella felt her face go flush.

"I think a weekend at my parent's house is one thing, but anything more than that would be pushing it."

Joshua's cellphone on the bedside table beside her buzzed. Bella glanced over at it and rolled her eyes. "Kind of early for calls, isn't it?"

"Would you like to check and see who it is, Bella?"

She handed him the phone. "Whoever it is calling your personal cell at this hour certainly isn't any of my business."

Joshua took the phone from her and looked at the display. "It's Jabari."

"Jabari? How's he calling? On your parent's phone?"

"On his new cell phone."

"Josh, you didn't."

"He needs one now that he's riding to school with Marcus in the mornings. Think of it this way, he'll never have an excuse as to why we can't reach him."

"So, I take it this phone has all the bells and whistles."

"I mean, it's got a full data package."

"And how are we going to monitor all of this activity? Josh, I don't think he's ready for that kind of responsibility. He's only eleven, and I really wish you would have spoken to me about this first. There are a lot of child predators on the Internet."

Joshua sat up in bed. "Calm down, alright? Take a look at this."

"I don't even know what I'm looking at."

"This is an app my computer guy put on my phone." Joshua pulled up a display on his phone. These are all the sites Jabari's been to in the last twenty-four hours. He pulled up another screen showing a bunch of horse sites. "No emails sent." Joshua pulled up another screen. "These are all the texts he's sent in the last 24 hours. One to Marcus, one to Mike, and one to my mom. 'Hey, Marcus, guess what? I got a new phone.' Marcus wrote him back at 9:40. 'Congratulations, Shorty. I did too. I'll save your new number.' He sent a text to both my mom and my brother this morning. 'Hey, Grandma Mel, can we have pancakes for breakfast?' 'Whatever you want, sweetie.' 'Hey, Unc, I think your girl likes me.'" Joshua chuckled at Mike's response. "In your dreams, Baby Keys."

Bella stared at him mouth agape.

"What?"

"You're cyber stalking our kid."

"Welcome to parenting in the digital age."

"Josh, that's a lot of work. Are you going to do that every day?"

"It took less than three minutes. I'll peruse through it weekly, but I've already assigned someone from my tech department to look through his phone records daily. He'll alert me if anything looks suspicious."

"You're paying somebody to spy on our son."

"To monitor his phone usage." Joshua frowned down at her. "Why you punking out now? What happened to 'the Internet is a scary place?'"

"I'm not punking out. I just don't want him to find out that we are doing this. Do you?"

Joshua rubbed his morning stubble. "It doesn't matter because it's not a secret. It's a condition of him having a phone. I get to monitor it."

"And you don't feel like this is an invasion of our son's privacy?"

Joshua smirked. "Bella, Jabari don't pay no bills around here. As far as I'm concerned, he doesn't have privacy."

"I don't pay any bills either, Joshua. Does that mean you're monitoring my calls?"

"No, because you're not my child you're my wife."

"Joshua, would you even tell me if you were monitoring my calls?"

"What, you think I'd lie about it?"

Bella studied him for a moment. Of course he wouldn't lie. He would flat out tell her to her face. And he'd be shameless about it too. Just like he was being now. In the past he had no problems tracking her credit cards or hiring a private investigator to discover her whereabouts. So monitoring her phone records would be child's play.

"Good point," she muttered.

Joshua handed her his phone. "You might as well program Jabari's new number into your phone. And if you want me to, I can download that app for you."

"Huh, no thanks. Feels a little too much like reading your child's diary to me. But keep me in the loop. I want a full report every week just like you. I just don't want to be the one doing the snooping."

Joshua's phone buzzed as another text came through.

"Boy, you sure are Mr. Popularity this morning." Bella read the message. "'Dad, what time are we giving Ms. Selena her horseback riding lesson?' Since when do you give lessons?"

"Since my secretary wants to impress my brother."

Bella stared at him.

"What? Don't you want Mike to be happy?"

"Of course I do," Bella snapped.

"Well it appears, at least for now, that Selena makes him happy. Text Jabari back and tell him 7:30, please." Joshua kissed the tip of Bella's nose and jumped out of bed. "And don't pout, we'll be back before breakfast."

CHAPTER 102

Bella was sitting at the desk in the bedroom reading Joshua's Bible when a freshly shaved, showered, and delicious smelling Joshua walked out of the adjoining bathroom. He wore a new pair of jeans and was, at the moment, shirtless.

Bella rolled her eyes. "You getting pretty dolled up for a date with a horse."

"What, you want me to go funky?"

"Yes."

"What you doing?"

"Reading."

A whiff of his aftershave tickled her nostrils as he peered over her shoulder. "The Songs of Solomon."

"There's no way you gon tell me that Ms. Selena Mason thought this was a conversation between a brother and a sister in Christ."

"I don't know, she's a pretty new Christian. She hasn't learned how to rightly divide the Word of Truth yet."

Bella read from the page. "'You are all together beautiful, my love, there is no flaw in you.' Joshua, the girl would have to be retarded to think that means anything other than what it says. Oh, and listen to this. 'How beautiful and pleasant you are, o loved one, with all your delights. Your stature is like a palm tree, and your breast are like its clusters. I say *I will climb* the palm tree and *lay hold* of its fruit.'"

Joshua pulled her up from the desk and held her tightly against his bare chest. Bella's breath caught in her throat as he began to recite the words of the scripture by heart.

"Come, my beloved, let us go out into the fields and lodge in the villages. Let us go out early to the vineyards and see whether the vines have budded, whether the grapes blossoms have opened, and the pomegranates are in bloom. There I will give you my love."

Bella cleared her throat. "You don't have to be a Christian to understand that."

"I see your point."

"Well then why are you smiling?"

He released her. "Cause I'm just glad you're reading the Bible, even if it is to find evidence against my secretary."

CHAPTER 103

Selena stood outside the barn waiting for Joshua. She muttered a curse under her breath when she saw Jabari running towards her waving excitedly.

"My dad just texted me. He's getting dressed, he'll be out in a minute."

Selena quickly replaced the look of disappointment with a smile. "We were all up so late last night that I thought for sure you'd be sleeping in this morning."

"Are you kidding? I wouldn't miss going out on the trails with my dad for anything in the world."

"So, Jabari, is anybody else joining us this morning?"

"Like who?"

"I don't know, your mom, maybe?"

"Oh no, my mom doesn't do horses. Ever."

"That's good."

"Uncle Mike says you don't have any family and that we should be nice to you. You're kind of like my mom in that way."

"What do you mean?"

"She doesn't have family. I mean, she does, but she doesn't talk to them. I've met her mom before, though."

"You mean your grandmother?"

Jabari nodded. "I've never met my grandfather even once. I don't even know whether they survived the hurricane."

"Why don't you just ask your mom about it?"

"She doesn't really want to talk about it. It's kind of a painful subject."

"Have you tried talking to your dad?"

Jabari shook his head. "It would probably just make him angry."

"Why would you say that?"

"Because one time my dad punched my mom's dad in the face."

"I see." *So the gossip sites had been right.* Selena had looked for the infamous footage of Bad Boy Joshua Keys punching the mega preacher in the face, but apparently either Joshua's people or the pastor's people had made sure the footage never saw the light of day again. "You know, Jabari, by your family being so high profile, I bet you could find out a lot of things about them on the internet."

Jabari seemed to consider this. "You really think so?"

"Oh, I know so. Do you have an email account at school?"

"Yeah."

"If you promise not to rat me out, I'll send you some links. But no one can ever know that I helped you with this. You understand?"

"I won't tell, Ms. Selena. I swear."

"Jabari, this is really serious. I could lose my job over this. Your father and your uncle both would be very angry with me if they ever found out."

"No, for real. I got you, Ms. Selena. I ain't no snitch."

Selena glanced around furtively for signs of Joshua then pulled out her cellphone. "Here, type in your email address. When I get to work next week, I'm going to send you a link to a site. Put your dad's name in and it will tell you everything you need to know. Just promise me you won't access it from your home computer or from your cell phone. Wait and open it up at school, otherwise your dad will see it. Deal?"

"Okay, deal."

"I'm counting on you, Jabari. We're friends, and friends don't let each other down."

CHAPTER 104

Bella and Joshua were sitting in the waiting area of Dr. Cadwell's office when his nurse, Linda, walked up and greeted them.

"Mr. and Mrs. Keys, come on back."

Bella and Joshua followed the woman down the long corridor to the patient examination rooms. Nurse Linda turned to look at Bella. "Did you already pee in the cup?"

"Yep. It was the first thing they handed me when I got here."

"Good. Your lab reports should be in by the time we sit down to talk." Nurse Linda pointed to the examination room across the hall. "Mr. Keys, you can wait inside if you like. I'm just going to get a weight check on the mama-to-be."

"So how were your holidays?" Joshua asked a few minutes later, once they were all seated inside the exam room.

"Good. What about you two? Did you two dance the night away for New Year's?"

"I was asleep before the Time Square ball dropped," Bella said.

"We spent a quiet evening at home," Joshua added.

Linda loosened the blood pressure cuff around Bella's arm. "Your pressure is a little elevated today. And I may need to run your lab results a second time. Did you eat anything out of the ordinary this morning before you came?"

"Why? Is something wrong?" Joshua asked.

"It's really not my place to say. I'm going to let the doctor talk to you. See what she thinks. Dr. Cadwell isn't here today. He's vacationing with his family in the South of France. His first real vacation in 20 years. So you're going to be seen by Dr. Bennet today. I should prepare you, her bedside manner isn't as bubbly as Dr. Cadwell's, but she's very good at what she does. It's just that her manner can be a little brisk sometime."

"Brisk?" Bella said.

"Just a little."

There was a brief knock on the door before a woman in a white lab coat walked into the room.

"Linda, are you finished?"

"I just added the last of Mrs. Keys' information into the computer. So yes, I can turn her over to you, Dr. Bennet. Good seeing you again, Mr. Keys, Mrs. Keys."

"Good seeing you again too, Linda," Joshua said.

"Well, as Nurse Linda said, I'm Dr. Bennet, Dr. Cadwell's partner. I'm going to be monitoring your case until Dr. Cadwell returns. I'm going to get right to the point, I've read your file, including your lab results from today, and I'm concerned by what I see. You're not putting on enough weight. In fact, you're losing weight. That tells me you're not eating enough. You're also not taking your prenatal vitamins, which are actually putting you more at risk than the child.

"Bella, when did you stop taking the prenatal vitamins?" Joshua asked.

"They were making my stomach upset and I kept throwing them up."

"Your iron levels are also ridiculously low," Dr. Bennet said.

"The iron pills were making me constipated," Bella said.

Dr. Bennet held out a folder to Bella. "Care to take a look at what children can look like when they are denied folic acid in the womb?"

Bella shrunk away from the folder. "No, Dr. Bennet, I don't."

Dr. Bennet sighed. "Look, Mrs. Keys, I know motherhood is inconvenient. Trust me, I've done it myself three times. But what I am really wondering is, do you even want this child?"

"Excuse me?"

"Do you want to deliver a healthy, full term baby?"

"Wait a minute, doctor. You need to take it down a notch. Bella's doing everything in her power to deliver a healthy baby."

"No, Mr. Keys, she is not. She has not followed any of Dr. Cadwell's recommendations."

"Of course I want my baby," Bella bit out.

Dr. Bennet's lips turned up into probably the closest thing she could manage to a smile. "Then we're on the same page and from this point on, I trust that you are going to do everything in your power to keep him or her healthy. Your labs show that you have protein in your urine. I want to hospitalize you."

"No. No way!"

"Bella, relax. Dr. Bennet, can you please explain to us in laymen's terms what that means?"

"When protein is found in the urine, it could be an early indication of preeclampsia, or what we call pregnancy-induced hypertension. Symptoms of preeclampsia could include fatigue, abdominal pain, headaches, nausea, and frequent urination. It is possible for this type of condition to keep the mother from passing enough blood to the placenta. This, of course, would affect the amount of oxygen and food that the baby receives, and we don't want that to happen."

"No, of course not," Joshua said.

"To the best of your recollection, Mr. Keys, has your wife been experiencing any of these symptoms?"

"Some, but I didn't think too much about it since she had many of those same symptoms when she was pregnant with our son, Jabari. Especially during the first trimester. So what are we talking about, total bed rest?"

"Actually, I'm more concerned at this stage about nutrition. If your wife doesn't eat, then the baby can't eat. If she were in the hospital, I could have her fed intravenously. That way I could personally see to it that the baby gets exactly what it needs."

"Josh, no. I am not going to let her put me in some hospital."

Joshua laid a calming hand on Bella's shoulder. "Doctor, what if you gave us a week to turn this around? Bella will take the iron pills and the prenatal vitamins and I will personally see to it that she eats."

Dr. Bennett was silent for a moment, as she considered Joshua's proposition. "Okay, Mr. Keys, here's what I'm going to do. I'm going to write your wife a prescription for 50% more rest, her body weight in water, and a low salt diet. You've got one week to turn this around."

CHAPTER 105

Joshua cut the engine, walked around to the passenger side, and lifted Bella out of the truck.

"Josh, what are you doing?"

"You heard the doctor."

"She didn't say I couldn't walk."

"What do you think bed rest is? If they put you in the hospital, I guarantee you won't be walking anywhere. They'll stick a catheter in you and make you pee in a bag. Is that what you want?"

"No."

"Alright then, get hard. Cause we've got exactly one week to turn this around."

Joshua carried her upstairs to the master bedroom and sat her down carefully on the large, four-poster bed. "I want you to sleep in here until the baby is born."

"I see. So now that the baby is in danger, I'm welcome back into your bed?"

"I'll be next door in your room so as not to complicate things. I spoke to Ms. C when you were in the bathroom. She's going to stop by the health food store on her way in today and pick up some non-binding iron pills and a children's multi-vitamin. Apparently, they work the same as the prenatal pills and they shouldn't upset your stomach. In the meantime, I'm going to make you some lunch."

"Josh, wait. I know what today is. Carol told me about the ribbon cutting ceremony for the new Hebron site. You don't have time to babysit me today."

"The ceremony isn't until 2 o'clock. I'll make you some lunch and by that time, Ms. C should be able to take over for me."

CHAPTER 106

When Joshua saw the fresh tears pooling in Bella's eyes, he set the lunch tray down on the dresser and walked over to the bed. He touched his hand to her forehead. There was no sign of a fever. "Talk to me, Bella. Are you hurting?"

"No, I'm f-fine."

"Then why are you crying? Look at me."

She stared up at him with watery eyes.

"You and the baby are fine. I know the doctor said some disturbing stuff to you today, but I don't want you to hear all of that. I mean, I want you to hear it, but—

"No, I-I get what you mean," Bella sniffed. "It's not her, Josh. I got a bad feeling in my gut about Jabari. He needs to know the truth. If he finds out some other way, it'll just devastate him."

"You mean about the baby?"

"No. I mean about his parentage."

"Okay," Joshua nodded. "I understand."

But he didn't. Out of all the things in the world to be concerned about right now, Joshua had no idea why Bella was fixating on this. Joshua could literally feel the anxiety rolling off of her in waves. And, what he was trying to do at the moment, was gage how much of her current anxiety level could be contributed simply to pregnancy hormones.

"I respect that and I completely agree. Jabari should know everything in due time."

"Joshua, I've been praying," Bella gushed. "Something's coming. If we don't get on top of this, it's gonna be bad."

Yep, Joshua decided. She was having a straight-up hormonal meltdown. Joshua pulled her into his arms and stroked her gently, just like he would a skittish horse.

"Prayer is good, Bella. You know I believe in prayer. And I think that timing is just as important. After you and the baby are out of the woods, we'll sit Jabari down and explain everything. I promise."

She moaned. "Josh, I gotta stop with all the lies. I gotta come clean!"

Joshua put his finger to her mouth. "Promise me, we do this together. Alright?"

She nodded, "I promise."

CHAPTER 107

Bella ate her lunch. After which, under the careful eye of the housekeeper, Ms. C, she swallowed an iron pill, a vitamin C tablet, and a children's multi-vitamin. Bella fell into a fitful sleep. She dreamed of Jabari standing in the doorway with tears streaming down his cheeks. Buckets and buckets of tears that formed an ocean between them. She wanted to swim to him and embrace him, but the words that were coming out his mouth were huge barrier reefs that kept pushing her away from her child. Words like "Internet" and "genealogy project at school."

No, I have to wake up. I have to get to my child and explain.

But each time, Bella found herself being pulled deeper and deeper into sleep. When Bella finally did awake, Jabari was standing in the doorway of the master suite with silent tears rolling down his face. Before he could tell her why, she already knew.

"So, is it true?"

"Is what true, baby?"

"All this stuff I read on the Internet today."

There it was, the first barrier reef, *Internet*. This moment felt like an out-of-body experience to her. She had just had this exact conversation with him in her dream a moment ago. This time she wanted to be careful how she responded so that she didn't create the huge distance between them.

"Um, I don't know. What did you read?"

"That your father raped you and you had a baby by him, and when Dad found out, he punched him out. That's why you left New Orleans and never went back. Is that part true?"

"Not all of it."

"Which part is true?"

"Jabari, weeding through lies can be so dangerous. Maybe—"

"Just answer the question. Is your daddy my daddy? Are you my sister?"

"No, Jabari, that's not true! Thank God, that's not true."

"Is Joshua my daddy?"

Bella blinked hard. "Of course he is."

"Then why don't I look like him? How come he's light skinned and you're light skinned and I'm dark!"

"Jabari—"

"Just tell me the truth!"

"I got pregnant in college."

"Does he know—" Jabari could hardly get the words out for the huge, body quaking sobs. "Does he know I'm not his?"

"Baby, you are his! He adopted you on the day you were born."

"And you're pregnant again, right? That's why you're throwing up all the time. How many months are you?"

"Seven."

"How can you be seven months pregnant if we just got here? How?!"

Bella and Jabari both jumped at the sound of the thunderous voice coming from the doorway.

"Boy, have you lost your mind?"

"Joshua, wait no—"

Bella threw back the covers and jumped out the bed.

"I got this, Bella, get back into bed," Joshua growled. "Jabari, I asked you a question."

"No, sir."

"No, sir, what?"

"No sir, I haven't lost my mind."

"Boy, as long as you live, don't you ever raise your voice at her again. You feel me?"

"Yes, sir."

"I could hear you two all the way out in the garage. Somebody tell me what the hell is going on."

Jabari looked at Joshua, tears of raw rejection and anger in his eyes. "The truth."

Joshua's eyes flew to Bella.

"I didn't. He read some stuff at school."

Joshua pointed his finger at Bella first, then Jabari, "You get back in the bed, and you, in my office. Now."

CHAPTER 108

Joshua studied Jabari as he paced the floor in his study like a caged animal. Joshua knew all too well what Jabari was feeling. He had experienced the sensation of rage hundreds of times. Right now, the boy had so much pent up fury inside of him that if he didn't extinguish it he would either a) implode or b) explode. Neither was a suitable option. Not for his son. As a black man growing up in America, Jabari would have to learn how to do battle with the monster called rage sooner or later. It might as well be today.

"Jabari, take a knee."

Jabari, who had never disobeyed his father in his entire life, stopped mid-stride and glared up at Joshua, considering his options.

"I said take a knee!"

Jabari dropped down onto the floor into a runner's stance.

"Now breathe."

Jabari greedily gulped down mouthfuls of air.

"Slow down, son. That air ain't going nowhere." Joshua watched the boy try to modulate his breathing.

"Jabari, your world has not changed. You have a little more information than you had on yesterday. But your world has not changed. You still got a mama and I'm still your pops. Now, I'll tell you anything you want to know. Anything you think you need to know. I won't hold anything back from you. But only when you calm down."

When Jabari's breathing had settled to a slow, even pace, Joshua stuck his hand out to him and assisted Jabari up from the floor.

Joshua took a seat in one of the high back leather chairs and motioned for Jabari to take a seat across from him on the wine-colored leather sofa.

Joshua gestured towards the mini bar. "You want a drink?"

Jabari shook his head.

"Ask me anything at all. Anything you'd like." Joshua removed the ringing cellphone from his pocket. Jabari waited for him to answer it, but Joshua turned it off and set it down on the table beside him. Jabari stared at the phone.

"Go ahead, ask your questions, son. There's nothing in this world more important than what we're doing right now."

"Is that why you didn't come for me this last time she ran, cause I'm not yours?"

Joshua leaned forward in his chair and glared at Jabari. "If we have this kind of conversation, we need to have it like two men, alright?"

Jabari nodded.

"When two men have a conversation, Jabari, and they come to a mutual understanding, they only need to have that talk once. You feel me?"

"You're saying we say it now and we leave it here."

"That's right. It stays right here. Now, the first thing I need to tell you is that I love you. Now that, I will say to you over and over again, as much as you need to hear it, every day for the rest of your life. I've loved you ever since the day you drew your first breath. I was there when you were born, I caught you in my hands and I cut your umbilical cord. I named you and right then and there I decided that even if things never worked out between me and your mom, you would always, always be mine. So when your mom left this last time, I want you to know that I did look for you. I searched months for you and I prayed every single day for you. I never gave up hope. Because I'm your dad. And you're my son. Period. End of story. That's the part we leave right here."

"I don't know how you can forgive somebody for doing something like this," Jabari said as his eyes swelled up with fresh tears.

"I forgive because God's law commands me to forgive. And because something good came out of that unholy union, Jabari. You."

"Are you gon get a divorce?"

"I don't know, Jabari. I haven't gotten that far. This ain't easy. I'm just trying to obey God for today."

"Who do I look like?"

Joshua smiled and rubbed one large hand over his face, "You look a lot like your grandfather, Lemech."

"You found out he was hurting my mom. That's why you left the New Orleans Hornets and moved to Houston to play for the Rockets."

"That's right."

"Did he ever try to see me?"

Joshua stood. He walked over to the mini bar and grabbed a root beer out of the fridge. "Your grandfather?"

"The other guy."

"No."

Joshua watched Jabari's shoulders slump and then added, "I was a different person back then, Jabari. I would have killed that man had he tried to make contact with you or your mother."

"What about now. I mean, could I see him if I wanted to?"

Joshua studied the bottle in his hand for a long time before answering. "If you decide you want a relationship with your birth father, I won't stand in your way."

A heavy sob caught in Jabari's throat. "What if I say I don't want no new daddy? What if I say I don't want no other daddy but you?"

"That would sound real good to me, son. Cause I damn sure ain't trying to share you." Joshua was across the room in an instant pulling Jabari into his embrace. "I love you, Jabari."

"I love you too, Dad."

Ms. C knocked on the door before she entered the home office. "I'm sorry to interrupt, Mr. Keys, but it's your secretary. She's called four times now. She claims it's urgent."

Joshua released Jabari and looked down at him.

"It's okay, Dad. I'm straight."

"You sure about that? Cause work can wait."

"I'm cool, Dad."

Joshua studied Jabari's face for a minute. "Alright, go on upstairs and wash up for dinner."

CHAPTER 109

Joshua had just ended the forty minute call from Selena when he heard Bella's scream. Joshua shot up the stairs to the second-floor bedrooms. He found Bella in Jabari's bedroom clutching what looked to be a handwritten note.

"He's gone! I came in here to apologize, but he was g-g-gone. He r-r-ran away!" Bella sputtered. "I have to go find him!" She bolted for the door and Joshua blocked her path.

"Hold on, let me see." Joshua led her over to the bed. Somehow, he managed to pry Jabari's note, which was now soaked with tears, out of Bella's vice grip. Bella howled like a wounded animal. "Bella, calm down. We'll find him. Okay? I promise." Joshua pressed her face to his chest as he read the note quickly. He pulled his phone out of his pocket and dialed Jabari's number. Joshua could hear the sound of the abandoned cell phone vibrating in the bedroom. He left a message anyway when the voice mail picked up, to calm himself as much as he did to calm Bella.

"Jabari, this is your dad. Hit me back as soon as you get this." Joshua dialed again, this time his brother's number.

"What up, bro, talk to me?" Mike said.

"Jabari ran away."

"What? Why?"

"He read some stuff at school today bout me and Bella and—"

Bella screamed another ear-piercing howl as she tried to free herself from Joshua's embrace.

"What the— is that, Bella?"

"I gotta find him. I can't leave her alone like this, Mike."

"Josh, listen to me. Stay put, alright? Stay put and take care of Bella. I'll find Jabari."

Author's Note

Yep, I did it again. In a nod to the old school series literature I use to love in my youth, I've decided to leave our beloved hero and heroine metaphorically dangling from a bridge. Clearly our story isn't over.

You've just read, *Opening the Floodgates*, book two of the *Redemption Price* series. Books one thru three of this series focus on Joshua and Bella and how the redemption plan of God plays out in their lives. Book four is the long-awaited spin off featuring Joshua's tall, dark, and handsome, older brother, Mike Dutton, AKA, The Man of Steel. Mike's story is our season finale, and I can promise you that it's one you won't want to miss! For now, check out part 3, of the Joshua and Bella saga, in *The Fire This Time*, available on my website: catrinajsparkman.com or an online retailer near you.

If you enjoyed this book, please tell a friend and also go online and write a review. Reviews go a long way to helping independent authors like me. I love connecting with readers so please drop me a line at catrinasparkman@gmail.com Until we meet again, blessings to you and your household.

Sincerely,

Catrina J. Sparkman

Discussion Questions for Book Clubs

1. Which character did you identify with the most? Explain why? Which character did you find the hardest to connect with? Explain why?

2. Tonya's roommate Nisha makes a comment about Tonya being 'too holy' for her own good. What do you think of Nisha's assessment of her roommate? Is there any truth in what Nisha says? Discuss what you think it means for Christians to be wise as serpents but gentle as doves in our society today.

3. After discovering the true nature of the relationship between Bella and Brady, Mike tells Tonya that Joshua is the victim. Tonya disagrees and says that Bella is the victim. Which character is right? Are there any victims in the story? If so, who?

4. Reflect on the confrontation between Rev. Leblanc and Joshua. Tell whether or not you think Joshua's actions were appropriate in the situation. Does Joshua still have unfinished business with Bella's parents? Biblically speaking, is Joshua released from honoring Bella's mother and father because of the abuse?

5. Discuss the conversation between Selena and her great aunt. What do you think about the older woman's assessment of Christians? Explain why you think a woman who obviously practices magic would offer prayers to the Living God?